Trust No Alpha

The Omega Misfits – Book #1

by

Wendy Rathbone

**Trust No Alpha: The Omega Misfits Book 1
Copyright © February 2020
by Wendy Rathbone and Eye Scry Publications.**

ISBN: 978-1-942415-29-9
TITLE: Trust No Alpha: The Omega Misfits Book 1
Author: Wendy Rathbone
Cover by: Wendy Rathbone

© All rights reserved. This book may not be reproduced wholly or in part without prior written permission from the publisher and author, except by a reviewer who may quote brief passages. Neither may any section of this book be reproduced, stored in a retrieval system, or transmitted in any form or by any means, electronic, mechanical, photocopying, recording or other, without prior written permission from the author, except as exempted by legitimate purchase through the author's website, Amazon.com or other authorized retailer.

Address all inquiries to the author at:
wrathbone@juno.com

Piracy ruins lives.
This book is legally copyrighted © and MAY NOT be uploaded to any electronic storage center, website, or other such device/location. Period. End of argument. We are a small, independent company — if you upload this book to an illegal download site, you are robbing my family and my cats and dogs, who really do need to eat. You know better. Please don't do it!

For Della, as always…

***

A special thank you to three readers who helped me come up with some character names:

Avril Marie (for Mathias)

Jeanette Cooper (for Trigg)

Debra A. Choyce (for Ian)

***

And I could never do this without my beta readers:

Jackie North

Tay Wellington

Chapter One

Kris

We waited in the long hall, the five of us, and it was humiliating.

"What's taking so long?" hissed Mathias, my litter mate, older than I by a mere five minutes. He paced back and forth by Father's huge, brass-hinged office door, his velvet robe swirling about his naked ankles.

"He always makes us wait," Trigg said. He was the third of our litter, born thirteen minutes behind me.

Next week, the three of us would turn eighteen.

Technically, we were triplets, but we looked nothing alike. Not like our younger brothers from Father's second litter, Bren and Mica, who were identical. At five years old, the two of them stood silent behind us, huddled together, arms around each other, eyes big as they waited, like us, for their turn.

"You know he and Doctor Pokemeintheass like to have a whisky first," I said.

My brothers snickered.

Mica's solemn brown eyes found mine. "I don't want to be poked in the ass, Kris," he said.

"You'll be fine." I ruffled my little brother's hair, then crossed my arms over my chest to stave off the trembling in my body.

I hated every single doctor I'd ever met. I couldn't help it. They always made me feel small and stupid and self-conscious.

We all wore similar black robes and nothing underneath. Though Father kept the mansion well-heated, somehow cool air managed to waft up the hem of my robe and chill my body. Or maybe it was nerves.

I clenched my muscles, not wanting my brothers to see me shiver. I stood taller than them all, and I kept my head back, my back straight.

I was Father's pride and joy and they knew it. I got straight A's in my lessons. I was the quickest, the strongest and the smartest. Not to brag, but I could take on my litter mates in any form of fighting and beat them in under a minute. An Alpha's Alpha.

Never show weakness. Father taught us that from the first day we were able to speak.

He took pride in us all. Called us his thoroughbred Alphas. But he often told me I was his favorite. Maybe he did that with all of us, but I liked to think I was his best son, the golden boy Alpha of the family, his chosen.

Father, who was a hundred and two and still in his prime, always threw Alphas in his line, no matter the Omega chattel that bore them. We had older siblings we'd never met who'd gone out into the world to seek their lives. I'd seen photographs of them. All beautiful. All Alphas. Just like the five of us.

At birth we'd been tested. We all had the Alpha gene. He raised us to be perfect, strong and unquestioning. Leaders.

Even though each of his litters had different Omega birth-dads, we took after Father. Sure, I was lighter than the rest of them, with blond hair, but I looked like him. I had his chin and his dark eyes. I had his stubborn streak. None of us had ever met our Omega-dads. It wasn't even a question.

Father always said, "Omegas are fit only to fuck and get with seed. They are the breeders. The incubators for perpetuation of our species."

His belief was they held no other purpose in life. No Omega could ever be a free man. The closest one might come to it was if an Alpha took him as a bond-mate. It happened, but Omegas were still kept from the world, not allowed to hold a job, or a deed to a property, or to own anything for that matter. The ones who never found mates were kept on chattel farms and forced to serve Alphas who were both in and out of the Burn.

And bear their young.

When my body eventually fully matured, along with Mathias and Trigg, I was expected do the same as Father, as most Alphas. When I experienced the Burn, I'd be sent to a chattel farm of my choice to rut through my fever. Later, when I decided to have children of my own, I'd pick an Omega of good stock and breed him. It was that easy, Father told us. Nothing to worry about.

The time was getting close. We three would come of age next week, and according to Father's meticulous calendar we'd each enter the Burn within a month of that date.

I wondered what it would be like. I knew what sex was. And orgasms, of course. But the Burn itself was different. What would I feel like? Would I be sick with a real fever? How would the experience be?

Father said it was like nothing else in the world. The pleasure was so intense sometimes you never wanted to come out of it and resume a normal life pace. Of course we Alphas could have sex outside the Burn, on any whim, but the Burn was special. Different.

"Gods, I hate this waiting!" Mathias slapped his hand against the wall, making a loud thump.

Just then, the door to Father's office opened. He stood on the threshold, an intimidating elder Alpha, tall and lean, with long black hair half-way down his back and graying beautifully at the temples.

"Mathias, did you just hit the wall?"

Mathias bowed his head, his own dark hair covering his cheeks. "Yes, Father."

"You're to be first, then," Father said, making a brisk motion with his hand indicating Mathias should enter his private study.

From my vantage, all I could see was the right side of the study where a fire roared in a hearth big enough to stand in. The oranges and golds and yellows lapped at the air, making it crackle. I sensed another person but couldn't see him. But of course the doctor was in there. Father's friend for years and years. A doctor who made house calls to the very wealthy. His true name was Doctor Poe. But I called him Doctor Pokeme all the time. He was awful.

Mathias slinked into the room past Father's stern form. I heard Pokeme's voice but couldn't make out what was said.

Father turned to look at the four of us who remained in the hall. "You four wait here. And not a peep, you hear me? Kris, I'm putting you in charge. If your brothers act out, I'll hold you responsible."

We all nodded.

Father was probably the richest man in the country. Maybe in the world. We liked to think so. We joked about it.

We were spoiled with everything we could want. We had the finest tutors, clothes, furniture, games, and toys. The downside was he kept us isolated in that big mansion.

We didn't go out much at all, and our only friendships in the world were online, which he strictly monitored. We had each other, though, and our litter-mate brotherly bonds were tight. But at eighteen, we looked forward to more freedom.

Father had already bought the cars he'd planned to gift me, Mathias and Trigg in just a few days on our birthday. Since I enjoyed art, I was to attend a high profile design school. Mathias had an aptitude for math and would go into accounting. Trigg wanted to be a physicist.

We'd all be able to still live at home as we made our way into the world, and slowly we'd become the great Alpha men our father could be proud of, perhaps even have our own mansions one day.

Beams of light spread like long shards of amber glass across the walls from the big window at the end of the hall.

The door to Father's office opened smoothly across the shining wood floor.

Mathias came into the hall and made funny faces at us, then mock fell into my arms. "Save me from that horrible man!" he whispered loud enough for us all to hear.

I caught him under the arms. "How'd it go?" I asked.

He stood up straight, his black hair flashing blue and white streaks from the sunlight that tried its best to break through my father's mansion windows.

"I'm in perfect health. Ready for the Burn. I can't wait!" He danced back, nearly bumping into Father who came to the threshold to beckon me in.

"Mathias!" Father's voice boomed. "You are finished here for the day. Go change out of your robe and return to your studies."

"Ohhh." But his groans didn't last. Father never tolerated whining.

As Mathias nearly flew down the hall to the stairs and back to our waiting tutors, Father smiled at me.

My heart kicked me in the chest, a combination of dread and duty.

"Kris, you're next."

All the hairs stood up on my body. I hated this. But Father's smile spurred me on. To please him, I would do anything. Even face the horrible Doctor Poe.

I entered the study, which was warmer than the hall, and heard the fire crackling, smelled the mix of burning pine and antiseptic, and saw the doctor standing by a folding bed with a clean, white sheet tucked around it. A small table to the side of the bed had all sorts of things laid out on it that made me want to shudder. Little bottles. A syringe. Gloves. Darker metallic tools that I did not understand the purpose of.

Doctor Poe, who was older than two hundred according to his online bio, had a ring of silver hair around the top of his head, and features heavily lined, the valleys around his mouth so deep they looked dark and bottomless. His eyes were pinpoints of black ice that seemed to bore right through the skin.

Scary as shit.

He said, "Hello, Kris. Good to see you again."

"Yes, sir," I mumbled. I didn't realize my hands made fists underneath the long arms of my robe until Doctor Poe reached out as if to shake my hand and I held my arms back, away from him.

I turned without touching him, but Father stood just to my right, and really there was no escape even if my body, with its flight instinct, couldn't quite understand that fact.

"All right, Kris," Father said kindly. "Up on the bed now. You know the drill."

I was allowed to keep the robe on for the first part of the exam.

I sat with my legs dangling, my bare feet swinging, feeling childish and disempowered. Doctor Poe checked my vitals, my eyes, ears and throat, and listened to my heart. He used metal tools which were cold against my skin and made me shiver. He took my blood into three separate vials.

I had controlled my apprehension in the hall, but in here I couldn't keep my body from jerking at the doctor's touches.

"Stay still." Doctor Poe seemed to take pleasure from correcting me.

Sadist, I thought unkindly. Even as I shivered, a sweat broke out on my brow.

Nervous, I wouldn't even look at Father who stood to one side, watching. He always watched. His sons were his precious treasures. He wanted to see them, make sure they were perfect, and he followed every step of every procedure the doctor put us through to satisfy himself.

I wanted Father's support, but I didn't like it right now. I felt too exposed. Too pressured. Too judged.

Now came the worst part.

"Stand and remove your robe," said Poe.

I slid off the side of the bed and undid the plush belt, letting the robe fall open. The velvet slid like liquid from my shoulders, and though the air of Father's study was warm, I felt as if I was encased in ice.

"Ah," Poe said to my father, as if I wasn't even there. "He is a perfect specimen. Fantastic muscle tone. Well-muscled flank. Excellent abdominals. I commend you on your care of this one."

"Thank you. I make sure all my boys have proper nourishment and daily exercise."

They could have been talking about farm animals the way they were carrying on.

The doctor ran a hand down my back. "His spine is straight and his back strong." He came around my front, looking down. "His genitals are perfectly proportionate."

Ugh.

Father's gaze followed his every move. I had learned early in life I was to remain still during this part, emotionless. I was never to make a scene no matter how uncomfortable I felt.

"Spread your legs," ordered Poe.

I could not look at Father as I obeyed. I knew what was coming next. The examination of my testicles.

Poe put his cool hand on them, lifting them a little. Massaging. It felt awful, and a dead spot began to take hold inside me and expand. It was the sensation I always had when seeing Doctor Poe.

"Excellent weight and size," Poe told Father. "He will produce many Alpha sons, I am sure."

My face heated.

Father said, "Yes, it is my hope. He is my most perfect son. I've not had one like him in a century."

I should have flushed from pride. Instead, I stood and endured their judgment of me like a good boy. A prize Alpha.

It was good to know I was favored, but gods I hated this. Not just the touching, but the assessment of my body. I had no privacy.

I tried to think of it the same way I thought of my math, science or history tests. The conditioning of the mind felt less intrusive, though, than trying to pass a test on the conditioning of the body.

It wasn't like they were asking me to lift weights or run a race. They were examining me: my skin, my outsides, my insides. And with touches that made me flinch. It would have been easier if they had merely tested my quickness and strength, all things I could practice to achieve. But the weight of my balls? That was something not under my own control.

I felt helpless. Embarrassed.

To make matters worse, they weren't finished talking about me *down there*.

"His cock has a nice girth, too, as well as length. What a prime specimen to carry on the Vandergale name."

I breathed in slowly and closed my eyes. I tried to think of the verses of an old nursery rhyme to calm me.

"His Burn will be magnificent," Doctor Poe said.

The piper makes a lonely sound.
His soul is waiting to be found.

I tried to remember the tune.

Dreamers wake, the dance goes round.
My little Alpha claims his ground.

"Kris!" Father's voice came into my thoughts like a knife.

I opened my eyes. "Yes, Father." It took all my will power not to clasp my hands in front of me to hide my nakedness.

"The doctor just asked you to lie down. Obey!"

I gulped. "Yes, Father."

"On your stomach," commanded Doctor Poe.

Doctor Pokeme.

Yes, that was what was coming next.

As I complied with the doctor's request, he said to Father, "He has matured faster and more beautifully than all your other sons that I can remember at this age."

"He has. Thank you. I am so proud."

"Well," Doctor Poe continued as I settled on my stomach, "just a few more things to check and I'll give him his STD vaccine and he can be on his way."

Yay, I thought without much enthusiasm. Then, *Fuck me.*

I swore when I came of age I'd never see another doctor again even if I was in pain and dying.

I heard the squirt of the lube.

Waiting was the worst. And Father watching. I couldn't have been more humiliated.

Cold. It was so cold. And the finger intruding into me was like ice and freezing wind and empty lands. As if I were marooned and exposed to the elements, waiting to die.

I knew it was just an exam. But still—anything could happen.

Anything could go wrong.

And go wrong it did. Very very wrong.

Chapter Two

Kris

The finger inside of me poked and prodded, jamming against my insides like a mean old man.

Wait, Doctor Pokeme *was* a mean old man.

As he moved his finger inside me, taking his sweet sadistic time, he grunted and hemmed.

Those noises. They were awful. He was already invading me like the enemy breaking through partisan lines, but did he have to make gross sounds as well?

I was angry at my father now because he did not do a thing to stop him.

I heard Father say, "Something?"

Doctor Poe hemmed louder.

"I don't like your look," Father said.

Good! Maybe he was going to do something about this pervy runt who should have retired a decade ago.

"I'm feeling nodes," he said.

My heart jolted at his words. I tried to lift my upper body.

"Down!" said Poe.

Father put his hand on my back. "Stay still."

Did I have tumors? Was I dying?

"Father--" I began.

"Stay still, I said!"

Tears prickled cold at the edges of my eyes. The finger inside me wriggled and poked until it hurt.

"Ow!" I couldn't help myself.

"Shh!" Father's hand pressed harder on my back.

I was helpless, like a bug under a microscope, and they were going to talk about me again as if I weren't even in the room.

"I need to open him up more," said Poe.

"What?"

Father reprimanded me again, but it did no good. I was in a panic now.

I felt a cold metal instrument inserted inside of me. It hurt. I could feel it twist and expand my opening. It was like being stabbed.

"It hurts," I complained.

"It will be over soon," said Father.

I could feel his heat as he leaned over me. Looking at me. *Looking.* At my insides. At my most private of all spaces.

The doctor's breath was on me, he was so close. He explained to Father what he was doing.

"It's a camera," he said.

A camera? Going inside me?

"But I can already see what it is," Pokeme said, a little softer, his voice gone cold.

I clenched my eyes shut. I crushed my lips together and sucked them in. My whole body was tense, aching, split open. Invaded.

"Egg sacks. Dormant but there nonetheless."

"What?"

I tried to understand what he was saying. Egg sacks? Alphas didn't have eggs.

"Your son is not a true Alpha."

Finally, the cold instruments were pulled from my insides. I was shivering uncontrollably.

"Not a true Alpha? How is that possible? He carries the Alpha gene!"

"He does. There is no mistake of that. I tested him many times myself. But the internal sacks have been there since birth. They only grew enough for me to feel them as he matured from puberty to adulthood. He has the organs of an Omega, even if they are non-functional. The hormones from those organs will stain him… in fact they are staining him as we speak. He will never be a true Alpha. He may never even go through the Burn. But even if he does, he will probably have an instinct to be bred, not to do the breeding himself. It's a great flaw and I'm sorry to have to tell you this."

"This is an outrage!" Father yelled.

I heard everything as if from a far distance.

"Does he have the breeding pouch, too?" Father asked.

"I will have to run further tests. If he does, it will be underdeveloped. He is infertile in that way. But it does not matter. These organs still make him legally Omega. He's not an Alpha. Even the smallest of Omega traits, as you well know, get flagged in the common record offices. They are red-lined. They will label him officially as Omega even if he cannot bear young. Even if he also has the Alpha gene."

It had to be a nightmare. I had to be projecting my fears and still asleep in my own bed, safe and sound. Dawn had not come.

Yet, when I opened my eyes I was in Father's study with the fire crackling merrily and the ornate wood furniture and rugs meeting my view. I could see the side of Father in his black suit as he stood by the bed where I lay, still naked. I smelled his familiar aftershave like a leafy soap scent.

Father, who always praised me. Father who thought I was the most perfect Alpha of all his boys, his most prized son. He loved me the most. He'd said so.

He had to help me.

"You may sit up, now, Kris," said Doctor Poe.

I sat up, still feeling the gooey lube on my ass and thighs. I grabbed my robed and pulled it around my body, tying it tight.

Now Father stood gazing out the big picture window beyond his desk, hands behind his back.

"Father," I said, my voice coming out like a croak.

"You will be silent," he said gruffly, not looking at me. "I need to think a moment."

I wouldn't look at Doctor Poe, but I could hear him arranging things, cleaning them, putting things away at my side. His clothing shuffled as he moved.

Tears welled in my eyes. This time they burned. Hot. Steaming the air in front of me and stinging as they overflowed. I held my breath to keep from outright sobbing.

An Omega? I was an Omega?

It wasn't right. The doctor had to be mistaken. I was the strongest, the fastest, and the smartest. I was about to experience my first Burn.

"Of course I will run tests," said Poe. "I will triple confirm my findings. But it is no mistake, Varian. Kris is and always has been part Omega. And by the definition of our society, he cannot and never will be an Alpha in our society."

Father cleared his throat but said nothing.

"Varian, you know what this means."

Father sighed. It was so loud I could almost feel its breeze. "I know."

"You must care for him for the rest of his life here in the mansion, or send him to a chattel farm."

The chattel farms? I would be sent away to that? My throat began to close up. I started to gag.

Doctor Poe, for all his sadistic streaks, could obviously tell when a person was about to lose their lunch. He quickly grabbed a bowl from his table of instruments and held it under my head as I emptied the contents of my stomach into it.

Father never moved to help. Never spoke.

Tears streamed down my face.

All Poe did by way of comfort was hand me a towel. How kind.

I stood, my robe falling about my body like a death shroud more than an expensive cover-up now.

I didn't know what to do.

Both Poe and I waited for Father to come away from the window and give us his orders.

Finally, he moved and turned toward us, but he never looked at me, never met my eyes. "You will run more tests. You will provide me with the results immediately."

"Yes, I will," Poe said. "I have his blood. I have other samples he provided before coming in here today. I will let you know as soon as I have officially confirmed my findings."

"Kris, you may leave now. Go directly to your room. Do not come out until I say."

"Father--"

"Go! Now!" Father rarely yelled. But he'd already yelled twice in five minutes. This louder tone was what let us know, as children, when he was displeased, or when discipline was on its way.

I couldn't help my emotions. Sobs escaped my throat as I ran for the door, my robe flailing behind me.

I opened it and fled into the hall where Trigg, Mica and Bren still waited.

"Hey, Kris--" Trigg began.

I ignored their curiosity and their looks and stares as I ran down the hall toward the sunlight, such a bitter yellow now as it washed against the clean walls and wood floors. I tried to keep from wailing aloud, but I wanted to scream until my voice echoed throughout the massive rooms that comprised the Vandergale Mansion. Once my home. Now my prison. My hell.

When I reached my room, all done up in frothy blues—my favorite color—I collapsed on the soft comforters of my bed. I buried my face and the tears wet my pillows. For a long time I thought I would never breathe right again. I thought I would surely die of this mortification, this death sentence to all the dreams I had for my life. I was doomed. And there was the horrific chance that Father would ship me off to the chattel farms.

I wanted to die. What did I have left but the pain and humiliation from all I'd held dear?

I clutched my pillows for dear life and rocked myself, but it did little to soothe me.

After awhile, I felt too weak to cry, too dried out. Dehydrated and depleted, I finally calmed enough to begin to think a little clearer about my predicament.

I sat up, straightening my robe around me. My first thoughts were for comfort alone. Maybe Father wouldn't send me away. He did love me after all. I was still his beautiful son. Still smart. Maybe I had value and he would keep me here to work with him, to help him in his business.

I had a lot to offer other than my failure to be a perfect, unflawed Alpha for my father to brag about.

Yes. After Father got over the shock of my diagnosis, he would help me. He would see that I was productive and useful. He'd never send me away. I couldn't imagine it!

I dried my tears on the sleeve of my robe.

I stood and entered my bathroom, turning on the shower. The lube from my exam was sticky now. I needed it off me, along with the touch of that sadist, Poe.

As I stepped into the shower, I caught a glimpse of myself in the mirror. Golden and sleek. Tall and broad shouldered. Muscles in all the right places. Alpha in every sense of the word. Yet inside me was something that had betrayed me. Something that had been there all my life and gone unnoticed. Omega organs. Atrophied but still there. Still Omega.

I didn't feel different. I didn't look different. But everything had changed.

When the warm water hit my skin, I felt relief for the first time in hours. The water cascaded over me creating a safe cocoon of liquid, a respite, a haven. I stayed under that fall of warmth for longer than usual, letting my body relax, forcing myself to keep my wits about me.

I needed everything I had going for me now to weather this. My strength of body as well as mind. My leadership qualities. My conviction and fortitude that I was still worthy as a human being.

But a sad little voice quipped inside of me. Was I worthy? Was I nothing more than chattel now? Or worse, for even chattel had a purpose. They could bear young.

I never would. I would not seed young, either, for it was taboo for an Omega to lie with another Omega. Maybe they did it more often than people liked to think, using protection, but if caught it was a scandal. And if the union bore children, they were said to be monsters. Sylphs, they were called. Some were so monstrous they were put to death at birth, although I wasn't sure why.

I left the warmth of the shower and dressed in a crisp, white shirt and brown wool trousers.

Feeling more myself, I padded barefoot into my bedroom.

There, in the center of my room, stood Father.

Chapter Three

Thorne

Autumn had killed the grapevine. Well, it wasn't exactly dead. It was dormant.

Thorne ran his fingers along the roughness of the ropey vine, in awe over how something so dead-looking could spring back to life in a matter of a few months just because of a turn in the weather. Dormancy, hibernation, the fairytale of sleeping for a hundred years… it was all so amazing how nature worked to keep itself going, to perpetuate life even in the harshest conditions.

The Virginia creeper turned bright red in fall. Apples dropped along with leaves of every hue. Trees became sticks like skeletal sentinels against the coming long night. The lucky ones, the roses, white, pink or red, all continued through sunshine and gloom, never deterred. Along with the pine trees and winterberries and oleander.

Thorne kept a garden for every season. He loved running his hands through fresh earth or even snow if he had on gloves. He loved the sounds of sprinklers churning water to thirsty life forms reaching for the sun, and craved the scent of lavender by the gate, and rosemary at the door. He had a pond just for his water lilies. He had a path primarily so his daffodils, in springtime, could mark the way.

Today it was cold, so he only stayed outdoors a short time. He was fifty, but that was still quite young by Alpha standards. The oldest Alpha on record had lived to be two hundred and ninety nine.

Thorne looked up at the darkening sky. Brown clouds edged in red were blowing in from the west. The weather report said it would definitely rain by morning, if not outright snow.

On a distant hill, the golden lights of the Vandergale Mansion started going on one by one, making the house look like a Christmas ornament year-round. He knew five boys lived there with their father, Varian Vandergale, but he rarely saw them.

Kids trespassed on his property all the time, taking shortcuts home from school, or to visit friends. But never the Vandergale children. Once in a while he saw them go by on some special outing in their sleek, Rolls Royce van, but as neighbors they were taciturn and unfriendly. Everyone knew the Vandergales stayed mostly to themselves.

For a long moment, he watched the house, thinking of the inhabitants within their vast rooms and vast wealth, shut off from the world on purpose. But why?

For Thorne, he'd had no choice. The world had thrown him away long ago. It didn't want him. It looked at him askance.

Marked *dangerous* as an Alpha, the blot had destroyed his career, not to mention his prospects for love.

Now he turned away from the pretty mansion on the hill and moved toward the back door of his house, but not before stopping one more time before going in.

Under the spreading oak he'd planted twenty-five years ago lay a grave, also twenty-five years old. The marker read: **Ian.** No last name.

Thorne sighed as he reached out to stroke the top of the marble marker. "The long nights are coming," he said softly. "Sleep well, love."

Twenty-five years later and the pain in his chest was just as strong.

No one understood he had not meant to kill his mate.

No one understood Ian had been the love of his life. He was an Omega with no last name. A nobody. And killing him had broken no Alpha laws because it had happened during the Burn.

But Thorne had to live with it forever. And be marked for it, as well. *Dangerous.* An Alpha who could not control the Burn for long enough to see to his mate's needs. An Alpha who blacked out when the need grew too strong.

His kind was rare. There were places—special places—set up just for those like him to go to when the Burn hit him. Where Omegas were quietly kept to be abused by those Alphas who couldn't control themselves, or Alphas who were sadists, rapists, murderers or worse.

He was none of those. It *had* been an accident. He'd blacked out. He had not been conscious when his mate stopped breathing.

The doctors said Ian had died of natural causes. Those natural causes included an undiagnosed weak heart and too low electrolytes. Thorne felt responsible. He had not seen to his mate's needs. He had not adequately observed the signs that his mate might be ill.

He could have gotten a lawyer and fought against being labeled dangerous. But he wanted the label. He felt he deserved it.

In the end, it didn't matter how Ian died. Thorne felt responsible. Never again could he trust himself around Omegas during a burn.

It was terrible. Horrifying. Mortifying. For not only was he branded, but he'd lost the man he loved most in the world.

Luckily, by age twenty-five he had managed his business well enough that he could sell it for enough money to buy a place and live frugally. He still did temp work and free-lance jobs in computer software.

Otherwise, he stayed to himself. He tended his plants, his sore heart, and Ian's grave. Beyond that, he had no purpose, no reason for being.

He got by, and that was all.

When the Burn came, he chained himself up in his basement with enough food and water to last it out. Sometimes the fever ran for only a couple of days. Other times, he was down there for a week.

Most Alphas went to the chattel farms and got it out of their systems in a day or two. But Thorne would never do that. He'd denied himself even those farms that existed solely for Alphas marked as dangerous.

He'd sworn he would never subject another to his rut. If he couldn't control himself, he didn't deserve to have others in his life. It was that simple.

Nodding once more toward Ian's grave, he entered his home and began to prepare his dinner.

Chapter Four

Kris

Coming out of the bathroom to see Father standing in the center of my bedroom, my heart flipped over and over in my chest. Nervously, I ran my hand through my long blond hair.

Father looked about as stiff and unmovable as he ever did. The legend of him—wealthy, strong, an Alpha leader not to be defied—stood before me, and would not meet my eyes.

I knew from my studies that this wasn't my fault. I had no more control over my biology than a star's flame in the sky. But because I was now deemed a second class citizen, I would be punished for my biology. Everything would change for me now.

"Father." I spoke the single word as a sentence. Swallowing hard.

Father put his hands behind his back and turned away from me, his head held high, his shoulders back. In a low, emotionless voice, he said, "What will happen is this. From here on out you are my property. You will remain here, your needs met, but that is all. You are never to leave here. You are not to leave your room without permission. A lock will be on your door at all times. Be assured, you are no prisoner. It is for your own protection."

I could not believe my ears. My voice came out scratchy. "Protection? From whom? You? My brothers?"

"Yes."

I blinked several times, trying to comprehend what Father was saying.

Father continued. "As an unmated Omega, you must know from your studies that you can't be around Alphas."

"But that's all about strangers, and Alphas in rut. Not family. Not Mathias and Trigg. And surely not Mica and Bren. They're only five!"

"You are an Omega. Even if you don't feel it, inside, deep inside, you are. You can't be around Alphas all the time unless you are mated and bonded to one. You can't trust them."

"But you are my father! And—and my brothers?"

"You can trust none of us." Father still would not look at me. "We're Alphas. When you're an Omega, you can trust no Alpha!"

Only this morning, I was to be one of them. An Alpha. Someone who Omegas could not trust. It felt weird. Wrong. Suddenly I was this other person. Not me. An Omega in label. Yet I still had my strength, my beauty, and all else that Father had taught me. And I had the Alpha gene.

"But Father, I don't want to be locked away." I did not whine. I stepped forward and made my argument. "I have so many plans. What if the organs were removed? Couldn't surgery solve this problem?"

Father sighed but still wouldn't look at me. "It would seem that way, but that's not how our society works. Of course I have the money to see you through such a medical procedure, but your records and our laws will not allow simple surgery to change the fact that technically, in our world, you are an Omega. These laws are in place for your safety and that of the whole community."

"It doesn't seem safe if you feel a need to lock me away."

"I cannot change the world, my son. But I can make your life comfortable."

But I didn't want comfort. Not if it meant being a prisoner forever. Father could ply me with designer suits and satin pillows and meals served on fine China plates, but my life had gone from pride of achievement and Alpha status to nothing in a few seconds of an intrusive medical examination.

I could still beat my litter mates at any game, or in any fight. I could still score high marks on tests far beyond my age and grade. I could stand beside the best of the best of Alphas and no one would be able to tell I wasn't one. Except for a few atrophied organs no one had ever noticed until now.

Hell, I didn't even smell like an Omega. Did I?

I'd never smelled one before, but Alphas bragged the scent of them riled up the Burn. Made them crave sex with them.

"Do I smell like one of them?" I asked Father.

"What?"

"Do I give off an Omega scent?"

"I have never noticed," he replied.

"But you've never been around any of us when you're feeling the Burn. You hide it from us. You go away for days at a time. Maybe you didn't notice anything about me because of that. Maybe—"

Father held his hand up for me to stop talking. "I have not neglected you. Or your brothers. No one, not even Doctor Poe detected your Omega status until now. It's dormant in you. Maybe it will never awaken. Maybe your Omega organs are dead. But the law is the law. You have Omega attributes. It marks you. Forever, I'm afraid."

"But--"

Father held up his hand. "I'm sorry, son. There is nothing to be done. You will be treated with kindness here. But you will obey all my rules. You will never sully the name of Vandergale and though your status will be public record, you will speak of it to no one. Not online. Not to guests if you see them within this house. Your brothers already suspect something is wrong. I will inform them myself, and they will keep our secret or be cut off from me permanently. But I think they love you enough to obey my will and not expose you. If public record does expose you, I will do everything in my power to staunch rumors and make the story quickly run stale. Keep your mouth shut and your door locked, and you will have a comfortable life."

My breathing grew more rapid. A comfortable life? Was he fucking kidding? What he meant was he wasn't going to throw me away to one of the chattel farms. He wasn't going to stand by and watch me raped by Alphas in rut. How *nice* of him! How *Alpha* of him!

Comfortable meant I wouldn't be raped. Fine. But it also meant I would be alone forever. I would not have a career. Own nothing. Inherit nothing. I would have no status. I would never find a mate. Essentially, I'd be a non-person in the wealthy home of a man who was ashamed of me, who wanted me hidden away, who never wanted me to drag his thoroughbred name through the mud.

I would remain the property of Father. I would remain a child forever.

The room spun in blues and whites. The lights of my Swarovski chandelier flashed in my eyes. The top of my head tingled. Something caught me as I swayed forward.

Father's arms. I felt six years old again. I wanted to scream. To sob.

Strong muscles lifted me. I felt my bed encase me with a soft embrace. The leaf-soap scent of Father surrounded me. His warm breath skirted the skin of my forehead.

"Kris," he whispered. "My Kris. You don't know how sorry I am." Lips brushed against the center between my eyebrows.

My breath caught. My eyes were tight shut. "Father--"

"I will visit you once a day. That is all I can do for you."

The sobs piled up in my throat, swelling it, but I wouldn't let them out. Not for Father. Not for myself.

I knew he would monitor all my activity, physical, online. Everything. I would be cut off from the world. This room, and this house when I was allowed out of my room, would be the entire universe for me.

Already I was suffocating.

Already I felt dead.

My life as I knew it was over. I was only just beginning to grieve.

Chapter Five

Thorne

In the shadows there was lamplight. On hard, concrete flooring sat a soft mattress with a foam topper, clean sheets, and lots of pillows. Beside that, Thorne had a computer, a TV and a fridge stocked with water, soda, snacks.

There was no reason to suffer in darkness and discomfort when an Alpha experienced the Burn. But for Thorne, though he had made himself a nice nest in the corner of his basement, some discomfort was necessary. He bound himself with enough length of chain to function, but not to run away and wreak havoc if he blacked out.

He did not trust himself not to sleepwalk his way to find an Omega during his Burn. Since he blacked out during his Burns, he knew his mating nature and urge had to be extreme, off the charts. There was no medication for his condition. No help. Since he refused the special chattel farms for his kind, this was his solution. Hole up for a couple days and let the Burn simmer and slide away.

Masturbation helped his symptoms wane a little at first, so he kept plenty of lube nearby to keep from chafing his genitals. During a Burn, he could orgasm as many as fifteen times a day. From the literature he'd read on the subject over the years, he knew that was excessive even for the wildest of Alphas.

He never wanted to be responsible for another's death ever again. To wake and find his lover expired beneath him… It was the worst of nightmares, and he vowed he'd never put himself in that position again.

Now he sat on his mattress in the corner and fastened the cold, metal cuffs about his wrists. Over the years he had thought about lining the cuffs so they wouldn't chafe, but he never did it. Deep inside, he felt he didn't deserve cuffs with soft linings. If he suffered a bit, after Ian, it seemed only right. It had taken him two years to even allow himself a soft mattress down here. And another two before he bought the topper and extra pillows.

One day, maybe, he'd get around to lining the cuffs with something soft like sheepskin.

Already the Burn was making his skin hot. Cold seeped in through the underground basement walls but he didn't feel it. His skin flamed. His hair stuck to his neck in thick strands, and itched where it found its way under his t-shirt. His bangs had grown long this fall, and hung in his eyes.

His cock was already as hard as a marble sculpture, pressing insistently against the soft, loose material of his sweats. It seeped at the tip with an itch that turned to pleasure.

He hadn't yet touched himself and already he was soaring on the ecstasy of the Burn which was such a powerful drug it left him in an orgasmic stupor, coming again and again, sometimes for days.

Thorne decided if there was a god, creating this kind of biology for humans to endure simply to perpetuate the species was mad. Even if there was pleasure, it was out of control. And it had created a society where Omegas like his beloved Ian were subservient to such madness.

It had been twenty-five years and he still thought of Ian every day, though the tears had dried long ago. He found himself forgetting more and more about him. He could no longer remember his voice. Sometimes he had to look at a picture of him to remind himself of the details of his face and hair.

The chains on Thorne's wrists ran through a metal O-ring cemented into the floor of the basement. He could have bound himself in his own bedroom, but he didn't trust his own strength. He might, given time, be able to break his bonds if he had affixed the chains to the wall or his headboard.

It was safer in the basement. Sturdier. And it blocked all sound. His way was safer for himself, and everyone else.

Thorne lay back and took deep breaths, letting the Burn simmer through his veins, basking in the pleasure. Guilt left a bitter taste, for his love was buried under an oak tree in his yard and he did not want to forget that for one moment, but the pleasure consumed all that grief and regret, and soon there was nothing but red-gold ecstasy.

His cock pulsed and he couldn't push his sweats down fast enough to take himself in hand and milk his rock-hard shaft.

His thumb rubbed over the leaking tip and his head spun. He rode a tsunami of ecstasy as he pulsed out his first orgasm, the rattle of the chains diminishing as he lost his breath and his eyes rolled back. He nearly passed out from the strength of it this first time.

He used the liquid from his first orgasm to lube himself, and squeezed his balls, then rubbed his still-hard cock with tighter pressure. It felt so good, so comforting. He didn't want to stop, and he lay in a doze stroking for half an hour until another pulse began, this time lasting longer.

A knot formed at the base of his cock. He tightened his fist around it and felt his own pulse beneath the stretched skin. He squeezed it and his cock jolted, spurting over and over.

If he'd been with an Omega for this part, his knot would have locked them together in a frenzy of pleasure, the Omega's muscles automatically milking him, squeezing everything from him in the act of breeding. At this point in the mating, a healthy Omega body would, in turn, be stimulated by the knot inside him, and the Omega's own cock would pulse and leak until the knot worked itself up the shaft and let loose thick spurts of potent semen for impregnation.

Alphas and Omegas could be locked together for as long as fifteen minutes in shared ecstasy.

It took a lot of energy. A lot of effort. Aftercare was essential after the knotting, which happened about fifty percent of the time during an Alpha's Burn. Aftercare was something he'd been unable to do for Ian.

Now, here in the basement, without the stimulation of another body, Thorne's knot moved up his shaft and released in a few minutes. He'd been prepared. He had a towel on hand, but the pleasure catapulted through him so hard he blacked out.

When he came to, another half hour had passed. He'd slept like the dead with no dreams, only darkness upon darkness and no memory of the evidence of yet another orgasm all over his chest and stomach.

He used the towel, wetting it in a basin of water, and cleaned himself.

He took about fifteen minutes to drink some water and eat an energy bar. Then he curled up under a blanket for a few minutes before his skin began to heat up all over again, and he came another three times, one of those times with another thickly-formed knot.

From sheer exhaustion, he napped. When he woke, he had the clarity of mind to turn on the TV for company and eat another energy bar.

Feeling his cock rise once more, he covered his palm with lots of lube and went at it again, milking himself through it. The lube was never enough in the end. He always finished out his Burns with sore genitals and chafed skin.

To help himself more, he had various toys. The fleshlight shaped like a mouth with soft lips and a tongue fed with lube by a plastic tube was the best and most gentle device when he was feeling overly sensitive. It even had a vibrate setting.

But he hated it. It looked crude, rude and unsophisticated. The toy of a sex addict. The toy of a whore. Thorne only used it in the last throes of the Burn when his hand ached from so much pumping, and his cock was almost painful to the touch. The softness and the vibration helped him get the last of the fever out of him, the last liquid he had to give.

When he put it on the *vibrate* and *auto* setting, he was able to lie back and let it do its job. He could close his eyes and soar to better realms. He could even dream a little of his favorite things: the beauty of sunsets, snow in his winter garden, a starry summer sky. Sometimes then, Ian's face would return to him, laughing, and he'd see him running through the long grass of the backyard, or turning to embrace him, kissing him with sweet, sweet lips that tasted like sugared plums and better times.

But the blackouts still happened with regularity. Despite his ability to enjoy the Burn and have multiple orgasms in such a short time, he could not control the intensity of the first hours and the first day. It was only when the Burn ebbed that he might feel some control, and relax into his final orgasms.

Thus, he still could not be trusted. Not ever with another person.

Now he looked up at the tiny window at ground level, watching as the light darkened to evening, turning the walls pink and lavender.

There was an earthen scent down here, more like a cellar than a basement, though Thorne did not use it as a cellar for food storage. The room was only for laundry.

It had a heater, though he never used it. During the Burn, he did not feel the cold even in the deepest time of winter.

He watched the outside ground and the little bit of long grass he could see darken with night's shadow.

The arousal returned, and another knot. More shadows darkened his vision as he grabbed hold of himself and rode into wild throes of euphoria.

Chapter Six

Kris

I went to my bedroom door after Father left, peering at the inside lock. Father had not turned it on the way out, so I tested the door. It would not budge.

That meant Father had used an outside lock I'd never known about. And I had no key.

This was real. Not a dream. No joke.

I was a prisoner. An Omega prisoner inside the home of the wealthiest man in the country.

I still couldn't quite comprehend it. It had happened so fast.

All control of my life had been ripped from me. And all on the word of a doctor I had not wanted to see in the first place.

I went to my bed and sat in the center, knees drawn up, pillows surrounding me. I tried to clear my mind.

The day darkened to dusk. I rested my cheek on my bent knees and tried to calm my swirling mind. So many thoughts and internal voices. Too many overwhelming scenarios and fears.

My heart drummed in my chest and would not slow. I couldn't relax.

It seemed I sat for hours. I had zero ideas how to handle this. And no ability to accept my fate.

The room's shadows swept me with their dusky edges, always a comfort in the past. But now they were sharp-edged and scary. They had pointing fingers and held accusing darknesses.

Had I done something wrong to deserve this fate? Maybe if I had eaten differently, or exercised harder. Maybe if I had a purer heart and hadn't spent so many hours masturbating in the shower when I found out how good it felt, I would have been spared.

It had to be something I had done, said a voice in my head. All my fault.

But I knew better. I'd paid attention in science. Biology didn't work that way. Genetic manipulation was still years off.

Beyond that, it was a random event. Your parents determined your DNA, and the details from that, beyond hereditary conditions, were a crap shoot. You could be born with one arm, or no eyes, or an underdeveloped brain. Or you could be an Alpha, with the Alpha gene, and have dormant Omega organs.

Fuck.

Hours had passed and I heard no sound from outside my door. I'd dozed for a time, and now my skin felt cold, my body stiff.

Night had fallen. I thought about my brothers sitting down to dinner with Father, chatting away as if nothing had happened, happy that they were all healthy and perfect, each one vying for the new place as Father's favorite now that I was gone.

Did they miss me?

Later, I heard the lock on my door turn. A servant I had never seen before left me a tray with a sandwich and a soda.

I took the food to my desk, set it down, and accessed my computer. Father monitored all our computer activity, any conversation or website we visited. All actions. None of us older boys could even log onto a porn site without him seeing it. Not that he'd ever say a word. Alpha boys were supposed to be curious and learn all they could about sex. They were, after all, the masters of sex, the dominant ones who bred Omegas because that's how it was meant to be. That was nature.

From Father there was no privacy.

The last time Doctor Poe had visited, when I was sixteen, he'd asked me in front of Father how many times a day I masturbated. I had flushed so hard I thought the room would burn down from my heat.

When I didn't answer right away, Poe had explained, in front of Father, that a healthy Alpha boy should "clean his pipes" at least twice a day. If I wasn't doing that, I wouldn't develop properly. Gods, even my tutors didn't say such stupid things. And I'd never read that in any book.

Poe had gone on to touch my cock, and pull it up as if to show it off to Father. When I'd jerked back, he'd ordered, "Stay still." His favorite perv words when examining us boys.

"You should be proud," he'd said to Father. "This one is developing above average in size. He's definitely cleaning those pipes more than once a day."

I thought I would sink down into the floor and die right then and there.

Pokeme was such an ass. I had no idea why Father respected him and kept asking him to come back and see to his boys.

And now? Pokeme had ruined my life forever. I had to blame someone right now, and as far as I was concerned, he was the enemy.

When I pulled up my messages, I saw I had two from my litter mates. One each from Mathias and Trigg.

My eyes heated as I opened them.

Trigg: *Kris, what happened this afternoon? Are you okay? You ran away so fast, and Father has forbidden us to go to your room. He told us he'd have a meeting tonight with all of us there, even Mica and Bren.*

What's going on? Are you sick? I'm going crazy not knowing!

Mathias: *Trigg told me you ran away from Father's study like the very wolves of legend were chasing you.*

Dude, did Dr. Pokeme ram too hard? What the fuck?

Father's having a meeting with all of us later tonight. Will you be there?

Trigg had always been the more considerate one. Mathias. Well, he was crude even as a little boy. Trigg showed his worry for me. Mathias deflected. But I loved them both. My birth triplets. My litter mates.

I stared at their messages, not knowing what to say.

Finally, I chose Trigg's message to answer first. When I set my cursor on the answer window and began to type, nothing happened.

My hands were shaking so I tried again. When I typed, a picture of a padlock with a red line through it showed up. When I ran my cursor over it, a message read:

Reply function on lockdown for messages on this system.

Father.

Tears welled again.

I tried the Internet and got on, but I could only see and read. I could not interact.

He'd locked my computer down tight. Only incoming was allowed. No outgoing. I was not only cut off from my own household, I was cut off from the world except for what I could read, watch, and see. How generously Alpha of him that I could still download movies or games.

Only the best for me, right?

I slammed my fist into the computer monitor over and over. It cracked. I picked it up and threw it against the wall, knocking over my tray of food in the process.

Blood dripped on my Alpaca rug. My only wish? That there was more of it. For I wanted to paint the room red.

Chapter Seven

Thorne

Thorne awoke to the sound of something dripping.

For a moment, he was confused. Where was he? Then it all rushed back when his chains rattled and he realized he had on only a soiled t-shirt. No bottoms. And he was cold.

Chilled skin meant the Burn had ended, for which he was grateful, but now, as he looked around the dimly lit basement, he saw that a hose on the washer had a slow leak. A clear puddle was growing on the floor six feet away, the surface reflecting the dark, wood-beamed ceiling and the clean, white walls.

Thorne rustled around beside the mattress and found his box of lube and toys. Also within, was the key to his manacles.

The manacles were a safety measure only. He did not know what he might be capable of during his black outs. He suspected he did nothing but perhaps rut against whatever was within reach of his mattress. But he did not trust himself not to sleepwalk and go hunting Omegas.

The TV muttered softly to itself.

As he unlocked himself from his chains, he noticed his wrists were chafed, but not badly. He checked his phone as well, noting he'd been down here only two days.

As Burns went for him, this had been a relatively minor one. Every time he had a short Burn and his cock didn't feel bruised and beaten, a spark of hope ignited within him. Maybe he was getting more mellow with age. Maybe he wasn't such a dangerous Alpha after all.

But those thoughts didn't last, as he always reminded himself his cycles in the wintertime were smoother, shorter. A tease to make him think he had any control over himself whatsoever. It didn't ever change the fact that his Burns came on every other month, and that in the spring and summer they could last up to a week.

That wasn't rare for Alphas. But his blackouts were. And those blackouts were what made him officially designated as *dangerous.*

Thorne wound the chains up into a neat little pile by the mattress, used the toilet in the alcove six feet away, then gathered up his trash.

Setting it all by the foot of the stairs, he delayed his usual shower and coffee to fix the hose leak. Over the years, he'd gotten adept at minor repairs. It took him five minutes. He grabbed a mop, cleaned the floor, and was upstairs and in the shower within ten minutes.

Now coffee percolated on the kitchen counter. He'd missed it, and the way the sun glimmered through his kitchen windows where he'd hung various stained glass knick-knacks in the shapes of flowers, cats and stars.

After cooking his usual bacon and eggs, he opened his computer and perused his favorite sites, including news, weather and gardening. He also loved to read, and belonged to a few book groups, but rarely participated. But now he checked those groups as well.

When he finished all that, he put on his favorite music channel and began his morning routine of cleaning the kitchen whether it needed it or not. Then he moved on to the rest of the house. Though he never had any guests, he kept the place nice.

His life was boring, but stable. He preferred it that way.

Snow might be arriving later in the day, so he checked his gardens. The spring and summer gardens were dormant now. But the fall and winter gardens thrived. He kept them well maintained. He picked a few roses for the kitchen table.

As he puttered about outside, he talked to himself. He was his only company, so he never thought it odd.

"I really should get a dog." "Should I make chili for dinner? Or turkey soup?" "Hmm. I don't smell snow and the sky is clear. Maybe I should subscribe to a new weather site."

Thorne sat in the cold by Ian's grave for about ten minutes, as he did almost every evening.

"Well," he said aloud, "I made it through another Burn. No partner. No chattel. No harm done."

The sun set early in these parts now. He glanced to the west, past the top of the Vandergale mansion, to watch the sky paint itself in strokes of brilliant pinks and oranges. A slow purple stain edged the tops of the mountains to the northwest. The mansion's lights came on. Some windows remained dark, others turned gold.

It seemed far away, yet it was just down the road, his nearest neighbor. He'd gone for walks and been by that giant house hundreds of times. Five boys lived there, yet he almost never heard a peep from them.

One time, as he'd walked down the road, he'd seen two boys on the front yard silently playing catch. One was dark, the other light. They were beautiful Alpha teens, healthy and handsome in every way. Maybe their father sent them away to school. Or maybe they had everything they needed stashed away in that massive home, from a gymnasium to a theater. Who knew?

But Thorne wondered. Shouldn't little Alpha boys—five in all—make some noise sometimes in their daily lives?

Well, they were different, after all they were Vandergales. Varian Vandergale was known for being reclusive and reticent with the media. Thorne could certainly relate to that.

Of course Varian would keep his boys on a tight leash. He would want to avoid all scandal. And he would want to mold them into perfect Alphas, which was how Varian saw himself.

Thorne had researched Varian, though not in depth. He wanted to be generally informed about his neighbor.

They were good neighbors in that neither bothered the other. But they weren't good neighbors for the simple fact that they'd never met. Thorne didn't care about that so much, but he couldn't help but be curious. When you had famous neighbors, you sort of paid attention.

Thorne like the quiet of his road, and the large properties and empty fields that brought feelings of serenity. The mountains in the distance, white-tipped, were tall and lonely, and the skies wide and deep.

But sometimes—just sometimes, there could be too much quiet.

It was then he almost wished he knew even one of his neighbors just so he might wave as they drove by. Just so he might hear one solid "hello" as he went for his walks near their vast and lonely estates.

Chapter Eight

Kris

The first night I was locked away—for my own protection according to Father—was the easiest. Much to my surprise. For it had been miserable and horrible, of course. But it had been the easiest only because things got worse from there.

Servants brought my meals, and not the usual servants I'd grown up with. These men were strangers, and refused to speak to me.

As promised, Father came to visit once a day. It was the only company I had, and I both looked forward to and dreaded those visits. They were always too short. And Father, at first, was taciturn at best.

Most of my requests—pleas, in fact—went ignored.

"Father," I said to him. "I've been reading about my condition. I am not the same as any Omega. My scent for example. It will never develop as an Omega scent. Therefore, I don't think it will be dangerous for me to be around Alphas as you say. I don't need to be locked away all the time. Can I at least have permission to walk around the house and yard? To see my brothers?"

"No. Your label alone is a temptation. And you may not be aware yourself, but your scent has developed. It's neither Alpha nor Omega but something else."

"But I wouldn't be a temptation too my own family, would I?"

"You would be to anyone. We are a well-known family and your status is on public record. I have managed to keep the media from finding out so far. But someone somewhere will stumble upon the information. It's only a matter of time before you, as my son, as a Vandergale, will be known as what you are to the world."

"I could go out in disguise then, hide my identity."

Father shook his head. "You aren't listening to me. Even now, son, I don't think you realize. You may not smell like a full Omega, but you do not carry the Alpha scent either."

"What's my scent like then?" For eighteen years, no one had ever told me this. No one had ever noticed.

"It's actually sweeter than an Omega's."

"What?" Horrified, all my muscles contracted.

"Your eighteenth birthday is tomorrow. Your official maturity date. It will only get worse. And you grow more beautiful every day. Your scent is different, yes, but will only be more enticing as you hit full maturity. Not unlike that of the Sylphs. Not Omega. Not Alpha. But something else. An abomination."

"I'm not a Sylph!"

"No. You've read about them, I'm sure. And the brain disorders that come with their birth and their condition. They are almost always institutionalized for life."

"I know a little. But I'm not one of them. A Sylph?"

"No. You are different still. Which is why you must remain under my protection."

Tears blurred my vision. It seemed I cried a lot these days. With reason!

I stood up and went to Father, putting my arms around his shoulders. "Please don't do this. Please find a way for me to have a life. If you love me at all."

I pressed my face to his chest.

I felt his body tense. He gave me one swift pat on the shoulder and backed away. He'd never been overly affectionate with any of us, but in my time of need, he showed almost less emotion.

"You must endure this, Kris. Survive it. I will see to all you need. I will expand your rooms, bring in exercise equipment, give you means to create whatever you wish, but it must be within these walls. It is for your safety."

I sniffed and wiped my eyes, looking up at him. "What if my Alpha side takes over and I experience the Burn. I've been reading up on my condition. It's rare and not well studied, but it's possible I will experience it."

"I will provide what you need for that as well."

"What does that mean, Father?"

"If it comes down to it, I will pay for the discreet services of an Omega for you."

The thought mortified me. But then again, I had known I would go to the chattel farms for my first Burn. It was the way it was done. It was expected. But to have chattel brought here to the house felt dark, seedy, almost criminal. It was done by Alphas, but not by Father. He kept all that apart from his life, away from his ordinary routines. As if the shame of the Burn might be erased, or at the very least kept separate, a dark secret in a dark cave for dark days.

The next time Father came I begged him to allow me minimal messenger access to my brothers.

He denied it.

Every day he visited, I asked for not things but connection. Could I have access to my tutors? Denied. To servants? Denied. To various online social groups under an anonymous handle? Denied.

He offered to redecorate my rooms in any way I pleased. He gave me tools for my designs, pencils, paints, easels, computer programs, and computers. But even if I made art, or became expert at anything I desired, no one would ever see or know about it. I could share myself with no one.

Within a month, my room expanded. Behind locked doors and firm walls I heard daily hammering, pounding, machines. When the extra room was presented to me with the double door entryway to it flung open, and I saw a beautiful area complete with gym and hot tub, I burst into tears.

My life was gilded, to be sure, but still a cage.

I had all these things, but most of my time I spent sitting by my tall bedroom window on a reading couch, looking out over the fields that surrounded the house, and to the hills and mountain ranges in the northwest that, at dusk, became silhouetted against fiery red and pink backgrounds.

I had lived all my life in the Vandergale mansion, kept in luxurious surroundings, isolated from the every day world, though we boys did go out sometimes on various Father-sanctioned trips. Still, I'd never felt stifled. But now that the doors were locked to me, and all my freedom and my dreams taken away, those same walls closed in until it seemed some days I couldn't catch my breath.

After my introduction to my new, expanded prison, Father came by for a visit.

He stood and admired the remodel. "It's grander than my initial plan. A fantastic space for you. Do you like it?"

My head down, I replied, "Yes, Father."

In truth, all of it was amazing. The hot tub was situated against a real rock wall. The gym area had every imaginable piece of equipment I could want. There was a living area with a wall-sized TV screen. Father had brought in expensive art and marble statues of his own favorite images of wolves and lions to accent the room. I even had a kitchen area with white marble counters and oak cupboards stocked with any kind of food I could want.

Growing up, Father had never allowed any of us to have pets. Now he turned to me and said "I have decided you may have a cat, if you wish it."

I wasn't ungrateful. But my depression came and went in unmanageable doses. The new room brought with it a devastating blow to my hopelessness. It was as if it was the final statement. *This is your life. You will have no other. No purpose. No freedom. Nothing further than the confines of these walls.*

The thought of bringing such a lovely and graceful creature like a cat into my prison paralyzed me. My vision darkened.

"I don't want a cat!"

"Well, if you change your mind."

My eighteenth birthday had come and gone. My gift, which was to be my own car, had been hidden away. I'd watched Mathias and Trigg drive up and down the road in their new cars, while I'd probably never see the inside of one again.

Father watched me, his dark eyes narrowed. "I should tell you that Mathias experienced his first Burn last week. Trigg has not. Yet." He took a deep breath, turned and headed for the door. "Just thought you would like to know." He threw those last words over his shoulder as he reached for the handle.

For months, Mathias had talked of nothing else to me and Trigg. Annoying as hell. He'd been the least nervous and most excited of the three of us.

"He is well, then?" I asked.

"Perfectly." Father's reply was like a dig. A little over a month ago I was his perfect son. His favorite.

Never again.

*

Father visited one morning in late November.

I'd been sitting on my couch looking out, watching the figure of a lone man walk slowly down the road that curved by our house. I saw him every day. A solitary figure, shoulders hunched, but with the height and broad form of an Alpha in good health, maybe not even to middle age yet, fifty or under.

He had to be our neighbor to the east, the one rumored to have killed his Omega mate years ago. My brothers and I used to imagine he was some kind of monster, horribly scarred and disfigured, an evil demon who perhaps killed and ate Omegas for pleasure. And no one could do anything about it except label such Alphas because whatever Alphas did to Omegas was not seen as criminal.

All I really knew about the guy was his name. Hawthorne. Like the famous novelist.

Every time I saw him walking the road, he was alone. Until I was locked away, I'd never noticed his routine. Never noticed him walking by. But now I looked forward to seeing him. At nine a.m. every morning, on the dot, he'd go by the house and disappear on down the curve that led to a little hill.

He did not look like a monster.

The door to my room clicked.

Father stood in the entryway, watching me. He was early. He usually came to see me in the afternoons. By then his work would be done. But he never stayed long.

I sat up. "Father. Hello."

He said nothing.

"Is everything all right?"

"Yes." He seemed to wake from a stupor and glanced about the room. "It's dark in here," he said. "You have all the lights off."

In truth, there was plenty of morning light from my window.

"You're here early." I slid off the couch and stood. "Are Mathias and Trigg all right?"

"Mathias and Trigg are fine."

"Good."

As I took a step in Father's direction, he moved toward me in swift strides, the crease at his brow deep and dark, his lean, still fit body sliding through the bedroom shadows like a sleek wolf about to pounce.

I backed up and the insides of my knees hit the edge of the couch.

I was tall, but Father stood inches above me. He stopped his approach abruptly, an inch from me, his face so close I could smell the heat of his breath.

"You smell like the fields in spring, but sweeter. Your hair is like honey. The nectar of you must be divine," he whispered. His hand came up and the flat of his palm curved at the back of my head.

Adrenaline rushed my system with a sting of panic. He smelled of fire and ash and smoke. My entire body tingled in knowing fear.

Father was in the Burn.

I didn't know what to do. Sudden moves, I knew, would be unwise.

Slowly, I began to edge to the side, pulling myself away from his touch on my head.

"Father, it's me. Kris," I said gently.

He blinked but did not move. "Kris. My favorite most beautiful son."

His right hand came around my waist. He brought my body into contact with his. I felt his arousal, full and hard against me.

"Father. Listen." I spoke just above a whisper. "You need to go. To the chattel farms. Now."

"Kris..." He stroked his hand from my waist down to my buttocks.

"You have to go, Father. Now!"

I tried to move away, but he only followed.

"The sweetest I've ever experienced. The very air of you," he said. "I must—must--"

His hand tugged my shirt from my waistband. Before I knew what was happening, he pulled with an abrupt shift of strength and tore it. The buttons popped. The seams gave away.

In the Burn, Alpha strength often increased.

I was stronger and quicker than Father by virtue of my upbringing and youth. But maybe not during the Burn. Plus, as angry as I was at being locked away, I didn't want to hurt him.

I needed to bring him to his senses.

"Father! You need an Omega. Not me! Father!"

I felt his arousal against my hip. The hardness so tight against me. The pulse. He blinked, still holding me close. His hand on my head and his arm at my back kept me right up against him. His breath steamed in my face. "Kris. Kris. I've dreamed. I've wanted."

"No! Father! This is wrong! This isn't what you want!"

He rubbed his cheek against mine. It was damp with sweat. With fever. His breaths grew more rapid. More tortured.

My shirt fell tattered to the floor. His fingers curled about my waistband, a death grip.

The button to my trousers popped open.

I could not let it go any further. Father was not in his right mind. I knew he didn't want to hurt me. And he'd never forgive himself if he did.

I brought my hands up between us and shoved.

He growled and tightened his grip on me.

I didn't want to do it, but I brought my knee up as hard as I could right into his groin.

He howled. His hands came to my bare shoulders, gripping so hard I could feel my skin almost tear. He pushed back until I fell to the couch, then pounced on me.

I beat on him. Punched him.

He grabbed my trousers and tore them down to my thighs. "Ah, you will bend for me now!" he roared.

I kicked and flailed. I landed hard blows on his face and into his stomach. They barely slowed him down.

The world narrowed to a black pinpoint as I felt him grasp my waist and try to turn me over.

Tangled in my trousers, I kicked them off. I lashed out, fighting like a wild thing.

Blood sprouted from Father's nose. I left a long scratch down one of his cheeks with my nails. When he shoved his arm against my throat, I squirmed back enough to grab his forearm by my teeth. I bit down as hard as I could.

He yelled until it echoed off the walls and surely that animal sound traveled on into the fields beyond the house's structure.

As he pulled his arm back in pain, I took the opening as my advantage. I reached to the side table and grabbed a heavy abstract sculpture. I brought it to the side of his head.

He crumpled to the floor and was still.

Naked, bloody, I knelt and felt for a pulse. There was one, but it was weak.

As I stood, I glanced around my ornate rooms. There was no way to call for help. Nothing I could do.

I ran to the door and pounded on it. "Help! Help! It's Father. Father needs help! Help!"

I pounded until my fists bled. Then in one last effort, I tried the handle. It moved and the door swung open. Father had not locked the door behind him when he came in.

I yelled into the hall. "Mathias! Trigg! Help! Help!"

As footsteps came running up the hall, I saw my brothers for the first time in weeks. Both were taller than I remembered.

I stood back and they came bounding through the door.

Mathias had his phone out in seconds, calling 911.

Mathias and Trigg stood beside Father, glancing about the room. Their gazes landed on me, naked and bloody.

"What the fuck?" Mathias asked.

"What happened?" Trigg demanded.

"It's Father. He's in the Burn. He's still alive. He tried to—tried to—" I couldn't catch my breath.

Trigg ran to me then, catching me under my arms as I lost my balance in my shock.

"Holy fuck!" Mathias was yelling into his phone as he fell to his knees by Father's side. I heard him talking. "Yes, he's breathing. Yes, I can feel a pulse. Just get here as fast as you can."

Trigg steered me toward the bathroom. "Fuck, Kris, you're hurt."

I gulped in huge mouthfuls of air. "I don't care. I just care about Father. I didn't want to hurt him. But he—he--"

"I understand. Mathias is handling it. Let's get you cleaned up first."

Trigg was gentle as made me sit on the closed toilet and brought a wet cloth to my injuries, wiping away the blood. He found a blanket and wrapped me up in it.

As he worked, he said, "I'm sorry about what happened to you. Father explained it to us, but that didn't make everything all right again. I've missed you."

"I've missed you, too," I said.

"He said he locked you away for your safety. But I guess you weren't safe from him. He had the only key to your room and loaned it out only to two new servants who delivered your food."

"But Father is always so controlled," I said.

"Around Alphas." He leaned back not saying the unspoken thought: *But you're not an Alpha.* "But who knows what he's like in the Burn. It's different for all of us. And he's always been very secretive about his personal life, you know."

I nodded. My eyes were dry. I'd almost been raped by my own father and I felt nothing. Nothing.

Trigg finished cleaning my wounds. They were superficial. I had scrapes and bruises, but nothing more.

"Are *you* all right, Kris?" He put his hand against my long hair, pulling it back from my face.

I nodded.

"I'm so sorry," he said. "So sorry."

"It's not your fault," I countered.

"But it's just everything. You were the best of us. And now." He stopped. Let out a huff of air. I could see his eyes brimming.

Together we walked back into my bedroom.

Mathias sat on the floor with Father's head in his lap still talking on the phone.

Trigg said, "I'll go to the front doors and let the paramedics in when they get here."

Mathias nodded, still talking to an unheard presence far away. I stood in the center of the room gripping the blanket about me.

I looked up, seeing my little twin brothers standing arm in arm at the doorway, eyes wide.

I went to them. "It's okay," I said. "Father will be okay."

They both nodded, eyes big and solemn.

But was it true? Would he survive? My body began to shake. Soon the paramedics arrived.

Father was taken away. Mathias and Trigg followed to be with him. Before they closed and locked my door behind them, Trigg said, "I'm sorry. Father said to keep your door locked at all times. It's for your own safety."

I said nothing. But the thought that came to my mind was, *Who will be in charge of the key now?*

After another shower, I dressed in new clothes and sat all day on my couch by the window. I saw the lone Alpha man pass by the house about an hour after my Father and brothers left for the hospital.

I was in a daze and could only think: *Hawthorne, Hawthorne. Is your life as lonely as mine?*

If it was true that he'd killed his mate, I wondered how he even lived with himself.

My stomach was too tight to eat. I wanted to hear about Father. Any news. But I had no phone. And I couldn't write to anyone on my computer. My life was now all about me seeing out but no one seeing in.

I still could not comprehend that Father had attacked me. I knew the Burn had caused his behavior, but I couldn't believe it. All of it was like some dream I could not wake from.

The silence of my rooms, vast now, made my head ache. I could have played some music, or turned on the TV. But I never moved. Not to prepare myself lunch or a drink. Not for any reason.

The sky stretched white today. It looked like it might finally snow later.

I clasped my hands over my chest and saw they were shaking. My body felt like a tumble of knots.

At long last, the door to my rooms opened. Mathias stepped in, glancing around before seeing me by the window.

"Kris."

I sat up. "How is Father?"

"He's fine. He's conscious. He wants me to tell you he won't be pressing charges."

"Won't be pressing charges?" A heat of fury went through my body.

"Well, uh, that came out wrong. He said he's sorry and it's not your fault. If you thought you'd get into trouble, you're not."

I fumed even though he'd clarified things a little more. "Has Father always been a dangerous Alpha?"

"What? He's not!" Mathias puffed out his chest as he sat on the edge of my bed facing me.

"He forced me." I stuck my chin up, pressing my lips together until they hurt.

"Technically you're an Omega. You must submit."

"It was Father! And fuck that, Mathias. It's rape."

"Not if you submit." Mathias's mouth twisted.

"If you submit but it's not by your own will, then yes it is rape."

"It's Alpha law. You don't get to use that defense. Not if you're an Omega."

"Well, I am using it as a defense."

Mathias leaned toward me. "You nearly killed Father!"

I swung my legs over the side of the couch, thinking I needed to get up, walk away. "Listen to yourself! What the fuck? I'm your brother! Was I supposed to just bend over for him? For Father?"

Mathias's brows lowered. He wouldn't look at me as he answered. "Yes."

"What do you know?"

"I know. I've felt the Burn now. There's a reason things are the way they are, and the laws favor Alphas."

"And what was it like? Did you go rape a few Omegas to get it out of your system?"

In a flash, he was up and pushing me back against the couch. "How dare you talk to me that way!"

"What way? We're litter-mates. You should be on my side!"

"You're an Omega now even if you also have the Alpha gene. It doesn't count anymore. You're not the perfect son now. You're sullied. You have egg sacks. You have a pouch somewhere inside there." He looked down at my stomach.

I lowered my gaze to where his hands held me by the shoulders. Then I looked back into his eyes with as cold a stare as I could muster. "Get your hands off me!"

"I could do anything to you and it wouldn't be a crime."

I couldn't believe what I was hearing. "Get. Off." My teeth clenched on each word.

"Now that I've had my first Burn, I can smell you. You do smell different. Sweet, actually. And fuck. That hair. It's like liquid gold. You're too pretty to be an Alpha. You always were. I don't know why we couldn't all see it from the start."

"Shut the fuck up right now!"

"And Father. Father said to say it wasn't your fault. But I'm beginning to think it was all your fault. The way you are. Fuck you're so—I dunno—incandescent or something. You've been seducing him all along, haven't you? You could be rightfully his. He could take you and there would be no crime. If I took you right now, there would be no crime."

"Oh there would be a crime all right. Because I would kill you!"

Mathias licked his lips, looked me up and down, then finally let me go. I was shaking all over, but I took a deep breath and controlled it. I would not let him see that he actually frightened me. Mathias. My litter-mate. And now the one who held the only key to my door.

He stood up from the couch, still looming over me. "I don't know how Father showed such control all this time. You should be grateful for his love."

"I am grateful!"

"I feel like I have the Burn right now. Maybe you incite it in Alphas."

I must have missed the moment when Mathias had turned from sweet little boy to nasty cold Alpha teen. Had maturity and the Burn changed him so quickly?

As kids, we three, Mathias, Trigg and I, only had each other for so long until Mica and Bren came along. We played together, laughed together, made pacts and had secret clubs. We were the trio who stuck by each other's sides. We would have died for each other.

That should not have changed. And yet, since Doctor Poe had seen the truth about me and revealed it, everything had changed. Mathias, who'd now been through the Burn, had changed as well. I didn't recognize him.

His words chilled me. I looked down to see the bulge in his trousers. "Are you saying you want to rape me?"

"You don't get it, do you? It isn't rape. You're an Omega."

"Any decent Alpha would ask for consent!"

"It's a gray area in the law, but only outside the Burn. During the Burn, there would be no official crime. We studied that subject together."

"That doesn't make it right! And you're not in the Burn right now. Besides, I'm your brother!"

He gave a bitter laugh. "You always thought you were better than me and Trigg. But now look at you. You're not number one anymore."

"Is that it? You just want a power play with me?"

"Tempt me some more and I'll show you what I want. For Father's sake, you deserve to be nothing more than a hole to fill. You don't deserve all this." He waved his hand about my rooms and all my new things.

We were brought up to be proud and perfect Vandergale Alphas. Everything Mathias was spouting we'd been taught side by side. I'd learned all of it just the way he'd said it and hadn't given it much thought. I was an asshole, just like he was. I believed Omegas were holes to be filled, and that the Burn Alphas went through meant they were superior and needed to be in charge and not held accountable if something went wrong. Our species would die out if Alphas weren't in charge taking what they needed, breeding the breeders.

These facts and ethics were in the text books I'd read, reinforced by tutors, and by Father himself.

The reality of it hadn't entered my mind. It was as if I'd been asleep my whole life until Doctor Poe revealed my physical Omega traits.

Mathias stood before me, dark hair, dark stance, and by rightful claim dominated the conversation, the room he stood in, and me.

But I knew I could still take him in a fight.

I turned my back on him. This man I didn't know anymore. This brother mine who held the only key to my rooms.

After a while, I heard him leave, the door slamming behind him.

One thought crossed my mind.

I have to get out of here.

Chapter Nine

Thorne

The snowfall came late in the day. It smelled faintly of cherry shaved ice.

Thorne made a fire in his living room hearth and settled back to read. He was still tired from coming out of the Burn just that morning, and wanted a quiet evening. A long night's sleep.

He opened his tablet and turned to his current book. But he couldn't focus on the words.

He kept thinking about his walk that morning, and how as he passed by the Vandergale mansion on his way home, his eye caught the shape of a face in the high window on the west side of the house. At first he thought it a reflection. But as he came closer, he saw the profile of a young man. He recognized the blond son he'd seen years ago playing catch in the yard.

At a higher spot in the road, he could see the face a bit clearer.

The boy seemed to be gazing out the window and over the landscape.

Thorne had not wanted to be caught staring, so he'd lowered his head, but his eyes still peered upward and he thought he saw pain on the boy's face, even from this distance, and such sadness that even his own heart, filled with sadness for so many years, could not quite comprehend it. This son could be no more than eighteen. He should be entering the first tier of Alpha adulthood, relishing in the throes of his first Burn. But the grief-stricken look he saw on that face had clutched at him. A pang of empathy knifed through him.

His throat went dry. His heart heaved like a heavy ball of lead in his chest.

He'd kept his pace. Followed the road. But all day he could not get the image of that boy out of his head.

Now, shaking his head to clear it, he forced himself to focus on the words before him. Soon his eyes grew heavy.

After a while, he took himself upstairs and to bed.

*

All night the snow filled the land. Quiet and white. Feathery and soft.

A fairy tale scene greeted Thorne when he woke near dawn.

Slowly, he went about his chores, peering out the windows every now and then to take in the ethereal beauty.

By nine, as usual, he set out for his walk. He wore snowshoes. Where he walked, the snow would have come up to his knees if he hadn't stayed on top of it.

On the road it was a little better. Wet but clear except for ruffles of packed ice down the middle line. A few cars had come by after the plow. It wasn't too icy, but the soles of his snowshoes had a good grip.

Thorne headed for mile marker one-fifteen three miles down. After he came upon it, he would circle it and head home. A six mile walk every day kept him in shape.

He wore his red scarf, black cap and red gloves. Beneath his black wool-lined coat, he had on jeans and a white sweater.

The air filled his lungs. Ice. Pine. Damp earth at the edges of the road where some of the snow was already starting to melt.

The Vandergale mansion dominated his vision as he strode west. Dark stone. Black windows. No lights. Not even a porch light glinted on the snow crystals of the front yard.

The mansion was silent. It felt abandoned, as if no life existed within.

Was everyone still asleep? Certainly Varian Vandergale, the owner of more corporations than he could count, kept to a strict schedule and regimen for himself and his boys.

But Thorne reminded himself he rarely saw life there. Cars came and went. Deliveries. Mail. But beyond that, he never saw boys running up and down the roads on bikes or skate boards. He never heard voices or laughter. Only that one time had he seen two of them playing catch in the yard.

Maybe they kept to a different schedule.

He sighed, remembering yesterday, and the sad face in the window. Would the boy be there again today?

Slowly, Thorne trudged through puddles and ice on the blacktop. When he was nearly past the house, he could not stop himself. He glanced behind and upward to the third story window reflecting the white day.

He saw nothing.

He remembered a few weeks ago when he'd seen construction workers busy on that side of the house. He hadn't paid much attention, but now he realized the work had been happening on the third story. And right near the window where he'd seen the boy.

He walked a few more steps, looking back over his shoulder to see if the glare lessened as he came further into the house's shadow.

Now he saw it. The faint glint of a face, and long light-colored hair. Instantly, the image vanished, as if the boy had ducked away.

Shy, then?

Thorne smiled. All Vandergale boys were Alphas. That shy trait was rare in an Alpha. Alphas tended to be all bravado, brash and narcissistic. It was how they were taught.

But after Ian, Thorne's own philosophies about that behavior had turned upside-down.

As he walked along the damp and shiny road, Thorne's mind worked the puzzle. His curiosity entertained him, for quite honestly, he had nothing else to think about.

The world was so bright today that even Thorne's sunglasses could not keep him from squinting. When he reached his designated mile post, he turned and headed back toward the Vandergale mansion and his own home across the road and to the south.

The walk made him hot. He opened his coat a little and a cool wind blew down his neck.

That boy in the window. He couldn't stop thinking about him. Which one was he?

On the way back, he kept glancing at the window but this time he saw nothing.

Once inside his own house, he opened his computer and began to research the Vandergales. . Even though they were his neighbors, he'd only researched them one time. That had been years ago. He'd only looked up the father, Varian Vandergale. Just one more rich Alpha with perfect Alpha sons.

But now he couldn't help but be curious.

As he recalled the last time he'd looked up the Vandergale name, there was actually little to find on Varian Vandergale concerning his personal life. His businesses were everywhere, and his picture. But not much about the man or the family.

He saw a brief bio, ancient, citing Vandergale's first family from over thirty years ago. The bio named quadruplet Alpha sons, all adults even then, named Darcy, Eliam, Felix, and Gavin. They'd all be at least Thorne's age by now.

The boy he'd seen in the window could not have been one of them. Alphas aged slowly, but even so, he looked far too young.

Thorne continued to hunt for more updated bios.

Finally he hit the jackpot.

Varian Vandergale was the recent father of identical twin boys, Bren and Mica. The bio was dated five years ago. But it couldn't have been one of them in the window. They were still too little.

Thorne read further. That was when he could finally place names to the two boys he'd seen playing catch.

The bio stated: *Vandergale is the father of three more boys, age thirteen, triplets. They are, by order of birth, Mathias, Kris and Trigg.*

Those boys would be eighteen now. It had to be one of them he had seen. He had three names to put to the face now.

It was a start.

At eighteen, all three boys should be going through their first Burns by now. And soon after, move off to further their educations and their careers. So why was he seeing the sad face of one of them in the window? And more than once?

Maybe one of the sons was ill.

Finally, finding no more information, he snapped off his computer. He needed to get his mind off this subject for he knew himself well, and he had the sort of Alpha personality that fixated on things until he couldn't focus, sleep or even eat.

He needed to distract himself.

Picking up his half-completed shopping list, he decided to go into town for groceries. It would kill a couple hours at the very least, and maybe he'd get himself a nice juicy burger at his favorite restaurant.

His four-wheel drive truck made it easily down the driveway through the snow. Once on the road, he went the opposite direction than toward town, and drove slowly by the mansion again.

What a stalker! he chastised himself.

Shaking his head, he turned away, gunning the engine and making a U-turn further up the road.

His stomach growled at the thought of a junk food lunch.

Chapter Ten

Kris

Later in the evening, Mathias returned to my rooms.

He walked around admiring all my new stuff. I didn't want him here, but at the same time I longed for contact. News. Anything but these closing-in walls.

"Any word about Father?"

Mathias shrugged as if it didn't matter. I hadn't known him to be this way. But then again, maybe I simply hadn't noticed until now. He was the most outspoken litter-mate of the three of us. The most daring and bold. But was the strongest. I got the best test marks from our tutors.

"He'll be home in a couple of days. You really whacked him good," Mathias said.

I did not reply. I already felt terrible enough. I loved Father. I had never wanted to hurt him.

"Where's Trigg?" I asked.

"Oh, there's news on that front. I guess all that happened this morning was too much. He went into the Burn. Accommodations were made for him at Zilly's. Only the best for us, you know. Father's orders."

"Fuck you, Mathias, you could have led with that. That's huge news. I hope he's okay."

"He'll be fine. They take care of Alphas real good over there. But you'll never know that now."

"Could you just leave?"

Mathias acted as if he didn't hear me. "I think maybe being around you ignited it in him. Father, too. You aren't really an Omega. You're different. Like a Sylph or something, although we all know you aren't that since the three of us shared a womb."

"No, I'm not a Sylph. And I didn't do anything to ignite Father's or Trigg's Burn."

"Well, you're igniting me now, you smell so good."

"Am not. And just shut up!"

Mathias sauntered over to me. "You can't talk to me like that anymore! I'm in charge. And you have nothing. Nothing. Do you hear? All this," he waved his arms. "It's not really yours. Father owns it. It's on loan to you until he figures out what to do with you. It's only because you're still his son you get this kind of treatment."

"I've done nothing wrong. You should have some feelings for me still, and what I'm going through."

"But Kris, you aren't who we all thought you were. You're a fraud. How do you think that makes all of us feel?"

"Mathias, just get out. Get the fuck out!"

"I don't have to."

I walked up to him and shoved him. "I can still beat you and you know it!"

For the first time since walking into my rooms as if he owned them, his eyes widened. Even if he failed at having empathy for me, he did have some capacity to feel apprehension. Maybe even fear.

"You'll regret this. You can't treat me this way." But even though his words came out threatening, he backed away.

He became braver as he crossed the threshold, turning. "One day I'll have my dick all the way up your ass. You won't be saying anything then, will you?"

My teeth gritted. "Never gonna happen!"

The door slammed. I heard the lock click into place.

My brother had never talked that way to me in the past. One tiny thing had become revealed about my nature, and now he despised me? This was insane!

I'd always been the natural leader of the three of us. Trigg was the sweet one. Mathias the rudest. But never too rude at our expense.

But now all the power dynamics had changed. Mathias had been through his first Burn. The cocky personality we often thought was cute had turned to full-on assholery.

First Father and now this. All in the same day. I needed to get out. And fast.

But I had no plan.

Any of my windows were out of the question as escape hatches. The side of the house was flat. The windows led to no balconies and no roof edges. I might be able to construct a rope of clothing and sheets, but I shuddered to think of repelling even three stories. I was a strong Alpha, but I was a bit afraid of heights.

I went to my bedroom door and examined what I could see of the handle and lock mechanism. On the inside it was unlocked, but that was of no help to me. I brought my tablet over and looked up lock-picking. Father had probably blocked anything like that from my repertoire online, but I had to check.

To my surprise, hundreds of sites came up.

Father had been remiss in his list of subjects he forbade me to research.

I watched some videos and after a while realized I did not have the proper tools on hand. But I was creative. Now that I understood how various inner mechanisms of doors that resembled mine worked, I could play at it.

Funny thing, though I did not use a printer for much anymore, I had one. And I did have some old papers in my desk drawers. Keeping some of those papers together were paper clips. They were just right for what I needed.

It took me a couple of hours to finally figure out the lock and pick it. When I succeeded, a surge of adrenaline flooded my insides.

It hit hard. I could really leave this place. Forever! But a small voice within said, *Do you dare?*

I stood by the door for a long time staring at it, thinking. I could not escape the honest truth. It wasn't safe for me here. It wasn't safe for me on the outside, either, but I could pass for Alpha and take my chances.

It was dark, past dinnertime. No dinner had been delivered to me. Now that Father was gone and Mathias had put himself in charge, he'd probably told the servants to ignore me. But thanks to Father's renovations, I had my own kitchen now. I had food in my cupboards and a fridge.

I quickly fixed myself a sandwich. I stuffed a small backpack with minimal clothing and necessities, as well as dry food and fruit. I put on my thickest, longest jacket and stuffed my pockets with anything small I could find that might be worth some money. I had lavish gifts from Father over the years: diamond cufflinks, some gold rings and watches, expensive tie clasps. I gathered all my jewelry into one pocket. In the other I put a small stash of cash I kept, saved from change for when Father took us shopping or on vacation. It wasn't a lot, but it might see me through hard times before I found my way in the world.

Yes, I was running away. It was the only way I could see to control my situation.

If I could pass for an Alpha I might be just fine. I realized I might be recognized if Father put out a search for me, but I gambled on the hope that he would not want the bad publicity. Though it was probably on record by now that I was labeled an Omega, Father would never bring that to anyone's attention.

In fact, Father's reputation seemed too valuable to him; he might not search for me at all.

My future was a scary prospect, but I allowed myself to think of only a single step at a time. Right now, I needed to move one foot in front of the other. I needed to wait until the house was silent and my brothers were asleep, then make my escape.

Tension pulled through my body. I tried to stay calm as I planned and packed. Even if I were caught, I could fight my way out. Mathias was no match for me. But if possible, I didn't want to risk anyone seeing me. It would be best for all, especially Bren and Mica who probably barely understood what was happening, if I simply disappeared.

I dozed on my bed for a while. I heard no sounds in the rest of the house. No footsteps outside my door. Nothing.

When midnight struck, I went to the door with my paperclip, my backpack, my jacket, hat and scarf, and released the lock.

The door silently opened.

The hallway was dark. Trigg and Mathias's rooms were at the end of the hall. Mine sat closest to the stairwell.

Walking slowly, listening to my every footfall, panicking that I might make the floorboards creak, I made my way to the stairs and down.

It was almost too easy.

Father had an alarm on the front and back doors, but we kids always knew the code.

Hoping it hadn't been changed, I entered the key code and the door opened. On the porch, I inhaled the fresh air from outside, air I had not breathed, except through open windows, for over a month. It smelled of freedom.

The night sky glittered with a crush of stars—so many—like broken crystals forever falling.

It was freezing but I didn't care. My walls were gone. I was out of that stifling house.

Even so, that first step was hard to take. I thought about my life here, privileged and secure. Growing up here kept us isolated, but we had everything we could ever want, every opportunity. After everything, I still loved Father. I loved my brothers, although Mathias was on my shitlist now.

Moving across the porch, I felt I was leaving behind my entire life. I blinked rapidly and my heart gave a jolt.

But I knew I had to do this. Things with Father and Mathias had escalated far too rapidly. There was no safe future for me here. No future at all.

I had all my hair pulled up into my cap. I tugged the cap down tighter over my ears and set out.

Town was east, and many miles, but I was fit and strong. I figured I would find a cash motel for the night and sort things out in the morning. What I hadn't planned on was how cold it was.

Even with my heavy coat, after about ten minutes of walking my muscles ached with cold. I couldn't feel my toes. Through my gloves, my fingers were numb.

The cold came at me from all directions like swords slicing through the air. My cheeks stung. I had not checked the weather but apparently tonight was going to be a vicious freeze. I could not remember ever being this cold this fast. But then I'd been raised in heated rooms with over-sized hearths always blazing in the wintertime. I didn't work outdoors. Father rarely let us out except in afternoons when studies were done, and then mostly only in the summer.

I had been one of those boys who went from building to car to building. I grew up in ornate rooms and plush leather car interiors.

The snow by the side of the road was packed high and glittering in the starlight. I had thought more of it would be melted from the day, but I'd been wrong.

My snow boots crunched on ice in the road. Everything looked shiny-sharp and dangerous. A frozen wasteland.

Already I had tripped on a patch of ice and slid for a few feet. I stomped around, huffing and puffing, but I barely felt it. When I did start to get some sensation from jumping and kicking my legs, it was pins and needles.

I'd never make it to town. I had not even come a quarter of a mile.

I'd been stupid to run away at night in the latest part of autumn.

What I needed was some temporary shelter. A shed or barn would do.

I glanced about. We had neighbors, but most were far away. Too far for me to consider in the moment as my breath turned the air white and my lungs ached.

This was a deep freeze. I could tell now. If I didn't think quickly, it would send me back home to my prison. It was better than freezing to death, but I would be defeated.

Our closest neighbor was Hawthorne, the dangerous Alpha we'd told stories about when we were kids. The monster who'd killed his Omega mate.

I saw the peaks of his house up ahead. It sat down a long, snow-covered drive, and I dreaded the idea of walking by it. Yet, if he'd been the man I'd seen out walking some mornings, he didn't seem like a monster. Or dangerous. But of course I couldn't tell. I'd never met him.

I kept up my pace, stomping up the road until more of the top story of his house came closer into view. That was when I saw it. A little garden shed out front and off to the side of the house. It was perfect. I had my little paperclip lock pick. I could spend the night there until the freeze let up, then be out before anyone noticed me.

It was the only idea I had going for me, so when I got to Hawthorne's driveway, I turned and trudged through thick snow, feeling on the verge of collapse.

I felt I was making far too much noise tromping through the snow, crunching layers of ice. But as I came up to the little shed, all the house lights stayed dark. The windows remained black.

My hands shook as I used my paperclip to open the padlock on the shed. I couldn't get them to stay steady. It was maddening. But finally, after what seemed like hours, the lock clunked open.

Inside the shed was pitch dark. One small window shined black to my left, but the starlight did not make it through. I had forgotten my key-ring flashlight. I realized I had not given myself time to plan ahead for this journey, but I could not stay one more night in that house.

I moved into the shelter, kicking something as I went. It thumped against the wood wall. Something else moved in response, like a cascading sound of cloth from up high. I hoped it was only a tarp.

I was shivering so much I could barely get the door closed behind me. Feeling around in the dark, I located some shelves at head level, and what felt like a stack of boxes. I slung my backpack off and slowly slid down against the stack, pulling my pack to my chest. My head slumped forward, my cheek hitting the icy coldness of the hard material.

Being under shelter felt more secure for now, but I could not seem to get warm. I longed for my rooms, and my own soft bed. But there was nothing there for me anymore. Going out into the unknown, homeless and alone, still seemed the lesser of two evils.

I took off my gloves and blew on my hands. Slowly, they began to itch and warm up. But my feet were like solid blocks of cold nothingness. When I tried to stretch out and move them, my heels scraped and banged on the wood floor too loudly. I was terrified of discovery by the so-called Omega murderer Hawthorne, so I kept them still.

Every time I shifted my weight to get more comfortable, something in the shed shifted. The boxes behind me rustled. To distract myself, I wondered what was in them.

I fell into a stupor-doze, dreaming of home, and not in a good way.

Every time I entered R.E.M. sleep, I saw my father barging through the doors to my room, lunging at me and tearing off my clothes, running his hands through my long hair and using it as a handle to tug me ever closer to him. I jerked awake, only to float right back into the nightmare in a darker version. In the worst and final dream, Mathias stood watching Father attack me, naked and awaiting his turn to rape me.

My own voice, crying out, startled me awake.

I opened my eyes to a brilliant light, white as the outside snow, burning into my retinas. I scrambled backward, my feet drumming hard on the hollow flooring.

My heart nearly burst from my chest as I heard a deep voice say, "What have we here?"

Chapter Eleven

Thorne

A loud sound from outside woke Thorne.

At first he thought the silence of the frozen night had been broken by ice cracking on the roof, or ice shattering and falling from nearby trees.

He was normally not a light sleeper. But tonight the quiet of the night around him amplified all sounds. It could have been anything or nothing.

But he could not get the thought out of his head that this thumping noise had been lower in resonance. Like the opening and closing of his shed door.

His bed was warm. He loathed getting up and going out in that cold. But as he lay under his covers debating what to do, he realized he would not get anymore sleep if he didn't at least get up and look out the window.

He gasped a shuddery breath as he pushed the covers aside and stood. He always slept naked, and turned the heat off as soon as he went to bed at night, his thick covers offering ample protection against lower temps. Now he regretted that habit, for it was fucking painful, that cold. Like the bottom of some forgotten sea. The time it took to get his robe around his shivering form seemed far longer than a few seconds.

Hugging his arms to himself, he walked to the window and drew the curtain aside.

The shed stood off to the left, a small dark square with a sloping roof in the middle of waves of white snow illuminated by starlight. It looked normal. The door was closed. The window dark. He listened intently but heard nothing else.

As he was about to turn away and shuffle back to his warm bed, he noticed something. Squinting, he saw a disruption in the smooth patternless snow. As his eyes focused on it, he saw the snow had been disturbed in a curving line that led from his driveway straight to the shed's locked door.

Thorne's intruder had left a trail.

"Well. Damn. Fuck." His words whispered through his bedroom as he quickly climbed into his warmest, fleeced pants and shrugged into a thick sweater and heavy boots. Grabbing his coat and scarf from the hook by the front door, he stepped out onto his porch.

He stared at the shed which sat dark and silent against the white landscape. Still, all the hairs on his body prickled. He went back inside and started toward his gun cabinet. But the pact he'd made with himself years ago stopped him.

I'll never be responsible for another's death as long as I live.

He went for his flashlight instead. If the stranger out there wanted to kill him, they would have broken into his house, not the shed. On this cold night he felt it only rational to assume they were looking for shelter and nothing more.

The light shone gold in the snow as he crunched a path over the ice to get to the shed. When he saw the brass lock hanging on the handle, open, he knew for sure now that whoever it was was still in there.

At six-three, he still felt somewhat vulnerable standing outside in the middle of the night about to open a door on an intruder. His gloved hand trembled as he reached for the handle. His flashlight wavered on the shed wall and the snow.

Taking a deep breath, he yanked open the door and shone the flashlight inside with full force.

A man in a dark coat, all bundled from head to toe and hugging a bag to his chest, jolted awake with a painful cry that stabbed Thorne straight through the heart. He skittered back among the shadows but Thorne followed him with his light, shining it straight into his eyes.

The light illuminated the man's face. He was young, his mouth open in shock, his wide gaze darting about.

"What have we here?" Thorne kept his voice neutral, flat. It wouldn't do to frighten the guy any more than he already was.

The young man's mouth opened and closed as if he were trying to speak. Or breathe. He had beautiful features from what Thorne could see. A strong nose and chin. Dark eyes that lit up under the flashlight beam. Scared, yes, but intelligent. Not mad. Not underfed or sick or in the midst of a Burn.

"Are you a runaway Omega?" Thorne asked. But he already knew it wasn't true. Though handsome, the man did not give off the right scent.

"You don't smell like an Omega."

The man seemed in shock. He sputtered a bit. He groaned. Then coughed.

"You don't smell like an Alpha, either. You smell better."

He wasn't going to accuse the stranger of being a Sylph, but that's what came to his mind as he tried to assess him. But he couldn't be. Sylphs were all madmen. And most didn't evolve an intelligence past the age of three. Plus, what did Thorne know about Sylphs and their scent? He'd never even met one.

"What's your name? What are you doing here?"

"I—I--" It was all the young man could get out.

Thorne took a step inside the shed, closer to the intruder.

"You don't have to be afraid. I don't have a weapon or anything. But you broke into *my* shed. So I think I deserve an explanation."

"My—my name's Kris."

Kris's pack had fallen to his side. He reached for it, his gloved hands gripping it hard.

"I—I'll just leave if that's okay w--with you. B--be on my—my way."

The poor guy was shivering like crazy.

"Kris with a K?" Thorne asked, his mind whirling, trying to put two and two together. He'd just read that name somewhere. Today. Online.

Kris nodded. "Y—yeah."

It came to Thorne quickly. "You're a Vandergale boy."

"H--how do you know? We've n--never met."

"I've seen your name on your father's online bio." He omitted that he'd just been snooping that very day. "There was no picture of you, just him. But you look like him now that I see you. You don't have his coloring, but you have his eyes. And it shows in the set of your jaw."

Kris sat very still, eyes glaring straight ahead, body tensed as if to bolt.

"You live just down the way." Thorne frowned. Wasn't this the very same sad face he'd seen several times in the window of the Vandergale mansion while he'd been on his walks?

"Kris, what are you doing out here in the freezing cold?"

No answer. Just that frozen, almost predatory glare.

"Are you running away?"

Kris started to shake his head. His gaze dropped to the pack in his embrace. His arms tightened around it.

Thorne sighed. All fear left him when he realized this was no stranger but only his neighbor's kid. A sad kid. A boy of eighteen who held the world in his fierce, but scared eyes.

"Well." Thorne spoke very gently. "I can't leave you out here. You'll freeze to death. And that wouldn't be very neighborly of me. Why don't you come inside and warm up and we'll figure all this out."

Kris didn't move.

"Come on."

Kris's chin lowered and he hunched down into himself.

Thorne held his hand out.

When Kris still didn't move, Thorne realized his own reputation probably preceded him.

"Ah, I see. Boys hear stories growing up of neighbors they've never met. Of men who live alone. You think I'm a monster? That I'll hurt you? Kill you?" He took a deep breath and flashed his light up at the cobwebbed ceiling of the shed. "Hmm."

Kris swallowed audibly.

Thorne bent toward him and met the boy's tight cold eyes. Voice firm, he said, "If I wanted to kill you, you'd already be dead."

Kris's eyes widened even more.

"Get up. Or freeze. I suppose I shouldn't care, but I do. Come along inside where it's warm." Thorne turned and flashed his light outside. He stepped out of the shed and onto the crunchy ice, then moved up the path and toward his porch.

He didn't turn to look and see if Kris followed. He didn't need to. Seconds later, footsteps crushed the snow behind him and followed him up the steps to his front door.

Once inside, Thorne went straight to his heater and turned the thermostat up. Immediately, warm air poured into the living room.

He pulled off his gloves, throwing them on his coffee table, and turned to see Kris, holding his pack at his side. The boy swiveled his body to shut the front door behind him.

Kris stood in the foyer of the living room, a stiff figure like some frozen black ice statue. All Thorne could see of his true form were his reddened cheeks, his dark eyes, the firm jaw, and how he stood nearly as tall as Thorne. But not quite.

Though Kris did not smell like one, he was definitely Alpha in stature and stance. Clearly he was in some sort of crisis. But not the Burn.

He'd read just today that all Vandergale boys were Alphas. Born and bred true, from pure bloodlines centuries old. Boys from the greatest of family lineages and wealth were always discarded at birth if they weren't perfect and true Alphas. No exceptions. No questions. That was just the way of their kind.

Therefore, Kris would be no exception. He was Alpha. He was a Vandergale.

But then what in all hells was he doing on the coldest night of the year in Thorne's shed?

The boy at the window. The boy who ducked away when he thought Thorne had seen him. No mistake about it. That was who now stood at Thorne's front door staring at him as if he were some sort of demon.

What the fuck was going on?

Throne shrugged off his jacket and scarf and hung them on a hook on the wall. Then he turned toward the kitchen.

"You need to get some hot liquid inside you. Do you prefer tea or coffee?"

No answer.

He didn't wait for the boy to decide. He figured this late at night, tea was probably best. He set the kettle on the stove and turned it on.

He tried not to be too curious, and refrained from checking to see if the boy had moved yet. He was going for nonchalance here. Trying to be the good host. After all, this wasn't just any boy. This was a Vandergale he was making tea for.

It had been at least a decade since he'd had anyone in his house. His last visitor had been a plumber when he'd had a flood in his kitchen. Most other upkeep and repairs to the house Thorne could do himself.

Thorne got out two mugs and his box of Red Zinger tea bags. As he busied himself, he called out. "Make yourself at home. Tea in just one minute."

No sound. He closed his eyes tightly. Then opened them again. When the kettle whistled, he poured the water and plopped in the tea bags. Steam rose into his face.

Putting the mugs on a tray along with sugar, some packets of cream, a plastic squeeze bottle of honey, and sugar cookies he'd bought on his last foray into town, he lifted it and took it into the living room.

It was ridiculous, actually. Did he think he was entertaining some wealthy guy? No. This was a runaway kid. But he'd still done the whole thing with the tray and the cookies. It felt right.

Kris stood, still in his coat, hat and gloves, inside the living room now. He saw the boy's pack sitting by the rug near the door.

Well, it was some progress even if the boy had set down his belongings and only taken a few steps forward.

"It's warming up in here fast," Thorne said casually. "I don't think you need your coat."

As if waking from a long sleep, Kris blinked slowly several times. He tilted his head up, chin out, and his eyes shifted, gaze moving about the room.

Finally, he lifted his still-gloved hands and started to unzip his coat.

Thorne set the tea tray on the table and said, "Drink it while it's hot."

Kris now held his jacket in his hands as if he didn't know what to do with it.

Thorne took a step toward him, reaching out. "I'll take it."

Kris stared at him, unmoving.

Tired of the game, Thorne grabbed the jacket from Kris and hung it on a hook by his own. He turned.

"Gloves? Hat?" He lifted both his hands in question.

Kris slowly removed his gloves to reveal strong, long-fingered hands. He dropped the gloves at his feet. When he removed his knit cap, Thorne had to bite down hard on his tongue to keep from reacting to all the golden hair that tumbled down onto the man's shoulders.

He wore a white sweater that fit tightly about his broad chest, and sleek, wool trousers that looked as if they were designed specially for his height and slender hips. Rich. Formal. The material stiff as if still new from the store.

Thorne took slow breaths. Kept his posture straight and tried not to show too much response to Kris's appearance.

Kris was quite probably the most beautiful man Thorne had ever seen, Alpha or Omega. And what was that fragrance surrounding him? Some expensive, luxurious cologne? It smelled of honey and wildflowers, bees buzzing and sunsets purpling the sky. It was strong. As if Kris had bathed in it. Maybe to disguise his normal Alpha scent? But why?

Thorne picked up Kris's gloves and set them beside his own along with the cap he plucked from Kris's frozen grip.

He pointed to a chair facing the couch. "Have a seat."

Kris looked down. Keeping his back straight, he moved and sat awkwardly on the edge of the cushion.

"Some people take cream in their tea. Do you?"

Slowly, Kris shook his head.

"Sugar?"

Kris nodded.

Thorne poured in an amount he himself liked, stirred and handed the cup to Kris.

Kris took it in both hands. The mug was hot but Kris seemed not to notice. Steam rose into his face, pinking the skin even more around his reddened cheeks.

Thorne went around the coffee table and sat on the couch, making himself busy by fixing his own tea. He took his mug in hand and leaned back, blowing on the liquid's surface.

"First, before we begin. I must ask you. Are you injured or sick in any way?"

The pale eyebrows moved up the sleek, high forehead. "Begin what?"

This was the first time Kris spoke without stuttering from the cold.

"The story."

"What?"

"Your story. Of why you're here."

Kris glanced down at his tea. He took a quick sip, pressing his lips together.

"I am not injured or sick. Just cold," Kris said without looking up. "I needed shelter."

"I understand."

"I didn't mean to intrude. I'll be out by morning." Kris added.

Seeing Kris's tension and sensing a more desperate air, Thorne kept his voice calm. "There's no hurry. There's no one else around. Just us. Of course I am wondering how far you thought you could get on foot. At night."

"I didn't know it would be so cold."

Though he remained unbending, poised as if to flee, Kris's voice was melodic. Sweet.

Thorne's stomach clenched. Listening to him was like music. He hadn't heard another voice echo off his house walls in so long. And Ian's voice? It had been the first thing he'd forgotten as if the sound in his memory had gone out like a spent flame. Some years later, the face of Ian became blurred as well until there was nothing to recall but a vague shape. He would always remember their good times and love. But beyond that, so much was lost to time.

"Won't your father wonder where you are?" Thorne asked.

Kris's chest rose in a quick breath. To hide his reaction, as if all his secrets might be too easily read if he showed any sort of emotion, Kris took a quick gulp of his tea, wincing at the heat.

A long silence passed.

"All right, then," Thorne said. "I have a guest room. It's dusty in there, but you're welcome to it."

Kris blinked rapidly. "You can't tell anyone I'm here."

That was enough confirmation for Thorne. The boy was running. But from what?

Thorne shrugged. "Who would I tell?"

Kris glanced about the room.

"Like I said," Thorne added. "I live alone. There's no one here. That means your secrets are safe. For now. But won't your father come looking?"

Kris shook his head. "He's in the hospital. For now."

"I hope it's nothing serious."

Kris took two deep breaths. "He'll be fine."

"May I ask what happened?"

"I hit him."

Thorne leaned forward. "Why?"

"He attacked me."

Two Alphas fighting was somewhat common. But father and son? The sad face in the window. The way Kris held himself, wary and suspicious. Something was very wrong here.

"Rumors say you're a dangerous Alpha. Should I be afraid of the same behavior from you?" Kris asked.

What behavior had been going on in the Vandergale mansion?

"No," Thorne replied.

"I mean no insult," Kris added, ducking his head a little.

"While your question is very personal, I will be blunt. Because of the rumors. Because you seem afraid. My last Burn ended yesterday. My cycle is every two months. So that's not a worry, either. Have I anything to fear from you?"

Kris shook his head once. "Thank you," he said, and sipped more tea. When he looked up again, a tiredness seemed to swell from his eyes.

"The guest bedroom is down the hall and to your right," Thorne said. "You should sleep. We'll talk again in the morning."

Kris put down his now empty mug and stood. "Your name is Hawthorne, right?"

"You can call me Thorne."

"Thank you, Thorne. I can't go home. This is a lot you're doing for me. I—I don't know what to say. So I thank you."

"You may sleep as long as you like. You'll find soap and shampoo in the room's adjoining bathroom. Don't hesitate to ask if you need anything. If you hear sounds in the morning, it will only be me. I'm an early riser."

"Thank you again. I will find a way to repay you."

"No need. We're neighbors, right? That's what neighbors do." Thorne forced a smile.

Kris opened his mouth as if to speak but nothing came out. All he seemed able to do was nod. He walked to the front door and picked up his pack, then grabbed his coat from the hook on the wall before disappearing into the light shadows of the hallway.

A million thoughts ran through Thorne's mind. Kris was in trouble, anyone would see that. But why couldn't he find help? He was adult. He had any number of resources, and no doubt unlimited finances. Perhaps he wanted to avoid a Vandergale scandal?

But it seemed like more than just that. Kris acted as though he was threatened. He'd said his father had attacked him. Not that they'd had a fight. But that he'd been attacked.

In the monolithic silences of the Vandergale mansion, within its stone walls and marble pillars, what had been happening? What in the world was Kris running from?

Chapter Twelve

Kris

I stared at the faint stripes of dusty cobwebs in the ceiling corner. The dawn light brightened the white curtains at the window.

Daytime. Decision time.

It hurt.

I had hardly slept at all, but at least I wasn't freezing now.

Hawthorne—Thorne—didn't look or act like a monster at all. In fact, he was quite handsome with his black hair cut just above his shoulders and his errant bangs never quite staying swept back. He had cool black eyes and angular cheekbones.

I knew from rumors and town talk that he was about fifty years old. And now that I'd met him, I was sure he was the man I'd seen from my bedroom window during the mornings going for a walk down the road.

Still, he was a stranger. He was an Alpha.

Father's warning to me soon after my secret had been revealed came back to me. *Trust no Alpha.*

But I had been raised to be an Alpha. No one had ever told me Alphas were scary. How could it be that we were anything but smart and strong and important leaders? I was one. I had had no other ideas for myself. Ever.

I'd never thought about being scary to another person. I was just me. How I thought of Omegas was how I was taught to believe. They were made for us. They had a purpose, which was to be there for us during the Burn.

If, one day, the chemistry felt right and I did, in fact, fall in love with one, he'd be my mate. Forever. That was it. I never thought Omegas might feel afraid, or want anything else. And their rights? It didn't occur to me they needed them since they had strong Alphas to care for them. Even the farms didn't seem odd to me, but normal… until I was threatened with being sent to live on one.

How could I have been so naïve?

Now nothing made sense, and the world had turned into a dark unknown.

I rolled under the heavy covers of the bed and pulled my pack up from the floor. Ruffling through it, I found my tablet.

I paged through news, looking to see if there was any report about me or my family. Nothing came up in all my searches but of course it was probably too early. Maybe no one had yet discovered me gone.

I figured when they did miss me, Mathias would do nothing and say nothing. He wouldn't want to act before confiding in Father. And Father was still in the hospital. But that didn't mean I wasn't paranoid that eventually word might get out that I was missing and a warrant placed on me for my arrest as a loose Omega.

I heard some thumping and creaking from the house, first over my head and then on the stairs. A few minutes later I heard kitchen sounds.

Thorne had said he was an early riser.

I showered, then picked through my wrinkled clothes to find something to wear. I settled on my trousers from yesterday and a pale yellow sweater

My hair hung in wet ropes about my shoulders, so I braided it into a single tail, then went toward the sounds coming from the kitchen.

Thorne looked up when he heard my step. "You're up."

My first instinct, primed and programmed to Alpha behaviors since I had learned to walk, was to again assess him. This stranger. This Alpha who could be a possible danger to me. I noted his posture, his size, his mannerisms. He was a couple inches taller then I, but older. I was pretty sure I could take him down in a fight if it came to it, but if he had more experience, or was trained in self-defense, maybe not.

But he did not look like he wanted to fight. Or attack. Or threaten me in any way. Instead, he casually scraped a pan of scrambled eggs onto two plates already heaped with bacon, then handed one to me.

"Your timing is perfect," he said.

"Or yours," I replied. I hoped he could not tell that my voice trembled.

He offered a smile. "I heard you in the shower. I started the eggs when I heard the water go off."

I took the plate without a word and followed him to a dining table set up by a window that overlooked his front yard.

There sat napkins, silverware, two mugs of coffee, two glasses of orange juice, and a plate of toast and butter in the center of it all.

My stomach growled.

He sat and appeared indifferent to me, focused on his breakfast, as I sat across from him and picked up my fork.

The eggs were amazing, every bite a fluffy freshness melting in my mouth. He'd cooked the bacon perfectly, too, not undercooked as some of our chefs at home tended to do when rushed to get us boys off to our tutors by nine every morning. It was crisp and salty. My mouth watered as I stuffed a whole piece into my mouth.

The only sounds that filled the room where the two of us chewing, and the clatter of forks on porcelain plates.

It was Thorne who broke that silence.

"I can drive you into town if that's where you're headed. You shouldn't have to walk all that way. It's fifteen miles in the cold."

I kept myself outwardly calm, but inside my mind was chaos. What was I doing? I had no destination. No plan. But I had some cash. A lot by some standards. And jewelry I could pawn if need be. But where would I live? From motel to motel until my money ran out? If I tried to rent an apartment, my background would be checked. I'd be found out.

I could not stop thinking how stupid I was that I hadn't planned better. But I hadn't had time. How was I to know Father and Mathias would be threats me at home? Even I didn't understand my own condition. Was I responsible for making them act crazy around me?

There was no way I could return home. Not now. Not ever. And there seemed to be nowhere to head to, either.

I glanced up at Thorne. He didn't seem affected by me but he could be hiding it. When he'd first found me, he had commented on my scent. Thus, he was aware of it.

Thorne met my eyes. "Do you have a destination?" he asked.

"A motel, I guess."

"All right. Any particular motel?"

I shook my head.

"So I'm assuming you won't go home."

"No."

"Can I ask why your father attacked you?"

What could I say? That my Father kept me locked away because I was wrong inside? That he'd tried to rape me because of the Burn and because I wasn't a real Alpha? That my brother had threatened to rape me as well?

It all sounded too crazy.

I put my fork down and stared at my food. "I've seen you," I said, my words coming slow. "Walking." I swallowed. "On the road some mornings."

Thorne's response surprised me. "You're the boy in the window."

"What?"

"That's how I thought of you because I didn't know your name." He met my eyes again. "I saw you, too."

"That's my room. Beyond that window. Where I live. Or, rather, lived."

Thorne nodded.

"I was accepted to a very prestigious school of design. Tursor. Have you heard of it?"

"I have."

"But—something happened." He was a stranger. I couldn't trust him. Could I?

"What happened to you, Kris?"

"I'm not going to that school. Or anywhere. That much has happened."

"You're an Alpha. You have the right to do whatever you want."

"Not anymore."

Thorne frowned. His eyebrows were sleek and dark, like Mathias's only softer, not as arched. Not as hard. He had a kinder air about him, at least for now. But when he found out about me, what then? He would see me as only an object to be owned, to be controlled, to be bred even if I was infertile. He would turn me in. It was law.

"My father locked me in that room."

Thorne tilted his head as if trying to read my mind.

"You think I'm some criminal now," I said

"No." Thorne kept his voice calm.

"I'm not an Omega so you can't tell me what to do." I hadn't meant for that to come out so strong.

"I never said you were an Omega and I'm not telling you to do anything," he replied.

"But I need to hide. I need to stay away from my family."

Very slowly, Thorne stood, his body unfolding like a graceful panther, and took his plate to the sink. I heard the water come on and the brush scrape against his plate.

I stayed seated, my hands fists on top of the table, my head bowed. It was taking all my energy to keep myself together, to keep myself from breaking down right here and now.

"Kris," Thorne said from behind me. "Do you want more? I have more eggs. And help yourself to the toast. There's jam."

I turned and glanced over my shoulder. "I'm fine."

After Thorne was done doing whatever he was doing in the kitchen, he came back to the dining table with fresh coffee and topped mine off. Then he sat, mug in hand, the light through the glass falling over him like a white aura. Part of the reason I kept looking away from him was because I didn't want stare. He was magnificent and my cheeks heated at his good looks. Never in my life had I looked at Alphas the way I was looking at him right now. My tutors were old. All the mansion servants seemed cool and unfriendly.

"It would be pretty stupid of you to spend your money on a motel room when I have a perfectly good guest room not in use, don't you think?"

I jerked my head up to see if he was joking. He didn't even know me and he was offering me a room?

I shook my head. "No. It's too close to home."

"We're back from the road. No one can see me from the road even when I'm outside working in my garden."

"But you don't know me."

"I know you're a Vandergale," he offered.

"Why would you do this?" I didn't know what to think.

"I may live alone. I may not interact much with others. But I am still a good judge of character. Vandergale or not, there must be a very good reason for what you're doing."

Did he have ulterior motives? Was he going to attack me when my back was turned like my own kin? I might have found him attractive, but that didn't mean I wanted anything to do with him. Or so I told myself.

"But it's not your problem. Why should you care?"

Thorne leaned back. His hair reflected blue in the winter-light. "Because of the boy in the window."

"That—that doesn't make any sense." But when he spoke, his eyes sparked beautifully.

"No. But I think maybe I, too, know what it means to be alone. To be misjudged. So I'm offering. It makes sense, too, if you think about it. Hiding in plain sight. No one would think to look for you here."

He was right, of course. No one would. Thorne's house would be the last place my family would think I had gone to. A dangerous Alpha.

"I thank you for the offer." It certainly solved a few of my immediate problems. "Maybe for a couple nights. I left in a hurry. I do need some time to think about my plans." It was a little intimidating trying to think around him. He was so calm and organized. So confident. For someone labeled dangerous, he sure seemed to have himself under control.

Thorne put his mug to his lips. "That's fine."

"I can pay you. I have money." I could rent his room. But I was still a prisoner. I would not be able to come and go as I pleased. On paper I had no rights. I did not belong to myself. I belonged to my father Varian Vandergale. And if he caught me, he'd bring me home and lock me away again. Or worse, consign me to one of the farms for the rest of my life. This arrangement with Thorne, though I didn't know him, sounded a million times better.

"I don't need money," Thorne said.

"Well, I can help around here, maybe."

Thorne raised one eyebrow.

"My father can never know I'm here."

"I understand that."

"I'm not dangerous. I promise," I said.

Thorne let out a cool laugh. "Well, that's one of us."

My breath caught. But after our little discussion, I felt somewhat bolder than I had been since he'd found me in his shed. "Are you a danger to me?"

"Don't worry. I take care of myself during my Burns. No harm will come to you."

How he said it sounded ominous. Yet he didn't seem like someone who would kill his mate. But right now I didn't care. Anything was better than staying under lock and key under the ownership and power of Father, and the threat of Mathias. I wasn't safe there. I wasn't safe anywhere. But at least here, with Thorne, there was only Thorne. And as I assessed him over and over again in my mind, I decided that yes, if I had to, I could possibly take him in a fight.

Chapter Thirteen

Thorne

Thorne hadn't expected Kris would be forthcoming right away. He knew he would have to be patient, and tame this runaway one day at a time. No one spilled all their secrets—if any—to a stranger.

Over time, he would fish until he learned the truth. But for now, he rather liked the idea of having a guest. He hadn't realized how lonely he'd become. For over two decades, his habits had become ingrained, thoughtless. He never thought to change. But this honey-scented boy intrigued him, and brought a bit of a zing back to his step.

When he'd offered his room to Kris, he had not planned his words. They came out into the air as if fated. He had surprised himself. It further surprised him that when Kris agreed to stay a little thrill ran through Thorne's body.

When Thorne said he wasn't a danger to Kris, it had only been a half-truth. There was danger all right. This young man was a danger himself. To Thorne. Thorne saw threat written all over him. In that long golden hair he'd so nicely braided. In the deep dark eyes. In the nervous way his hands fisted and unfisted against everything he touched. The way Kris moved was liquid. And he wasn't a slim small thing, either, but more like an equal to Thorne's stature. Someone who could stand up to him, if need be. Someone whose mind appeared awake.

A couple times a week Thorne went to town for supplies. And sometimes a drink. He met a lot of drunks and a lot of Alphas who liked to talk big and swagger. That was what bars were for. But none appealed. Unlike Omega to Omega couplings, Alpha to Alpha relationships were not against the law. They just didn't form the same kind of bond an Alpha and Omega could have. And since Alphas were natural tops, there usually wouldn't be any of that kind of fucking going on unless the Alpha had that kink. Since Thorne had sworn off Omegas, his only prospect for sex was another Alpha.

But it never happened. He wasn't attracted to his own kind.

But Kris was different. Alpha but something else as well.

It was the first time Thorne had felt anything stir him since Ian, and that memory was so long ago he'd almost forgotten the sensation.

So yes, there was danger here. Danger that Thorne might end up craving what he could not have. Danger that Kris might be the rare one in a very long time to break his heart.

*

Thorne entered the family room, which doubled as his study.

Kris looked up from where he sat on the couch, his tablet in his lap.

"I free-lance my tech skills to a few companies for extra income." Thorne waved his hand toward his computer. "I've got a little work to do this morning."

"Oh, sorry. I'll go in the living room."

"Stay if you wish. You aren't bothering me."

Kris relaxed somewhat, but his shoulders remained stiff. "Don't you usually go for a walk this time of the morning?"

"Yes. But it's freezing today. And--"

"And you don't trust me enough yet to leave me alone here," Kris finished for him.

"That's not what I was going to say."

Kris raised a pale eyebrow.

"I was going to say I don't go every day. Maybe five days a week."

Kris's stare moved nervously about the room.

"Maybe after lunch it will be warmer. I can at least show you the yard. Back. Front. The gardens are mostly under snow right now but I can show you the beds. And the winter garden has some green." He took a deep breath. "No one will see you if you stay close to the house. Only the upper story is visible from the sides. If you go too far out front, though, you can see the whole of it. Keep that in mind."

"I don't mean to be a burden on you." Kris spoke up suddenly. "If you won't take my money, maybe there's stuff I can help you with. Around here."

Thorne smiled to hear him offer again. He could tell Kris, despite his fear of his Father, had been raised well-mannered and educated. But even so, none of that could account for a good heart. Thorne believed you were either born with one, or not. Sometimes the Alphas with good hearts could become ruined, but the ones without—there was little hope they might grow one.

The world was fucked up, but Thorne was doing his best to survive it. And so was Kris. Even if it meant they were both pretty much fated to be alone, they were doing what they could. Running away never solved anything, but sometimes it took one away from worse fates. There was something to be said for that.

Every moment since last night when he'd found Kris, Thorn wondered what had really happened. He worried that Kris might actually be hurt and not telling.

Well, he would do what he could for him. That was all he could ask of himself.

Thorne turned to his computer and switched it on. He worked in silence for about two hours before deciding to take a break. His stomach growled. Breakfast had been hours ago.

He turned to Kris. "Hungry?"

Kris had brought his stocking feet up on the couch and was leaning back against the arm, reading. And by some odd miracle, actually relaxing. It was heartening to see. Like the eye of a hurricane while all on the outside was in turmoil.

"Yes. May I help?"

So polite. "You may."

They ate toasted cheese sandwiches and soup.

Afterward, they put on their coats and scarves, and Thorne led Kris out the back door and showed him the yard.

"My property stretches back that way over ten acres to those trees." He pointed.

"It's beautiful," Kris said, crunching through the snow to stand beside him.

Their breaths rose in misty clouds above them and mixed together.

Looking at Kris with the white landscape all about him made Thorne's heart lurch. He'd never seen an Alpha like him, his features streamlined but fine and graceful at the same time. He had the broad shoulders and muscles of an Alpha, with the leanness of youth. His movements were both calculated and flowing, like a cat.

The air was cold but Thorne's skin heated just to gaze at him. It wasn't the Burn but something else. Something more.

"Can we walk back that way a bit?" Kris asked.

"Of course." Thorne made a path through the snow, expecting Kris to follow, but Kris made his own path, sinking in snow to his calves.

The pines were taller on the back acreage, and thick. Their scent filled the air. They bore themselves proudly and made thick shadows on the damp ground where the snow did not reach their trunks. A slow wind rustled overhead, then stopped. The silence all around them was deafening.

"I love the forest." Kris's voice came soft. "Father sent us to summer camps when we were boys, but as we got older that stopped."

So that was one reason why Throne didn't see them outside much in better weather and on summer days.

A secluded life. Thorne loved it. But Kris was still young, bursting to break free. For some reason, though Alpha and a Vandergale, he obviously thought he never would be free. Thorne yearned to know why his father had attacked him, and why he begged to be hidden.

Thorne's empathy had not awakened this much in so long he had forgotten what it felt like to experience so open and vulnerable a feeling. He was in good shape but found himself winded as they walked through the thick snow not because he was tired, but because thoughts of Kris sucked the breaths from his throat.

They didn't even know each other. And here Thorne was, mildly obsessing. It was only lust. That could be taken care of discreetly. Privately. And Kris need never know about his attraction.

"Sometimes I come out here and just stare at the trees for hours," Thorne said.

"It's pure here. Unsullied by—by everything." Kris turned all the way around, gazing at the land.

"Yes."

He liked to hear Kris speak as if melding to his own thoughts. Finally relaxed. Taking a break from his problems.

But after a while, Kris grew seemingly impatient. "It's cold," he said. "Let's go back?"

Thorne turned and followed his deep tracks back to the house.

Kris spent the afternoon going back and forth from the family room to his guest room, his laptop in hand. Impatient. Trapped. Airily beautiful.

Thorne finally decided to ask him outright what was on his mind.

"I can't find any updates on Father. I'd just like to know. But I can't contact my brothers. My tablet is—limited."

"Let me see that." Thorne held out his hand.

Immediately, Thorne saw the parent-lock on the device. There would be a password. Probably extraordinarily complicated.

He'd worked for years in computer science with various firms. He recognized the trap.

He raised the tablet face out so Kris could see. "I'm familiar with this. Give me an hour. You're still using your father's wifi which he can track, so I'll switch you to mine. I can also set you up on this with an anonymous IP. I'll give you a way to spy on your family's online correspondence."

"The private stuff?"

"Yes."

"It's illegal."

"Yes."

"No one will catch us?"

"No one will catch us."

Kris drew his lower lip into his mouth. His chest expanded. He let out a hard breath. "Do it."

Thorne nodded. Body tingling again. It was his pleasure to help Kris. Too much his pleasure.

He swiveled in his desk chair. For a moment his face passed through a late afternoon glare coming through the window. The sun lit up the dust motes on the air. They swirled about him, lazy dust devils mostly unseen but navigating the world in their own patient way. Like Thorne and his mind slowly waking, slowly swirling, encompassing new things into his life.

Chapter Fourteen

Kris

A brush of fingertips. That's all it was when Thorne handed me back my tablet. But it stirred something inside me. Heat. Warmth. Contact. And a weird deep hollowness that undulated like some insidious disease.

"But what if--" I started to say.

"Trust me when I say that IP cannot be tracked back here."

Trust him. Of course I didn't. Even if his house was immaculate and his pine-filled backyard swelled with the beautiful music of otherworldly silences. Even if he was careful and controlled and smart and gorgeous. No. I didn't trust him.

Dangerous Alpha.

But those slightly rough fingertips against my palm… An itch began inside me I couldn't scratch.

I hadn't even been here a full day and yet a big part of me wanted to trust him. Wanted to be near him at all times. As if it wasn't Thorne that was unsafe, but the whole wide world around us.

I was still in shock, I decided. Not thinking right.

Yet during the afternoon, I followed him from room to room, and when I realized what I was doing, I went to my own room to get away. To calm myself.

It was quiet and pretty in there, the walls painted pale lavender, the bed heaped with worn pillows. They were pale and shabby but very soft, like they had belonged to someone a long, long time ago. I had the thought they might have been his Omega mate's pillows, and Thorne had not had the strength to toss them.

The curtains were white, but the valances were a lacy dark green, which actually looked pretty against the pale purple walls.

I hopped on the bed and leaned back. I needed to stay clear-headed. I needed to learn more about his home and his situation before I could allow myself to relax and accept that I could stay here for a while and plan my future path.

I tried to take a nap but couldn't sleep.

When I got up, Thorne had finished fixing my tablet for me so I could spy on my brothers' messages to each other.

I couldn't have been more thankful.

I immediately found that Mathias had messaged Trigg earlier in the day.

At hospital. Father is in the Burn. They've given him medication to relax him.
This afternoon he'll be released and I'll take him to his favorite: Zilly's Farm.

Trigg had replied.

Father just had his Burn a month ago. What's going on? Do they know?

Mathias:

Triggered by stress. By Kris.

Trigg:

By Kris? How? He's not even a true Omega.

Mathias:

You haven't been around him since Father locked him away and he turned eighteen. It's weird. So weird. He stinks.

Trigg:

Like what?

Mathias:

Like burnt honey or something. But it's also sweet. Maybe you will understand after your first Burn, but he almost smelled like a fucking bitch Omega ready and waiting to take it up the ass.

Trigg:

You're so rude.

Mathias:

Not kidding, dude. My cock was hard just being around him. He's dangerous. I wanted to do things...

Trigg:

To your own brother? Mathias!

Mathias:

I thought I was having another Burn. Maybe it was a good thing we have him here. He's nobody now, a non-person. He could be kept around to be used as we need him.

Trigg:

Such a jerk! Cutting you off now...

But later, I saw more messages between them.

Trigg:

Mathias! Did you leave Kris's door unlocked.

Mathias:

Uh, no way, dude.

Trigg:

I found the door unlocked. I can't find him!

Mathias:

Don't tell anyone! After I drop Father at the farm, I'm coming straight home!

So they'd finally found out I wasn't there. I looked at the time stamp. That last barrage of messages was only an hour old. Took them long enough to discover I was gone.

I got up from my bed and went to find Thorne. He was in the kitchen by the oven. It was on and something inside smelled delicious.

His head turned and his dark eyes seemed to see right through me. "Have a good nap?"

"No." I waved my tablet. "I just spied on my brothers. They only found out I was missing an hour ago. And Father is in the Burn."

Thorne's eyebrows came together as a sheen passed over his gaze. "So no one missed you all day."

"No. And the servants, if they noticed anything, would report to Mathias. They're loyal to Father, so they won't say anything without his permission."

"I'm sorry."

"For what? Father wouldn't let my brothers near me these past couple months. It makes sense they wouldn't notice or care about me." My stomach churned. I might have felt a little disappointed that they didn't notice I was gone, but more I was mad. At them for being so shallow. At myself for never having seen it clearly until now. If I never saw my family again it would be too soon.

"They must care about you, they're… your litter-mates."

"I thought so. Trigg maybe does. And my little brothers always looked up to me. I haven't seen them in weeks, not since before I was locked away. I probably will never see them again."

Thorne sighed. "It's been only a day. Not all problems get solved in such short a time."

Frustrated, I took a seat on a stool by the kitchen's island. "I should tell you because you deserve to know. This problem won't be solved in a day, a year or forever. So I'm not looking for solutions."

"All right. I'm not offering any."

At his flat tone, I jerked my head forward and up, but he'd turned away to fiddle with something on the stove. Was he annoyed with me?

My pulse jumped. I hadn't told him everything. It was none of his business, really. But then again, it was. Thorne was putting himself on the line to help me. Even if he thought it was nothing, that no one would ever know, or trace my new IP to here, he was still taking a risk. Vandergales were powerful. No one stood up to us and won. Ever.

I put my elbows on the countertop and rested my head in my hands. I was determined to begin whether he wanted to hear me or not. He deserved to know the truth.

"A week before my eighteenth birthday." I kept my voice low, my eyes averted toward the countertop between my elbows. "Father called in the doctor for our six month check ups. I hated it. Every time. I hated it." I paused to keep myself from giving away any emotion. "But I wasn't afraid. I felt fine. Healthy. Ready for my final maturity. My first Burn."

Maybe I didn't show it, but all the words caught in my throat at that word. Burn. It had always been something to look forward to in the past. A rite of passage so to speak. But now it seemed like something dirty to me. Something awful and wrong. Something I might never experience except on the other end of things, like an Omega.

I could not suppress the shudder that undulated through my body from shoulders to toes.

Forcing myself to dissociate from that, I continued. "The doctor examined me and found something—something inside me. Hidden all this time. Dormant. Atrophied. Omega organs. Useless, but still there. Those organs redefined me to him, to Father, to myself. Staining me forever."

Thorne did not look at me, but he stood motionless, facing the stove, focused and listening.

I swallowed against a dry throat and continued.

"I'd always been raised to be the perfect Alpha. In my mind I still was. And on the outside, I was perfect. Everything Father could be proud of. I stayed in shape. I got good grades. Nothing had changed in that way. And yet everything changed when the doctor diagnosed me. Even Father's money could not hide this, I was told.

If they surgically remove the organs I would still be marked. If Father paid the doctor off never to file his report on the results of my exam, it wouldn't work, they said. When I turned eighteen my differences would show up in odd ways. I didn't know this until I researched it for myself. The doctor was an asshole and no help to me. He seemed more concerned for Father to have to go through this."

I let out a loud breath. It sounded like a groan.

"It is a lot for an eighteen year old to suddenly be saddled with." Thorne's quiet voice stroked its way through me. Strangely calming.

"Anyway, I looked it up. The scent is one of things that is a giveaway. I would not produce an Alpha scent to the world. I might or might not experience a Burn. With people like me, it's fifty-fifty. And my looks would change a little. I'd grow softer, not harder, no matter how much I exercised or how much muscle I put on. It's the hormones, you know. Also, people like me? We are usually solitary. We don't seek mates because we aren't full Omegas. We don't have the natural Omega instinct to—um—how to put it—to bottom, or to procreate."

I glanced out the corner of my eye to see if Thorne had any reaction. He stood over the stove, his hands clutching two hot pads, his head bowed.

I cleared my throat. "So that's it. That's my story. Father locked me away. Then he tried to—well, he attacked me because of the Burn. And Mathias, my brother, is an asshole, which I can see much clearer now than ever. He blamed me for Father's attack on me. I knew I had to get out. If I wasn't safe there, Father would have me sold to a farm, or have me institutionalized."

Still no response from Thorne.

"That's my story."

Silence.

"Well?"

Thorne turned from the stove and looked at me. As he started to reach for me, I immediately glanced down again at the countertop, swaying away from him.

"It must have been terrible for you," he said. He grabbed a cloth and began wiping down the top of the stove.

"It was. It is." My chest felt tight. My eyes hurt.

"It's interesting, though."

"Interesting?"

"Fascinating, actually. I don't mean to insult you, but I was thinking that you may have been hasty deciding something you read online defines you solely and fully. That you are doomed to never mate. That you are alien to this world."

"But I am!"

"Because of some paragraph on some random website?"

"No. Because of what I told you. And my Omega designation, even though I'm not one. Even though I'm infertile."

"Who says you're infertile?"

"My internal organs are undeveloped. So there's that."

"You could sire children with a pure Omega, though. So that's an untruth right there, that you're infertile."

Frustrated, though he spoke the truth, I shot back, "You know what I meant!"

He didn't answer.

"I didn't mean to yell."

"You've faced a lot in the past few weeks. I'd yell, too."

His weirdly calm tone immediately made most of the tension drain from my body.

"Thank you for that," I said. My eyes were stinging again.

At least he didn't think of me like Father and Doctor Poe and Mathias, like some useless thing and a burden to the family.

Thorne surprised me by setting down his rag and walking over to me. He leaned against the counter about a foot and a half away and said, "I can't imagine what you've been through—what you're still going through. It's a terrible thing. Now all I want to do after you telling me all this is help you even more. I'm not sure you believe me, but it's the truth. I'll help you any way I can. And as a start, how about we dispense with our unwanted labels for the time-being and have a good dinner?"

I blinked back tears of relief, hoping he didn't see. "That sounds good."

"And Kris." Thorne added. "Don't define yourself by what you read in the cold context of online know-it-all websites. When you're like me, away from the world for a couple of decades, you start to see the bullshit all the more clearer. Sure, there are stupid laws in place making everything worse, and people suffer for it. But who you are inside? No one can touch that."

His words were like balm to open wounds. "Thank you for that. It helps."

"Ah, if only I ruled the world, right?"

He was making a joke? Trying to get me to laugh?

I wasn't ready. Somehow, he knew it. He turned away as if he did not expect any response, and said, "Baked chicken, mashed potatoes, green beans. How does that sound?"

"Sounds wonderful." I cleared my throat.

"Excellent. It will be our first meal as the new rulers of our own little world."

Chapter Fifteen

Thorne

Here I am practically insisting he trust me when I can't even trust myself, Thorne thought.

They ate at the dining table by the kitchen window and watched the sun bruise the sky as it set against the snowy mountain peaks.

Despite his major problems and anxieties, Kris maintained a good appetite. Thorne found he liked feeding him. Liked seeing another person other than himself eat his cooking for a change.

Kris was quiet at dinner. After his long speech full of secret revelations, he was probably exhausted which was completely understandable and fine by Thorne. It had taken a lot for Kris to tell him so much so soon.

Thorne was no stranger to the quiet. Their rapport, even when not talking, felt natural. Maybe it was the attraction he felt toward the young man. At any rate, he was glad for the company.

Kris got up from the table when they finished.

"I'd like to help. Do the dishes or something."

"All right."

Kris picked up his plate and Thorne's. "What do I do?"

Thorne chuckled. "Have you ever done dishes before?" he asked, already knowing the answer.

"Not really. I had a small kitchen in my locked rooms, but a servant cleaned it every day."

"Well, it's pretty easy since I have a dishwasher. Bring them over to the sink."

"Okay." Kris helped clear the table, then stood at the sink looking down.

"We'll rinse them first and I'll show you how I load them in the washer."

For a spoiled rich kid who probably had his meals served to him on golden platters and thinking food came like magic from the air, Kris never complained. He didn't do a great job getting the dishes rinsed, but Thorne was not one to criticize.

After the kitchen was clean, Thorne said, "What do you like? TV? Movies? To be left alone?"

For a moment, Kris looked confused. He said, "You don't have to entertain me."

Thorne shrugged off an urge to lightly smack his upper arm. "I've been alone for years. Sure I've been to town a couple times a week, but I don't normally have guests in my home. It will be a treat to watch a movie with someone else in the room. Strange, but a treat."

Kris looked skeptical. "Okay. A movie, then. I don't care what."

Thorne brought up something on a subscription channel, got them a couple of beers and plopped himself on the couch.

Kris looked at the bottles. "I've never had beer before."

"What?" Thorne grinned. "Well, you'll probably hate your first. But you get used to it after that."

For some reason, that didn't sound right to his ears, how the words came out, their double meaning. But he ignored the flush that grew against his cheeks.

Kris popped off the cap and drank. He did not make a face, but he didn't smile, either. Well, in fairness, he'd not done any smiling since he'd arrived.

During the course of the movie, Kris drank the entire beer and did not comment. But Thorne could tell he was perplexed by the taste of the drink.

By the time the credits rolled, Kris's eyelids drooped.

Thorne said, "You can stay. Watch whatever you want. I know it's early, but I'm turning in."

He wasn't tired, but he'd read a book. He needed to do something to distract himself from the distraction of Kris. And it was Kris who needed rest. But he wasn't going to order him to it.

Kris blinked. "Oh yeah. I think I will, too. Thank you for dinner."

"You're welcome. Have a good night."

Once Thorne was in bed, tablet in hand, he grew instantly restless. He couldn't stop thinking about Kris. He liked Kris, and it was good to have him here. And it wasn't good.

In his mind, he listed the good things first.

One: He'd been lonely so company was a nice change.

Two: Whether the boy would admit it or not, Kris needed his help. Thorne had promised himself twenty-five years ago he'd never be responsible for seeing harm come to another, and though Kris's dilemma was not his fault, he'd be contributing to another's downfall if he did not at least try to assist him.

Three: The boy in the window. That image had haunted him. Now he had a name and a face to put to the image. That made him smile.

Four: Kris's presence gave him pleasure.

Which now led him to his list of the not-so-good reasons why he couldn't stop thinking about Kris.

One: Kris's presence gave him pleasure. Nothing wrong with that. A companion for a meal and a movie. Someone who desperately needed help. It felt good to be able to provide that help. But those pleasures weren't the problem. It was another secondary pleasure he hated to admit even to himself. Attraction. Racing pulse. Arousal. The scent of Kris alone might be the cause, but combined with Kris's unselfconscious beauty, and his desperate situation, Thorne could not help but respond. There was danger there. To both of them. Not good.

Two: If, and that was a big *if*, they were ever discovered, the Vandergale wrath was nothing to lightly dismiss.

Three: Kris had not yet entered his first Burn. He had been eighteen for many weeks now. Maybe due to his rare condition the Burn would bypass him, but Thorne could not count on that. It would be stupid not to make advance preparations. Just in case.

Four: If Kris's presence had disturbed the cycles of his father and brother, Thorne should not assume he was immune. Already he felt odd arousals and proprietary affection for the young man, things he had never experienced between Burn cycles except for his mate Ian. He needed to prepare for the chance that Kris might trigger an early, unexpected Burn in him.

Thorne knew how to handle his own Burns. He'd been doing it unassisted for what seemed like forever. It was number three that had him rattled. If Kris entered his own first Burn here, Thorne would have to help him deal with it by either drugging him, which went against all his tenets and ethics, giving him toys, or providing an Omega for him.

This was something they really needed to discuss. Because of Kris's anxieties and moods, Thorne dreaded it.

He fell asleep mulling the problem over and over in his mind.

Later, he would add number five to his not-so-good reasons for being unable to stop thinking about Kris.

Five: He dreamed of him.

*

In the whispering distances of a glacial void, he sat by a hearth looking down at himself, icy and wet wearing nothing but his robe. At the same time the firelight danced merrily over his skin. It burned.

Huddled on the stone at his feet, stunned and with his fine clothing torn along his back and his hips, Kris lay at Thorne's feet, eyes closed and mouth gasping for air. He shivered. His arms wrapped tightly about his waist and he rocked back and forth, his knees drawn up.

Thorne reached out. "Kris." His palms touched fire. Coal-hot searing pain swept through him, making him jerk back. But he knew if he didn't touch him, Kris would die. Kris would end up like Ian beneath an old oak in a plot six feet underground.

He grabbed for him again. Pain from Kris's burning body caused the void and the fire and the hearth to spin. He yelled until the echoes creased the blackness around them, and pulled Kris up into his arms. Thorne's own skin blackened but he would not let go.

Kris's clothing turned to ash and fluttered from his golden body. He lay in Thorne's arms, the boy in the window, a dream pieta, head lolling back, blond hair dangling everywhere.

He was the stuff of dreams for sure, the golden boy that did not really exist. His arms were raised over his head, the muscles round and hard. His cock lay against his stomach, pink, beautiful, stiff. The tip was as red as the roses in Thorne's front yard.

Kris's knees bent. His legs spread. Beneath his tight ball sack the globes of his buttocks spread just enough to see the pale gold aperture that led into his body, hairless, clenching and unclenching in need.

Thorne cried out again. "Kris!"

Everything blurred. Gone was the hearth and the fire. Gone the void. Gone the pain. When he glanced down again, his arms embraced emptiness.

*

Thorne woke to the taste of salt in his mouth and the acrid scent of his own sweat. His cock throbbed hard against his abdomen. He sat up, immediately assessing the rest of his body, and especially his mind.

The loss of control he felt during a Burn was missing. He wasn't paralyzed by raging lust. His mind seemed clear. Tension ebbed. His muscles relaxed as he took deep breaths. Brushing over the base of his cock he felt no impending knot.

This wasn't the Burn.

It was just a dream.

But hell and damn what a dream!

He got out of his bed and into the cold midnight air, naked, and padded to the bathroom. His skin prickled. His cock didn't like this one bit and threatened to deflate. But the images and sensations of the dream were still strong. The appendage bobbed demandingly.

Thorne turned on the shower until it steamed and stepped under the hot flow of water.

He put his whole head under the warm spray, eyes shut tight. But he could still see the flexing hole, the beautiful penis, the flaxen locks, the tall and shining body in his arms.

Happy to be under a warm fall of liquid, Thorne's cock throbbed and reached outward for assistance to further its pleasure.

Eyes still closed, Thorne touched himself, first cupping his balls, then curving his thumb and forefinger around the base of his cock and milking upward. He thrust into his hand and came in seconds, his seed spilling into the drain, the shower filling with more heat and steam.

The orgasm coursed deep and hard, as if to leave scars on his already scarred psyche. But the whiteness in his mind that accompanied it was agonizingly good, and the afterglow a sought after peace that men always hunted but could not contain.

As if to thank him, his cock relaxed until it dangled limp between his legs. Sleeping.

Frowning at himself, and wondering when he had started to think of his own dick as a separate intelligence—no, not intelligent but a thing comprised pleasure and need—Thorne stepped from the shower and quickly dried off.

Back in bed, he curled under the blankets and brought a pillow tight to his chest.

The dream images had ebbed a little, but not enough. It took him a long time to fall back to sleep.

Chapter Sixteen

Kris

I heard Thorne get up in the middle of the night and turn on the shower. I managed to sleep some, but had awakened from a weird dream I could not recall. I was on my back under thick blankets when I heard the footsteps above me and the pipes in the walls hum.

I grabbed a pillow and put it over my head to try to blind myself from imagining my dangerous Alpha neighbor naked, stepping into the hot water, and all that black hair streaming wet around his head.

Of course, I hadn't ever seen him naked, but I have a great imagination, damn it. And pillows don't block images in the mind.

I still wasn't sure what to make of Thorne. I had told him my story, but he remained vague about his own past, and his story about losing his Omega mate. All I had to go on was rumor.

Instinct told me whatever had happened, Thorne could not have done anything intentionally. He was too caring. Too controlled. And he honored life.

After the speech he'd given me over dinner about not defining yourself by your label, I knew he was not one of those cocky Alphas who thought they owned all Omegas as if they were slaves. He wouldn't have hurt anyone if he could have helped it. That made me wonder all the more how his Omega mate actually died.

How could I have lived down the road from him my whole life and never even been half-curious? Or wanted to get to know a neighbor who lived so close by?

It was an impossible scenario all the way around. Father liked to remain undisturbed in his work and the raising of his perfect Alpha sons. And Thorne chose isolation. Never the two shall meet.

Exhausted from the last couple of days, I turned onto my side and curled up, willing myself to sleep. It was hard not to think of

Thorne above me in his own room trying to go back to sleep as well after a midnight shower. Hard not to feel his presence in every breath I took, in the walls of the room and the sheets and blankets and worn pillows that surrounded me. Everything here was Thorne's. Everything was marked by him invisibly by virtue of being in his home.

I fell asleep with one thought: *Was I marked now too?*

*

Days passed in slow, quiet succession. The snow stayed on the ground though the weather cleared. The temperatures remained low.

I kept to myself, but Thorne and I ate together. He cooked. I helped him with small chores around the house.

We took more walks in the backyard but never went far.

One day, alone, I came around from back to the front yard, which I mostly avoided unless there were trees to block me from view of Father's house, and saw the slight bit of snow-melt over the last few days had revealed a headstone under a huge Live Oak. The name read *Ian*.

I had not known Thorne kept his Omega mate's body and had it interred in his front yard. I couldn't stop staring at it, immune to the cold as it seeped through my coat and sweater and into my bones.

After awhile, I heard the front door open and footsteps on the porch.

"I see you found Ian."

I turned to see Thorne standing at the top of the porch steps. He was all in shadow except for his chin and nose. He looked angry but I knew he wasn't.

"I'm sorry."

His head tilted until I saw his eyes, soft at the edges, lids downcast, the moisture within glimmering.

The pit of my stomach widened. A weight settled. This was wrong. All wrong. Ian should be here with Thorne. They should both be standing on that porch together smiling down at me, happy neighbors sharing happy times. This grim grave should not exist.

"Come in out of the cold," Thorne said. "I have a fire going."

Without waiting for my response, he turned and went back into the house.

I stayed behind a few more minutes.

"Ian," I said to the air. Nothing more.

*

It was difficult at first to meet Thorne's eyes, to look at him, though I found myself staring all the time. I was used to beautiful Alphas. My brothers were quite handsome, though Mathias was sharper and cruder than the others. But Thorne was no child like they were. And he wasn't old like Father. He was mature and refined and elegant. He had a control about him, and an intelligence that drew me as much as his physique and darker coloring.

It was hard to look at him because every time I did something inside me jolted with a strange need. It made me feel like a stupid child. Like I couldn't control my body or my thoughts.

Whenever I did look at him, I caught myself staring. Sometimes he caught me staring. Then my face would flush hard and fast, and I'd look away, or rush from the room.

At night I'd hear his footsteps creaking above me and he'd enter my dreams, vague scenarios with Thorne always surrounding me, his presence, his energy, his warmth. Voices echoed in my dreams. I couldn't make them out. Except in one dream I heard my name called and a distinct sentence.

Kris, you're safe with me.

Dreams. They fed fantasies and lies. Thorne, no matter how he had gotten the designation, was labeled a dangerous Alpha. How could I know I was entirely safe?

Thorne still hadn't told me the details of Ian's death. Though well-mannered as Father had taught me, I still wanted to pry. I kept telling myself it wasn't my business. But it was. I lived here now. I needed to know I was not in more danger than I had been if I'd remained at home.

On my sixth day as a guest in Thorne's home, I was scrolling every news feed I could find for the Vandergale name and scandals. I'd found nothing so far.

Still tracking my brothers' messages, I figured out they had not told anyone outside the household that I was gone. Father's messages, after he returned home from taking care of his Burn, consisted of business as usual, and hiring private detectives to search for me.

There were two by the name of Scard and Toley. I kept track of them as well.

I had been worried those first days that my tracks in the snow leading to Thorne's shed would be found. Thorne said he'd already taken care of it. The man thought of everything. Plus, he'd gone to town for supplies on my third day here, and had done a bit of shoveling to get out. His tire tracks from his truck combined with the shoveling showed nothing out of the ordinary.

But today Thorne came to me, a strange look on his face.

"I got an odd message today."

I looked up from my position on his couch. "What?"

"A man named Scard. Does the name sound familiar?"

I nodded. "One of Father's private dicks."

"Well, he does ask about you specifically, saying you are missing from the neighborhood and your father is looking for you."

"Did you answer?" I knew he would have to answer in order to deflect any suspicion from himself.

"I told him I'd never had interaction with any Vandergales, though they are neighbors of mine." His smile showed white teeth, and lit up his whole face.

"Good."

"But he wouldn't let it go, and he sent another message saying he had researched me and found out my designation as dangerous."

Thorne sat on the couch by my side. My insides fluttered but I ignored it. I hadn't been feeling well all day. A stomach upset. So I ignored it.

"He outright asked me if I preyed on runaway Omegas."

Immediately, I was angry. But Thorne still smiled. "What do you think I should say?"

"The truth." I paused, still horrified that some stranger would ask such a rude question of a man who'd only showed me kind assistance. "Well, the half-truth, that is. You haven't told me details of why you have the designation, but I can see you're no predator. Tell him that truth."

Thorne leaned back into the cushions and stared upward.

"It's an insult to you," I continued. I had the strange impulse fantasy that if the man Scard was standing before me right now, I'd punch him in the jaw. Hard.

"Maybe."

"But it is insulting. He doesn't even know you." I leaned back into the couch, mirroring his posture. My head spun. I hadn't eaten much today.

"Do you?"

"Do I what?"

"Even know me?"

"I—don't. Yet. But I am getting to. You're an honorable man."

Thorne said something but his voice rumbled and I didn't catch the words.

"What?"

"Kris, can you hear me?"

"Of course I can hear you," I replied. I turned my head and saw him watching me with scintillating dark eyes. Those eyes, so deeply brown I wanted to sink into them, into that steady, strong gaze, and float. Just float. And not have to worry about hired men searching for me, or Father's seeming lack of concern in any of his private messages I had spied on.

It hurt. It all hurt. My diagnosis. My family's response to it. My entire identity stolen away. My future dissolved to nothing.

Over the past days, that pain did not decrease, though Thorne did everything he could to make me feel welcome and at home here.

But today my mood and my stomach made it my worst day so far.

Thorne continued to watch me and my body liked the attention but tensed at the same time. The blood rushed in my ears like the sound of a nearby ocean.

"I asked if you are feeling unwell." Thorne's voice came into my brain like an echo.

"I'm fine. I just feel a little stomach upset."

I saw Thorne through a blurry gaze get up and walk into the kitchen. The air felt cold, then warm.

I heard footsteps first, and saw him return. He held out his hand and a bottle of water. "Aspirin," he said.

"I'm fine, but thanks for these." I took the pills and swallowed them. The water went down cool and clean against my parched throat.

"I'm worried about you," he said.

My mind cleared a little as I processed his words. "Why?"

"You're flushed."

"Well, you have a fire going and the heat on. It's maybe a bit hot in here." I stared at the leaping flames in the hearth and felt the needlelike touches as my skin broke out in a sweat.

"The heat is off."

But it was so hot. I glanced at him, frowning.

Thorne reached out and placed the back of his hand against my forehead. I started to jerk back but his skin was so cool against my own that I forced myself to relax just to feel it for a few seconds longer. Heaven!

"What other symptoms do you have?" he asked. His voice was like a whisper all around me.

"I don't know. I'm just mad at Father, you know? I can see no indication that he cares. He simply wants me back under his roof, under his control."

"Some see anyone that holds other than Alpha status as a lesser being, inferior." Thorne's voice calmed me. The tone was like music, resonating in my ears like a grounding, comforting force.

Thorne continued. "Or they are embarrassed by Omegas, by their out of control Alpha need for them. It is of note that your father never had a mate, never bonded."

"I wondered." My throat felt dry and I drank more water. "I never had the courage to ask him."

"Hmm."

The sound he made vibrated my whole being. I turned to look at him and he had a lavender light surrounding him. It was a play of the firelight, but still it looked beautiful.

"Do you think that's it? I'm just a fucking embarrassment?"

"You will drive yourself mad if you ask questions like that."

"I think it's true. Father taught us Omegas are nothing but breeders. They live to breed. Like stock on a farm. Don't most Alphas think that way? Isn't that why the compounds that house Omegas are called farms?"

"Yes. It's true. It is an unkind world to the other half of our population. The expectations of Omegas to be unintelligent and weak and need Alpha guidance, the jokes at their expense, their lack of protection under the law if they are abused. But not all Alphas think that way. You were raised one way, but I was raised another. There are others like me."

"Tell me about how you were raised."

"I had two parents, one Alpha, one Omega."

"You knew your birth-Omega?"

"Yes. He was wonderful. As was my Alpha father. Both my fathers loved me and taught me about acceptance and love."

I could barely fathom it. At times, when I was little, I had fantasized about having two parents, about knowing my Omega birth-dad. But I told no one because the way Father, my brothers and my private tutors talked about Omegas it was better our way, and no loss not to have one around disturbing our perfect lives, tantalizing us, interfering with Alpha rule and Alpha behavior.

"Your Omega father… what was he like?"

"Very loving. Attentive. Intelligent."

I must have reacted in some way I wasn't aware of, because Thorne said, "Does that surprise you?"

I shrugged.

"It's a crime that you've never met an Omega."

"I have. Or, rather, I've seen them in town when Father or our servants took us shopping. With their Alpha mates. But that's it. I never thought it through any further until now." I must have sounded like an ass.

"Well, that's not the same as meeting one."

"I guess I figured I'd meet one when I needed to."

Thorne nodded. "Most Alphas are taught that if they aren't raised by both parents. The Omega serves one need only, to service an Alpha through the Burn."

"And that's how they're also taught on the farms so they don't know any better, either?"

"Unfortunately, yes. They are taught how to make an Alpha happy and whole, how to defer to him, how to serve him in every way if they are chosen for the mate-bond."

"Where are your parents now?" I asked.

"My dad, my Omega father, contracted a rare infection. I was twenty-one. It was before I met my Omega mate. My dad was in the hospital for a long time, weeks. He didn't get better. He fell into a coma and died a few weeks after that. My Alpha father was so distraught. The breaking of their bond weakened him. Two years later he died of natural causes. Both were in their 70s and should have had much longer lives."

"I'm sorry."

"Well, it happens. I met Ian soon after my Omega dad's death. I had four good years with him. But only four. That's nothing in our life-spans."

I wanted so badly to ask the details of Ian's death. I waited for Thorne to be forthcoming. He was not.

"Well, life sucks. The whole thing isn't fair." I slumped down on the cushions. It felt like the flames of the fire grew larger, whipping about the room. "Whoa." The word escaped my mouth as I tried to straighten.

"What?"

"Didn't you see that? The fire just blew up, sparking out to almost the end of the table."

Thorne was silent, his gaze on the hearth.

"Tell me you saw it. Like something in the air ignited it, stretching out the flames."

"Kris, you are a little feverish, I think. Other than the stomach upset, do you feel all right?"

I swallowed against the dryness in my throat. The roar in my ears was still there. And Thorne still had a pale purple aura. All over my skin prickled with sweat. I became very aware of my cock, like a heavy weight between my legs.

"Just a touch of flu." But I had never had the flu. What was I saying? I knew deep down I didn't want what I was truly thinking—and maybe Thorne was thinking it, too—to be true. So I behaved as if my hoped for outcome was real. I denied.

"I think maybe an early bedtime, then." He spoke softly, the cadence like a stroke of reassurance. "I'll make some tea and bring it in to you."

Again I swallowed against a too-dry throat. "That sounds wonderful. With honey, please."

He smiled indulgently. Then said, "Go on."

I got up and felt a lot better when I walked away from the hearth and into the cooler air of the hallway. So refreshing. I pulled my sweater over my head to allow the air to absorb into my hot skin. My hair fanned about my shoulders, sticking to my skin wherever it fell. I hadn't braided it today, so I had to reach back and gather it up, holding it to my head with one hand. Colder air pressed under my arms, feeling almost too good.

I leaned into my door, which stood open, and pressed my damp forehead to the wood.

I thought of Thorne in the kitchen making the tea, getting out the honey. Flames caressed the edges of my vision. I realized I should have asked for iced tea. And another glass of ice just to pour over my skin.

A cold shower. That was what I needed. I'd do that as soon as Thorne brought the tea and left.

I entered my room and tossed my sweater onto the seat of a chair. My pack sat, half-opened, on the top of a wooden dresser. I had not completely unpacked it because I felt nervous thinking I might stay here longer than a couple of weeks. What if things didn't work out? What if Thorne turned out to really be a monster who had killed his Omega mate?

I'd brought the contents of my coat pockets into the room and hidden them in the top drawer underneath some t-shirts. I had cash and jewelry. It was worth quite a bit, though maybe not to someone like Father. But to me, who had nothing, it was enough to see me moderately fed, clothed and sheltered for several years if I was on my own.

I sat on the edge of my bed and kicked off my shoes. Thorne had loaned me a robe but I couldn't see it anywhere. Still hot, I didn't want to put it on, but Thorne was coming. It was only polite.

I leaned down and felt for it under the bed. I wasn't usually such a slob, but maybe it had fallen.

Nothing.

As I pushed myself up into a sitting position, I heard a creak at my door.

Thorne stood at the threshold with two mugs in hand, the steam rising to fill the air with tiny dots of moisture. I could see those tiny dots clearly, reflecting the light of my room in a rainbow spectrum.

"May I come in?" Thorne asked.

He looked like a savior of perfection right out of my more private fantasies, his hair mussed a bit at the forehead, his trim figure all in black and silhouetted against the hall light. Pantherish.

I nodded, unable to find my tongue for a moment let alone my voice. I was bare-chested and still sweating and slightly embarrassed.

He stepped toward me and handed me one of the mugs. I made myself focus on the hot liquid, blowing on the surface.

"A good night's sleep will probably do you well."

I could only nod, not speak.

"Well, then, good night."

He moved back toward the door and asked, "Do you prefer it open or closed?"

I had been too long behind locked doors. "Open," I croaked out.

Thorne's footsteps receded down the hall. My body lurched as if it wanted to get up on its own and chase him down. The urge was unique to me, and worried my mind.

I couldn't stop a tremble of fear that ran through me. The Burn. I might never experience it, some texts said. But what if I did? What if I was on the edges of it right now?

"It's the flu," I said aloud to the empty room. "It's the flu."

Over and over I convinced myself of my own personal diagnosis by stating it aloud.

I drank about half my tea before I got up and went into the bathroom. I turned the shower on cold, shucked my trousers and stepped into icy water-flow.

My body nearly convulsed at the sudden cold. But at the same time it calmed me. The water hit my genitals and my cock instantly shriveled.

As I cooled down, I gradually turned up the warm water and washed myself thoroughly, including my hair.

By the time I stepped out, I felt almost normal. My stomach had relaxed. My muscles unclenched.

I dried my hair, combed it out, and then padded naked to my bed through the cold air and got in under the thick blankets.

Everything seemed better. Normal. Fine. The sheets were soft against my skin, and smelled faintly of floral detergent. I fell quickly to sleep.

Chapter Seventeen

Thorne

Thorne was reluctant to leave Kris alone. He had been under the weather all day. Now his symptoms resembled that of an Alpha's first Burn.

Kris was already confused and traumatized by his discovery that he wasn't a pure Alpha. This, on top of living in a new place and experiencing the Burn as a virgin, would make matters far worse for him.

Thorne had secretly researched Kris's condition. More than half the boys with his medical anomaly did not ever experience the Burn. He had hoped for Kris's sake it would never happen. But if it did, Thorne had already thought of various options to help him.

He could phone for an Omega house call, something he'd never done for himself in twenty-five years. Or he could let Kris make his way through it blind, supplying him with lube and toys to at least make him comfortable.

The other option, one he craved but dared not hope for, was to be allowed to see Kris through the Burn himself. As an Alpha, he was fearful of bottoming for anyone, and had never fantasized about doing it. But he could help Kris in other ways. Many other ways.

He climbed into bed hoping he'd been wrong with his instincts about Kris. He heard the shower go on. Maybe that was all Kris needed to relax himself, and to assuage a fever from a simple case of the flu.

As Thorne lay in bed staring up through the darkness at his shadowed ceiling, he heard the shower go off. Kris would be in his own bed now, probably exhausted, curling up under the covers to fall to sleep.

He'd be naked and Thorne tried very hard not to think about that for he'd already seen too much tonight-- Kris nude from the waist up as he accepted the tea Thorne had made. Kris's perfect body gleaming with fever, flushed and sweet-scented. The honey and wild-flower scent of him. The beauty of his body, his features, his cascades of tawny hair. It might drive Thorne crazy if he let it.

He shook his head. "Enough!" he told himself. It would do no good to develop this attraction. No matter how he was labeled, Kris was an Alpha. Since he'd found out he wasn't pure, he knew better than to trust any Alpha. He'd still be attracted to Omegas, not Alphas.

Kris was an anomaly, and one he must accept he could never have.

He turned onto his side but it was difficult to fall asleep. His worry for Kris would not leave him alone.

Tossing and turning for an hour, he finally switched on his light, grabbed his tablet and began to read. At least reading took his mind off the boy downstairs. He relaxed against his pillows and focused on the story at hand which had nothing to do with halfling Alphas or runaways or first time Burns.

After about an hour, Thorne's eyelids drooped. His tablet, still glowing its white light into the room, fell against his thigh as dropped off to sleep.

It seemed only a short time later that a noise woke him.

Thorne sat up, listening.

The house was so quiet that any crack or creak would amplify its sound.

After a minute of silence, he heard a rustling from downstairs followed by a quick groan. If Kris was just having a nightmare, he didn't want to disturb him. At the same time, he knew this was only wishful thinking on his part. This might be a nightmare for him, but not the kind that haunted you in your sleep.

After another half a minute, he heard a person say, "Fuck!" A loud crash followed, then another, "Fuck!"

Thorne jumped up, threw on his robe, and sprinted down the stairs taking two at a time.

The voice from the guest room continued to curse.

Everything on the first floor remained in darkness. Thorne turned on the hall light and the shadows scattered. The white walls and brown wood floor came into view and only the corners still held any edge of dark.

He approached the open guest room door where light flowed in making the objects within take on sepia tone. But everything was visible including the over-turned table and lamp, the bed, and Kris flopped back on the edge of the mattress naked and aroused, skin glimmering, chest heaving.

In that moment, all Thorne's fears and dreams coalesced. The Burn. It was happening to Kris for the first time. And he was under Thorne's care.

Already he felt his cock hardening at the sight of Kris. Even though Kris was an Alpha going through an Alpha cycle, the boy was part Omega and the scent of him was like nothing Thorne had ever breathed.

He ignored his own excitement. He wasn't the one who needed help. It was Kris who was going to need help. And not as an Omega, but as an Alpha.

Chapter Eighteen

Kris

I woke clawing at the covers, shoving them down my hot body. The sheet stuck to me, I was so wet.

I sat up in the darkness forgetting for a moment where I was. My mind was trying to make out the faint outlines of my window and bathroom door as if I were in my bedroom in the mansion. But nothing seemed right. The darkness prowled about me, unfamiliar and menacing.

I pushed the blankets to my feet and the cold air hit me. It helped a little, but it wasn't enough. My lips were chapped. And I was so aroused I could barely focus.

My hands reached about in the darkness for a light, my tablet… anything familiar, but all I could feel were pillows and blankets and an empty floor.

I let out grunts and groans of frustration. I kicked at the covers at my feet, and whirled my hands about in the dark, hitting something. It fell with a crash to the hardwood floor.

Where was my lamp? My tablet?

I pushed my legs over the side of the bed but when I tried to stand I was hit with dizziness and fell back onto the mattress with a loud curse.

Something moved upstairs and I realized I wasn't alone in this strange place. Someone else was here. But my mind still would not supply the name.

"What the fuck is going on?" I said to the unfriendly dark.

My cock flopped wetly against my belly. When I touched it, I nearly came unglued. The sensitivity was amazing. Shocking.

Some thoughts came to me. I'd been sick. I'd had a stomach ache and a fever or something. The flu?

I heard more sounds in the house. I still couldn't find a light. I lay flopped on the bed and the dizziness continued, lighter than outright vertigo which I'd had once as a child from an ear infection, but still enough to make me confused and frustrated.

Suddenly something brightened the room. I winced, then squinted about, recognizing the place as the guest room where I'd been staying for the past week. The glow of light came from the hall and through my open doorway.

Memories returned. I'd said to someone only hours ago to leave the door open. Too many locked away secrets in my body, my life, and the confining walls I felt trapped within made me want air and light. If it wasn't almost winter, with snow all around, I would've had the window wide open to any breeze.

A figure appeared in the doorway.

"Kris?"

It all came tumbling back. Thorne had found me and brought me into his home as his guest. Thorne—the neighbor down the road from where I'd grown up, the solitary loner, the dangerous Alpha.

"Fuck," I replied. "Oh fuck!"

"It's all right." He kept his voice soft and entered the room. "I thought maybe last night, but now I can tell."

"What?"

"The Burn. I can smell it now."

Of course I knew. But I hadn't wanted to state it aloud. Now my pretending had come to an end.

"Fuck!"

What would happen next? I didn't know anything about my condition. I'd been trained as an Alpha, but I wasn't one. Or was I? If this was my first Burn, then did I need all an Alpha required? Would Thorne drag me to an Omega farm and leave me to rut through it?

Suddenly, I was as scared as I was suffering. Embarrassed. And so lost.

Thorne smelled like pure Alpha as he strode into the room, woodsy and leather-spiced and fiery. I breathed him in deep and my body responded.

I'd been taught I would want the sweetness of the Omegas, that their fragrance would heighten the Burn which in turn would make them respond by wanting me, by bending over for me with their bottoms already slick from their natural inner lubrication.

But Thorne's scent filled me up and drew out my hunger. I'd never known an Omega, but I knew him, and I was attracted to him. Was this even natural?

And worse, what if Thorne saw me as a mutation, something to be pitied more than anything else, someone who was a burden on society rather than deserving of love? That would mean he was helping me because he felt obligated and nothing more.

I hated that thought, especially since he was so caring, even tender toward me. But that made me even more fearful of becoming such a disappointment to him.

I startled back on the bed, my hands gripping the sheets, my knees bending, feet flailing against the side of the bed. I was naked and exposed. My cock throbbed at the exposure and my more polite self scrambled about to try to cover myself. But the blankets were gone, half-fallen off the foot of the bed.

Thorne's figure rushed toward me and I cowered back.

"Kris," he said. His voice washed over me like a caress.

My mind whirled. What would he do? I couldn't help but see Father coming at me and remember the panic of that, and what I'd had to do to him to protect myself.

Thorne had been warm and open and generous. I never wanted to hurt him.

"No." My voice squeezed from my throat. "I didn't mean for this. I'm so-sorry!"

How pathetic I sounded. Alpha training forgotten. Desperation driving me. The pull of disorder and lack of control.

"Kris, it's okay. It's a natural occurrence. All Alphas go through it."

His voice rang like bells in my ears. *All Alphas...* But I wasn't an Alpha. Not entirely.

Thorne reached out to touch my shoulder and I pulled back.

"Okay," he said calmly. "I won't touch you."

But I wanted his touch. Badly.

As if reading my mind, he asked, "What do you want? Can you sit up for a second? Can you focus?"

Again I tried to hide myself. I scooted my butt across the mattress but fell back, the sensations in my body sending me spinning.

"I can call a service. Have a ready Omega delivered."

It sounded all wrong to my brain. An Omega ready for me? But I was an Omega. Technically. I had seen how Father wanted me without a care to my own horrified feelings, and how Mathias treated me. I would be no better if I took an Omega now.

"It's what's done. It's not shameful," said Thorne.

Then why I was ashamed? Slowly, I shook my head. My right hand covered my crotch, but even the touch of my own palm was nearly unbearable, enflaming my flesh, making my cock jerk. I was terrified of coming right in front of Thorne. It seemed so horrible that it might happen, and my body flushed even more all over because another part of me wanted him to watch me, to see me.

He'd protected me so far from all I had feared, making sure I was safe. I knew his hands would be cool, and his touches encouraging, like the way he cared for his gardens, how he made one for each season and made sure they thrived.

He honored life. But what if I disgusted him?

I turned my head away from him.

"Kris, focus."

"I don't want an Omega. I can't! I just can't!"

"I'm sure you've been taught to prepare for this. You can opt to take care of yourself, as I do, but it is a more difficult road."

He was close. Too close. His breath smelled like tea with sugar. Take care of myself? I couldn't even stand!

"I don't—I don't think I can--" I let out an uneven moan. But it wasn't a moan of pain, but of pleasure so intense it took over and confused my thoughts.

"It's all right. Take deep breaths."

Thorne had been through this. Thorne was coaching me. The thought was both humiliating and evocative. But he could help and I wanted it. But did *he* want it?

"I don't want anyone else to see me like this. I don't!"

"All right." His voice soothed. "I promise. No one will see you."

My moans turned softer and caught in my throat. I was partially on my side, my face on the pillow turned away from him. The light from the hall wavered over the curtains on the window, turning them pale amber.

The trembles in my body might seem like shivers to any onlooker, but I wasn't cold. I was made of hottest flame, of the very heat-death of the universe. Red edged my vision now.

Thorne began talking to me again. He stood over the bed but he didn't touch it, or me.

"I have things that will help. Lube. Devices that can aid you."

Devices? I had been a curious teen. I knew the things he was talking about. Sex toys. They would be inhuman. Cold. Not the sort of cool relief I craved. But what choice did I have?

I gave him a reluctant nod.

Thorne's footsteps receded and already I missed him. The room opened all around me like a void, sucking me in, spitting me into nothing so that I would fall forever until I disintegrated to stardust.

I gripped the sheets harder and wished for Thorne. He would hold me up. He would keep me from falling. He'd never let go because that's the kind of person he was. Someone who held onto what he valued, and never forgot them. Never left them behind. Even Ian, who had died due to something Thorne would not reveal, was someone he wouldn't abandon. His grave in the yard was a testament to his loyalty.

Father had warned me. *Trust no Alpha.* But he meant Alphas like himself. And like the boys he raised. Myself included.

I heard footsteps return.

Thorne's soothing voice. "Can you turn? Just a little?"

Fire washed over me as I tried to prop myself on my elbow and turn my head. My cock pressed hard against my hip, pointing toward the sheet.

I blinked to clear my vision. In blurry tones of brown and gray, Thorne stood by my bed pulling things from a sack in one hand, and laying them in a row beside me on the bed.

"These are all clean and disinfected. I keep everything in good shape for when I need them every couple of months."

The lube was unopened and new.

The toys were soft and shiny and didn't look as scary as they did shameful, but I didn't like them. I didn't crave them.

"This," said Thorne, setting one device I knew was called a fleshlight beside the lube, "has new batteries. Here is the *on* switch." He picked it up again and turned it in his hand.

119

I could only see his tapered, long fingers, and the inside of his palm, not the toy as he held it. The toy did not exist for me.

"If you want anal stimulation there is this. Many Alphas don't, but some do."

The plastic penis had a soft, rounded head, and looked rubbery along the shaft. Again, I focused on Thorne's own hand, the perfectly trimmed nails, the map of bluish-green veins on his upper hand. Strong. Alpha.

I closed my eyes, not wanting to comprehend all this yet knowing I needed to. I took slow, shallow breaths.

He had a few more things. Sheaths. Vibrating rings. All things I didn't really think about, ever, or want.

Thorne named them for me in a neutral tone as if sharing sex toys with a young naked and suffering Alpha experiencing his first Burn in the guest room of his home was a normal event.

It boggled my mind.

I turned away.

"I can leave these here for you, Kris. If you think you are clear enough to use them."

"I don't want them." I could not believe how ungrateful I sounded.

"Well, you decide. But they are here for self-care."

On one shaky hand, I tried to sit up. I half-fell, then pushed hard with one arm while using the other to swipe at the toys. I shoved hard, pushing them all off the bed in one swing.

"I don't want them!"

The toys clattered to the hard floor, a hollow, sour tune. Maybe some of them even broke. But I didn't care.

Thorne stood motionless, still watching me, his brows lowered.

I glared at him. "You should just lock me away like Father did! I'm useless. Nothing. Disgusting."

The frown on Thorne's face stretched to pity, which I hated even more. "Every Alpha goes through this--"

"I'm not an Alpha! I don't want an Omega. Or toys. I don't want anything!" *But you.*

"Your mind is not clear."

"I don't care!" I turned away from him again, looking toward the window, thinking about climbing out of it and running forever through the snow and into the shadows of the furry pines on his back acreage.

Right here and now, I honestly wanted to die.

"I will not allow that." Thorne's quiet voice was like a secluded waterfall in a peaceful glade. It poured over me.

Had I just said my last thought about wanting to die aloud?

"I can't." My voice just above a whisper. "I just can't."

"Because you won't allow help?"

I shut my eyes tight, not answering.

"My help?" he asked.

My breath froze in my lungs. My heart seemed to stop. The entire world went even quieter as if everything at once had stopped. Stopped breathing, stopped moving, stopped existing.

The light against the curtains wavered. The room began to dissipate as I heard him say, "Will you allow my help?"

I felt even I had stopped existing at those words. I wanted this dream—this nightmare—to lift, but it grew even deeper.

Something touched my shoulder. I started to flinch. Stopped myself. The offer was too good. My cock throbbed in response.

But he'll hate you after, a voice inside me cried out. The voice of my self-critic, it held the tone of Father.

The mattress moved, then sloped with a new weight upon it. Gravity caused my body to roll slightly toward him. I felt velour against my upper back, and the scrape of the sleeve of his robe.

Thorne's robe. I'd awakened him from sleep. He'd come from his own bed. He probably had nothing on underneath it.

The thought flamed through my veins and an ache formed within me deep and rolling, like a void folding in on itself.

"Kris, if you cannot hold on to control, let me catch you. I'm here for you. I won't let harm come to you."

A stubbornness rose up to combine with the horror that Thorne was forced to deal with this. But when his hand on my shoulder moved down my arm and his fingers brushed the skin of my bicep, all my insides became liquid and I turned, the sheets sticking and wrinkling beneath me, to press my shoulder into his broad chest and slide my hip against his thigh.

He'd brought his legs up onto the mattress, one stretched out, the other bent. My head bowed, my chin almost touching his shoulder as he reached out to pull me to him. His hand pushed under the pillow behind me.

I was shaking so hard and trying to keep my body slightly bowed so my erection wouldn't bump his hip. But my cock knew what it wanted and it strained for touch. For him.

The Burn turned my vision to rose and obsidian. My mind became red glass and shattered.

I could hardly take a breath. Thorne's clean Alpha scent flooded my senses, along with his calm exterior, and his relaxed energy. I wanted to cling to him. Thorne. The man of the house. The Alpha who could keep me safe, dangerous or not.

He would help me dream the world back to life. He would bring me up and out of myself to the exquisite beauty of time-honored life.

I was on the verge of bursting.

His fingers trailed down my arm, over my chest and stomach, then down down down…

…and set me free.

Chapter Nineteen

Thorne

Thorne saw Kris's body arch and the muscles tense. Dim light played over the curves and lines and crevices of his body, moving as he moved, painting him in earth tones of tan, blond and highlights of pale pink. Such a perfect Alpha, but not. The air had a burnt-honey scent. The heat of Kris reached him all the way to the threshold of the door.

Kris's eyes widened: fear, fight, and confusion lit them, but the will he had was unbroken. Thorne also saw pain in how he held himself, covered himself, pain that would be mostly internal. He had Varian Vandergale to thank for that, and all the Alphas of this fucked up world who thought they could treat Omegas like chattel.

Kris was ashamed of the situation, but mostly of himself. Thorne felt shame himself, but not because of his biology, but because of his lack of control. His blackouts during his own Burns were something he could not help, but shame still ruled him.

He understood Kris more than Kris might imagine.

His desire to help overtook him. He spoke to Kris in soft tones. He showed him the toys he himself used to drain the Burn from his body. Kris shoved the toys to the floor. The clatter startled them both.

Anger sang in Kris's eyes along with the Burn. But the soft browns had also darkened with hollow need. The pupils dilated wide.

All of Kris's body language, along with his confusion and the fact that this was his first time cemented Thorne's decision to offer himself in assistance. His presence, his body, his comfort.

From the moment he'd found Kris in his shed and caught his unique and beautiful scent, he'd wanted him. But that could be denied, delayed and controlled. But it was now he realized he cared for him as well. The boy in the window. The half-Alpha half-Omega who had come into his life and begged to be hidden, to be safe.

His body surged at that need to protect. To care for. To love. He wanted to bond him. It had been coming on for days, more than attraction and desire, more than lust. Thorne wanted Kris by his side, in his arms, melded to every cell of his body. All the time.

It had only been one week but he knew. His body knew. His dreams knew.

But he would not push himself onto Kris. He would help Kris. It would fill him with joy he'd not known in a long time. But he would keep that joy to himself. Kris had enough to deal with at this time.

His first touch to Kris's shoulder got the response he had hoped for but not expected. Kris moved up into his touch, and the silken heat of his skin flared up into Thorne's fingertips and palm, coursing through him.

Beneath his robe, Thorne's cock came fully erect. The air sizzled. Beyond the curtains, fog from the heat of the room would no doubt be gathering on the windows.

Thorne leaned his hip against the side of the mattress and slid himself onto the bed, bending his knees and rolling up alongside Kris's fevered body.

Kris gave a short gasp and turned his glimmering body on the sheets, pressing his shoulder into Thorne's chest. His knee grazed Thorne's thigh and the hardness of his cock poked his hip through the soft cloth of the robe.

Thorne snaked his hand underneath the pillow beyond his head and embraced Kris, keeping his touch loose and light. But Kris responded by pressing harder.

Thorne knew the Burn responded to another's touch even if the person in the Burn was not fully mated to the one he touched. He'd felt it himself. It was why Alphas were able to so easily use Omegas and discard them afterward. In the Burn they couldn't resist them. Afterward, it was easy to turn away from a stranger if you had developed no feelings for them. Relationships had little to do with the Burn. Compatibility was key.

But Thorne was now no stranger to Kris and Kris moaned at the intimate contact.

Thorne took dominance. It was his nature, but also Kris was incapable at the moment. Moving into the sweet energy of Kris so near to him, so trusting, he ran his palm down his arm, over his chest and stomach, then further into primal heat.

Kris's head was bowed, his ear near Thorne's lips as Thorne whispered, "Your need is immediate. Let me help."

Kris bucked against him.

"Say it. That I may touch you. That I have your permission to give you release from the Burn."

Kris's lips opened, glistening. His eyelids fluttered, finally lifting and showing dark orbs that drew Thorne's gaze even as he said in a strangled voice, "Yes, yes," over and over.

Thorne's fingertips brushed lightly at Kris's cock which lay stiff against his stomach. Over the tip and along the underside his fingers skimmed.

Immediately, Kris arched up. He bent his knees and his legs spread as he leaned fully back onto Thorne's robe-covered chest.

Gorgeous, Thorne thought. *Beautiful. Radiant as sunlight on a silver lake.*

Kris was a prize. His father had known it. Which was probably why he'd wanted to keep him, own him. Like a work of art. A masterpiece. But also to keep him safe.

Varian Vandergale may be an ass, but he was right about one thing. Alphas could not be trusted. Especially around such a man as Kris. Enticingly beautiful but not fully Omega, the worst Alphas would be tempted to treat him as even less of a man. Or like a Sylph, to be feared and locked away in an institution or worse.

"Kris," Thorne said. "I'm going help you now. Try to relax. Let yourself go. This is a very natural thing."

He stroked Kris's stiff cock as Kris lifted his hips, exposing himself, presenting himself, not quite Alpha, not quite Omega, but filled with need.

Kris was damp with sweat and Thorne milked him easily, unable to look away from the beautiful sight, the pink tip flooding with clear moisture. The cock throbbed in his hand. He rubbed his thumb over the tip and Kris cried out as white streams jetted out of him.

It hadn't taken much for his first time. He'd been held back and repressed for too long.

Thorne's cock twitched in empathy, in need, but he ignored it as he milked Kris until the spurts stopped.

"Uh, oh. Oh! Sorry!"

That Kris could be coherent enough to apologize was astounding.

"No apologies. Relax and let me help."

Kris sighed, his weight pressing Thorne's arm beneath him, and the side of his chest.

His hand moved to Kris's balls, gently massaging, soothing.

Kris moaned and tossed his head. One hand reached up and clutched Thorne's upper arm, digging in.

As was normal during the Burn, first Burn or otherwise, the erection did not go down. For Thorne, an erection was nearly constant during his Burns. Even after his blackouts, he would come to still hard, and need more stimulation to keep himself clear-minded enough to remember to eat and drink.

For Kris, they had only just begun.

Thorne massaged his balls, thighs and abdomen. Kris responded in such lovely ways, his cock head flushed and dripping, his chest heaving, his mouth open and his eyes shut so tight the long lashes pressed a line into his cheeks. He rubbed his chin and the side of his face in Kris's thick golden hair, inhaling him and sending his own mind spinning.

The mating urge—more than simple lust—outside the Burn had never happened to him before. But he had it now. The desire was more than sufficient. He had to tamp it down. It wouldn't be fair to Kris who wouldn't understand it in this moment anyway. He would not try to bond him. He didn't know if he'd even be able to since Kris was not fully Omega. It would be worse than rape.

But he could ease the Burn for him. That he could continue to do, and *would* do because he cared for Kris.

"I—I need something. Oh fuck." Kris bucked. "It's too much."

Thorne's gaze traveled from his face down to his hard cock. His free hand cupped Kris's balls, assessing the tension. They were tightly drawn and the base of Kris's cock was affected.

Thorne wrapped his hand around the base, testing. Yes, there it was. Kris's first knot was forming. And so quickly!

He squeezed slightly and Kris cried out in a low, long tone. The pleasure of the Alpha knot was like nothing else. Omegas did not knot, but they had other things going for them. But Alphas were at the mercy of this manifestation when the mating urge became imperative.

It was a soul-deep need, more than just about getting off. It could make Alphas drunk or crazy, or because of the rare condition Thorne suffered from, black out. The blackouts were frightening to Thorne mainly because he could not know if the urges in his body continued on auto-pilot, and not being conscious of his actions, he feared hurting another the way he had hurt Ian. He had not known Ian was in distress, and had continued to fuck him well into his blackout. When he'd awakened, Ian was dead. The doctors said Ian had died of natural causes from a weak heart, but Thorne took full responsibility.

With Kris, though, he could safely assist. Thorne wasn't in the Burn. He wasn't going to black out.

He wrapped his hand more firmly about the knot and brushed his lips across Kris's damp forehead.

"You're knotting. I will squeeze it to make it feel better, but you need more."

Kris said, eyes rolling up, "That's good."

"I'm going to hold you tight as it moves. It will take a few minutes, okay?"

"Okay." The word led to more moaning.

"If you'll allow it, I can suck you and that will help the pressure relieve and you can come."

It only took Thorne's brief suggestion to make Kris moan louder. His cock flexed, the knot growing.

Taking that as a *yes,* Thorne pulled his arm from beneath Kris's head and curled his body until he could bend over Kris. The knees spread further. He held his hand tight at the base and Kris's beautiful cock stood straight up, flushed and swollen, an amazing asset to such a lovely young man.

Thorne had loved to do this act with Ian, who could come from Thorne's ministrations like this three times in one night, and still beg for more.

He banished all thoughts of his dead mate from his mind, for now he needed to focus on Kris.

Squeezing the knot, he breathed on the head of the cock before darting his tongue out and licking at the wet hole and all around it.

Kris bucked, but Thorne held him down with his free hand on his hip and sucked the tip between his lips. His grip loosened on the base, then tightened as he kneaded the knot and encouraged it to move as he lowered his mouth and sucked in more of the shaft.

Kris's knees tried to come together as if to hold him in place. They bumped his shoulders. The heels of his feet slid back and forth on the wrinkled sheets.

Loud groans filled the room like howls.

Thorne would have been insulted if Kris hadn't made such sounds, since this was something he excelled at. He hadn't done it in a long time, but he hadn't forgotten how.

He sucked hard, knowing Kris needed it, and felt the knot begin to move. He bobbed his head. When he came up, he licked and sucked at the tip, then went down again, trying to give Kris what he needed.

It worked. The knot, as his hand massaged it, had moved at least an inch up the quivering shaft. Thorne wet it all over with his tongue and went back to sucking, alternating between drawing him in soft, then hard, then soft again, letting the pre-cum fill his mouth with its sweet flavor, not quite Alpha spice and not quite Omega sweet, but a combination that was heady and addictive.

The knot moved another inch. Kris was amply endowed, so it would take another few minutes to get it to release.

Thorne ran his hand up and down the base, milking beneath the knot now, encouraging it upward, then squeezing it again and again.

Kris's legs, now sprawled straight, thrashed. His upper body tossed and turned right to left.

He came off Kris's cock with a pop, and said, "Let it come. Just relax. It's natural. It's all good. All beautiful and good."

Kris moaned a word Thorne could not understand. He went back to laving the tip, then sucking, his hand never stopping its work on the knot.

It came up faster now. Kris was on the brink, his hand clawing Thorne's robe at his back.

Another minute maybe. Then Kris might relax for awhile before it started all over again. It would give Thorne time to get him water and energy bars, if he could get him to eat.

His saliva made the cock slick to the touch. His palm slid easily over it faster and faster as he suckled the head.

The knot gave a sudden huge throb and moved up to the ring below the head of the cock. Thorne's lips could barely fit around it as it burst within and flooded his mouth with come.

He kept sucking even as his mouth filled and he could swallow no more. The spurts were youthful and strong, pure Alpha, the texture thick, the flavor salty sweet.

As he took his mouth away to lick at the underside of the cock and squeeze the rapidly deflating knot, more spurts shot into the air in time with the throbs of the knot. It wouldn't end until the knot completely deflated.

Thorne put his mouth back over the tip, catching more come. He loved it, loved that Kris allowed him this, that he could bring pleasure to another in the Burn. He had not been attracted to Alphas in the past, but Kris was Kris. He couldn't get enough

He sucked hard and Kris yelled, the spurts increasing as if a new orgasm had begun where another left off. But it was all one, all due to the Alpha knot.

He squeezed under the head of the cock until he'd gotten it all, the spurts slowly dying away to short squirts, then dribbles, then nothing.

When he pulled back, petting the penis which was finally losing tension and going down, he lifted his head.

Kris had his head tilted back, eyes shut, and his mouth was gasping for air.

Thorne patted him on the chest. Kris had a few short gold hairs on his chest that shone in the hall-light like filigree. Thorne reached for his bag and saw the scattered toys around the floor. In the bag was a clean towel. He wiped himself down, then Kris, and brought the cover up over Kris and turned to slide from the bed.

"Just rest for a minute. I'll be right back."

Kris mumbled something.

"What?" Thorne asked.

"Don't go."

"I won't. I'm just going to get some water."

Kris nodded once, then turned on his side away from Thorne and curled up, hands over his head.

When Thorne returned to the room with bottles of water and some energy bars, Kris was still in the same position he'd been in when he'd left him.

Thorne came around the bed to face Kris and sat beside him. He put his hand under his shoulders to help him sit up. "Here. Water. You have to drink."

Kris reluctantly sat up and took the bottle but would not meet Thorne's gaze. He put the bottle to his lips and guzzled the entire contents. Thorne took the empty from him and held out another.

"More?"

Kris shook his head, looking down and away.

"It's going to happen again. And again. I'll be here with you."

Now Kris looked up frowning and so delicate in his emotions right now, which played across his face in various movements and twitches. He was still aroused, fevered—one always was in the Burn—but he was also embarrassed in his desperate neediness.

"I know this can go for days for most Alphas. How—how long will it last for me?"

"I don't know."

Kris blinked, eyes suddenly tearing up. "You'll be sick of me in days."

Thorne reached out. He couldn't help himself. He pushed strands of blond hair from Kris's still-damp forehead. "I could never be sick of you, sweetheart."

"Sweetheart?" Kris glanced back and forth from his lap to Thorne's face.

Thorne's palm cupped Kris's cheek. "Yes. To me, you are."

"I'm a mess."

"You're an amazing young Alpha going through the Burn."

"But I'm not."

"You are."

"Not Alpha, I mean."

"You are Alpha or you wouldn't have been able to form a knot, let alone enter the Burn. And you are more. So much more."

"You're just saying that to make me relax. Because this isn't ending. It's just starting."

"No. I'm saying the truth. You're a delight to me and don't you ever forget it."

Pale lashes fanned the air as Kris took that in, chest still moving with his more rapid than normal breaths. "You are so good to me," he whispered.

"And I will continue to be." Thorne watched him wrestle with his new being, his awakening. "How did it feel?"

Kris looked away. "Good."

"And it was your first time knotting. Well?"

Kris's mouth tightened, opened, closed, then opened. "I'm speechless."

Thorne let out a small laugh. "Fantastic. That's how it's supposed to feel."

Kris glanced up. "Don't laugh."

"Why not?"

"This isn't funny."

"It's not funny. It's wonderful. You're crossing an amazing plateau. We should be celebrating, having wine and steaks and ice cream for dessert." In all honesty, he was trying to get a smile out of Kris. It was harder than getting him to come, that was for sure.

Kris simply shot him a pained look and lay back under the covers staring sightlessly upward.

Thorne let him rest for about half an hour. He spent the time picking up the scattered toys from about the room, and setting out more clean towels and making sure lube was within reaching distance for more milking. Even with lube, Kris's cock would chafe after hours of handling.

After seeing to all that, Thorne sat on the side of the bed and watched Kris nap, his eyes twitching, his body moving restlessly even in sleep.

When Kris woke, he jerked and moaned and it was time for another round.

Thorne maintained gentle touches and realized he was making love to the boy and not just servicing him. He cared, and he could do this no other way.

The second time Thorne sucked the knot from him, he positioned himself at the foot of the bed between Kris's legs and Kris held onto his shoulders and head as he brought him to a minutes-long orgasm that fountained out of him. Kris bucked and shot long white ribbons of come with every throb. Thorne kept sucking and letting up, then sucking back down again, squeezing the knot until it passed.

His technique drove Kris crazy, and he thrashed for long minutes until he was flushed and winded and soaking wet.

This time, the aftercare consisted of a shower. He helped Kris into the hot water, getting his own robe wet but not caring. He held him as he soaped him down, then knelt and sucked him off again without a knot forming.

Kris clutched hard at his hair, pulling, but Thorne didn't care. He only cared about the needs of this man. And bringing him as much pleasure as possible to make this a good memory, a positive light in his life to look back on from the future from wherever he ended up.

Back in bed, Kris rested for about an hour this time, and Thorne napped beside him, his hand on Kris's chest.

Five times before dawn Kris came. Three of those times included a knot.

He was the most gorgeous sight when he came, golden hair splashing about his face and shoulders, eyes rolled back, mouth open in a lovely sideways oval. His knees would bend and part, swaying, the thigh muscles tensing, and the tip of his cock would turn to a dark, dusky red as the shaft contracted with the orgasms, exploded with seed. His chest rose and fell, the skin over the pecs and at the center pink from exertion, his nipples hard and pointed. For Thorne, his heart threatened to break just watching him.

By morning they were both exhausted. They slept side by side and did not see the dawn brightening the windows.

It was nine a.m. when Thorne woke to a growling stomach. He left Kris sleeping and got up to make breakfast.

He brought eggs scrambled soft and toast with melting butter into the guest room on a tray and set it on the bed.

He was amazed when Kris moved to sit up, the covers bunching about his waist, and started eating.

Getting food into a young Alpha during his first Burn was a feat. Many Alphas lost as much as fifteen pounds during their first Burns because they could not keep food down.

Luckily, Kris's appetite flourished and he managed another nap after eating.

Thorne took that opportunity to run upstairs and grab another shower. He had denied himself any sexual release while tending to Kris. Now he held his fully erect cock under the hot water and closed his eyes, seeing image after image of Kris blissed out in pleasure, head thrown back, Adam's apple bobbing, cock spurting long, fast arcs of white come. He rubbed only a few times before he came into the stream with a fast and much-needed release.

His first robe had been soaked by the shower he'd given Kris, and he'd changed into another after that. Now, running out of robes, he slid into a pair of sweats and a white, short-sleeved t-shirt. He stayed barefoot, then padded downstairs to make sure the heat was on. It was for himself, not Kris. Kris didn't feel the cold right now. He might happily rut in the snow if Thorne allowed it.

When he returned to the guest bedroom, Kris was awake, the covers pushed aside, his cock hard against his belly again. He looked up, hand stilling where he was touching himself, and immediately his face flushed. After everything they'd done that night, Thorne wanted to laugh.

He came forward, happy to see that Kris didn't flinch when he reached out and ran his hand down Kris's bare shoulder.

"Ready to play some more?"

"Play?" Kris asked, frowning.

"I didn't mean to offend you. I love this. I love pleasure with you. Is that wrong?"

Kris kept his frown but finally shook his head. Thorne understood. Kris didn't fully trust him yet. He had not figured it would be easy.

As if in answer, Kris scooted over without protest, allowing Thorne to sit beside him on the bed.

Thorne had a sudden urge kiss Kris, but held back. Several times in the night, he'd wanted to. Even after sucking Kris's cock, it felt too intimate, which seemed ironic to him. But there it was. That feeling. The urge to kiss. And the desperate anxiety to wait. Wait.

He reached out and tipped Kris's chin up so Kris would look at him. "I want you to know I will do whatever you need. I've never had another man inside me, but even that."

"No!" Kris's eyes widened. "You're not Omega. It would hurt you!"

Thorne let out a chuckle. "Many Alphas can take pleasure from physical stimulation that way."

"That's not what I was taught." Kris continued to shake his head. "I wouldn't be able to control, either. No. Just no."

"Hmm." Thorne brushed his hand down Kris's stomach. "More of the same, then?"

Kris fell back onto the pillows, head turning away as he said, softly, "I love it when you suck me."

Thorne began again by licking the sweet, pink head as Kris, unable to hold back, thrust up and into his mouth.

Chapter Twenty

Kris

Thorne's eyes roving over my body. Thorne's hands. His body warm against mine. And ah damn that mouth. That mouth.

He really knew what to do with it.

My cock had been comforted more times by that mouth in the past day and a half than I could count. Always warm and wet. The lips plush against my sensitive skin. The tongue going everywhere, all over, up and down, over the head, delicately licking the hole. And when he sucked long and hard, up and down my shaft, it was so very perfect.

I couldn't stop wanting him. I couldn't stop knotting and coming for him.

Sometimes, after my knot fully released, he would take his mouth away from my sensitive flesh and suck my balls. I had to grit my teeth to keep from screaming, it felt so good.

I knew what orgasms were. But I never thought this would be so… so utterly heart-stopping. It almost made me want to hold onto the Burn and never come out of it. It was amazing. And Thorne, well, he was my savior once I got over my hesitation and shame, once I got over the worry that he took care of me out of pity and for no other reason.

He called me sweetheart, which took me right out of reality and into a fantasy world where we were a bonded, mated pair. I imagined it. But I kept those thoughts secret from him, of course.

When he offered me his body, I wanted it so badly I almost said yes. It had never been so hard for me to turn away from something in my whole life. I wanted him. My cock wanted inside him. Wanted to mate. To fuck.

But no, no. It couldn't be. We weren't right to be mated. I wasn't Omega so it probably wouldn't work. And he needed an Omega who could give him a true life as a bondmate some day when he decided he might want that again. He did not need me, mostly Alpha, my Omega parts not working, barren.

I woke from another short nap. It was late afternoon of the second day of my Burn.

My first thought was, *Where is Thorne?*

I listened hard through the silence of the house and heard distant kitchen noises. I smelled roasted chicken, herbs along with a little garlic in there somewhere.

My stomach rumbled. For the first time in hours and hours my cock wasn't hard. I was clean from yet another shower I'd had before my nap. My hair hung around me in unbrushed locks but smooth and freshly washed.

I got up and found some clean trousers and a blue knit pullover shirt. The house was warm as I padded down the hall toward the cooking sounds. I felt fairly strong for having been in bed for two days. My thoughts came easy, less darkened by fear and low self-esteem.

This was a welcoming home, and Thorne a friend who'd done things for me far beyond what friendship entailed. He'd been gentle but thorough, caring and soft-spoken. I remembered every detail, even the most feverish ones. Sweetheart, he'd called me. And once he'd said to me, "Come, love." Or was that maybe spelled luv? I didn't know.

When I thought of Thorne and pictured him doing the things he'd done to me, my chest swelled. Something in the pit of my stomach turned over, deeper than mere arousal.

Thorne looked up as I entered the kitchen. His lips curved up. "You're looking much better!"

My heart skipped to see him greet me with such affection. But of course we'd shared affection. That was for sure. But could it be anything more than that?

"I feel more like myself now. Thank you." My voice came out low and still damnably hesitant.

"Sit. I'll feed you a good meal. You earned it."

I earned it? No. He earned everything. He earned my honor and devotion forever. My loyalty would never be in question concerning him.

I sat at the table which faced the front yard. I saw that in two days the snow had melted off quite a lot. There were now large brown patches of earth showing through the pristine whiteness. The late afternoon sky was darkening to lavender with pale pink smears through it.

"Thank you," I said again as Thorne set a plate before me filled with roasted chicken, cooked mushrooms, green beans and a baked potato.

"Eat up," he said. "You need the calories."

I dug in and it was the best meal I'd ever had for two reasons. Thorne was a good cook, but I was also ravenous.

Thorne had done so much for me I kept searching my mind for how to pay him back. What could I do?

I pondered as I ate. We talked very little but the silence did not feel awkward. Everything in the moment was right and good.

I helped him with the dishes afterward and we went into his living room to watch a movie.

Sitting together on the couch with space between us seemed entirely wrong. I was afraid to make any move. Stupid, I knew, since we'd touched so often so recently.

I barely saw the movie, or heard it. A breeze blew now and again against the windows and I heard that clearly as if my ear was pressed to the glass panes.

After the first movie ended, Thorne put on another until I was too sleepy to continue. I felt weird going off to bed alone down the shadowy hall, but that was our routine, our set up. After the Burn we needed to establish that routine again, and our usual boundaries.

He seemed unsure as he stood. "You will come to me if you feel anything wrong, won't you?" he asked.

"Yes."

"Please. Don't hesitate. You don't have to knock. Just come to my room and get me and I'll be here for you."

The hollow place in my stomach tightened with want, but not the same need I felt during the Burn. When I did not immediately answer, but stood poised at the entry to the hall, he came up to me, brows narrowed.

"Say you will, Kris."

I swallowed against my dry throat. "I will." My voice came out rough.

In bed, feeling clean and free of the weight of the Burn, everything seemed right. Yet everything seemed wrong. I kept reaching out just to feel the solid warmth of a body nearby only to grasp at air and the new sheets I'd put on before climbing in for the night.

I was tired but couldn't sleep. I kept turning over and over. I wanted Thorne next to me. I wanted to hear his breath and smell the salt of his skin. I wanted his hands on me. Not just sexually. But the touch of him. The presence of him.

I heard the boards creak overhead as he walked about his room getting ready for bed. I saw him disrobing in my mind, something I had not seen while he'd ministered to me. He'd kept his clothing on, or a robe the whole time. He'd never taken his own pleasure, I realized, and a flush crept up my entire body.

I imagined him sliding naked into his bed, alone in the dark, a man who had given everything to me. To me, a complete stranger less than a week and a half ago.

I curled into myself. My fingers formed fists. I grabbed a pillow and hugged it to my chest. My mind rushed over more memories and details of the past couple of days. I tried to breath deep and slow but I couldn't calm down.

Finally, I got up and paced the room to the window and back toward the door. Twice. Then I had a thought.

I flipped on a lamp, went to the dresser and opened the top drawer, moving aside the underclothing to get to my treasures beneath. Packing to run away, I'd brought with me all the valuable jewelry I owned in my coat pocket. Now I pawed through it. It clinked against the bottom of the drawer, jingling as I pushed aside gold watches and bracelets, sterling silver tie clasps and cuff links, and a large assortment of rings.

I picked up one of the rings and held it up. Father had given it to me, along with lots of other expensive things, one Christmas. The gold setting held a large emerald stone. I'd worn it many times on my middle finger until I tired of it.

It was worth a lot but how much I couldn't say.

Palming it, I grabbed my robe and shouldered into it, then headed upstairs.

The ache in my stomach tightened as I approached Thorne's closed bedroom door. He'd said to come to him if I needed to. Well, I couldn't sleep with this debt weighing on me. So here I was.

He'd said not to knock. But I did it anyway. A tentative tap.

I heard rustling inside the room, then footsteps. The door opened.

"Kris?"

Thorne had on his robe, hastily tied. I could see the edge of one muscled thigh and further up, the shadow of something promising.

"I'm fine, really. But I couldn't sleep. I had to see you. I had to give you something."

He held the door open and beckoned me in. I had not been up here before. The room was laid out much like mine with an adjoining bathroom right above my own. His bed had covers in lots of earth tones, and there was a plush chair by the window, a tall wooden dresser, and two mirrored closet doors. A black rug alongside his bed cushioned my bare feet as I entered.

"You sure you're feeling all right?" He put the back of his hand to my forehead like a loving parent, or a loyal companion. Or maybe like that of a sweet lover if I dared to think it.

I nodded against the warmth of his skin, wanting him to touch me more but pushing that thought from my mind.

I spoke quickly as I always did when nervous. "I said I wanted to pay you for the room and everything, that I wasn't going to live here rent free. You've done so much. And I just… just need you to have this or I won't sleep. I couldn't sleep thinking about it."

Thorne glanced at my cupped hand. "You don't need to pay me."

"I have to or I won't sleep. Don't you understand?" My words came out in a single breath. "Here." I held out my hand.

He took the ring between his thumb and forefinger, holding it up to his face. His lips parted in a slight gasp. "Kris, this is worth a fortune!"

"It is?"

He smiled at me. "It is. It must mean something to you. You shouldn't part with it."

"I want to. I want you to have it."

"But a ring?"

Then I realized how it could be interpreted. How I hadn't thought this through. Rings were binding for some people. Like proposals.

My face heated. "I guess it's weird. I—I don't have much cash but I do have some you can have. But I still want you to have this."

"I told you I don't need money, sweetheart."

There it was again. The endearment.

"I know but--"

"And you didn't have to come give it to me now."

"I'm sorry."

"No, I didn't mean it that way," Thorne said. "Don't apologize. But this can't be the only reason why you can't sleep."

I chewed my lower lip and peered at him with my eyelids half-closed. "Why do you call me sweetheart?"

"Because I care. It just came out and seemed to fit."

"No one's ever called me that."

Thorne frowned. "You are important to me, Kris. Very much. It's a term of affection."

"Affection." I repeated the word, liking it, but it wasn't enough. I wanted more. So much more. "How much affection?"

Thorne sighed. "A lot. Perhaps more than you're ready for. Especially from someone like me."

"Someone like you?" I kept repeating his words back to him, but I couldn't help it.

"A dangerous Alpha."

Trust no Alpha. Father had drilled that message into my mind. But maybe there were some Alphas, even ones termed dangerous, who might be trusted. A little, at least.

"I don't think you're quite as dangerous as people think. Or maybe even as much as you think. You certainly don't seem dangerous to me."

"But I haven't told you the whole story."

"No, you haven't."

Thorne turned away. "Maybe some other time, all right?"

"All right."

But I stood without moving in the center of his bedroom. When he looked over his shoulder at me, he asked, "What?"

"I still can't sleep."

"Do you know why?"

I gave a firm nod.

"Tell me."

"I think I got too used to you being there. Beside me, I mean. You know, when I slept." My face heated because there were so many other things he'd done that I had loved. That I wanted again. But I couldn't bring myself to hunt the words to state that. My tongue would fumble, I just knew it.

Thorn walked to his bed and sat, not looking at me. He slid under the blankets. Then he raised his covers and looked up at me. "Come on."

"In your bed?"

"Yes."

"Just to sleep?"

He looked me up and down, his eyes dancing. "For now."

I started forward.

"Wait," he said.

"What?"

"Turn off the light."

I reached for the switch. Darkness poured around us but I could still see his shadow on the bed, and the covers lifted up in invitation.

I started to climb in still wearing my robe. He must have felt it for he said, "Lose it."

I shucked it off and tossed it to the floor. Then I slid smoothly into Thorne's arms, realizing he'd removed his own robe as well.

My body pressed against his as he scooted until his arms were around me.

I gave a little cry, a weird sound that escaped low in my throat.

"Hush, it's all right," he said softly.

Slowly, I lay my head against his chest. My body began to relax, first my shoulders which I'd been holding so taut, and then my arms, my chest, my stomach and legs. His body against mine was hot, but not too hot, and felt both delicate and strong. His skin was soft but his muscles were big and hard. The fragrance of tea and fresh earth and autumn washed over me, along with the lavender shampoo we both now used.

I took a deep breath. It felt like the first true, relaxed breath I'd taken in days.

I closed my eyes. With Thorne's arms encasing me, I fell into the most refreshing sleep I'd ever had.

Chapter Twenty-One

Thorne

Kris's skin warmed against Thorne's own. He fit perfectly into Thorne's embrace. His silken hair flowed about Thorne's chest and arms as he held him, as he fell into a deep and restful sleep.

Thorne's cock grew hard again; it was a sweet arousal, not needy.

He could wait. He could wait forever for this beautiful young man if he had to.

He closed his eyes and let himself fall into sweet relaxation, his mind rejoicing that he held a lover. His lover. Even if it might be too early to think it, he couldn't stop himself.

Many times throughout the night he woke, shifting himself and Kris into more comfortable positions. Kris would wake, yawn and murmur his name, then curl against him and fall back to sleep.

Once Thorne woke with his hand on Kris's hip, his fingers caressing up and down the curve at the top of his buttock. He cupped it protectively and fell back to sleep.

When the window began to lighten with early dawn, he woke again and realized as Kris re-settled in his arms after squirming to half-wakefulness, that something great was happening to them.

They were mentally bonding.

Things had gotten out of control. But oh how beautifully fate had turned. Chaos became gentle love as if by magic.

He wanted this. But his impending Burn in a few weeks had him worried.

He fell back to sleep staring at the emerald ring he'd placed on the bedside table, the greens of the precious stone glimmering in the pale morning light.

*

When Thorne woke again, Kris lay facing him, eyes open and watching him. No more fear or pain or fever darkened those sweet brown orbs. No more misery. He saw a peace there, a soft affection and maybe more.

Thorne wanted to move his head forward just enough to kiss him. After everything, for a kiss to seem so daring was ridiculous. But he couldn't overcome the idea that it was too soon. Too early.

Kris stared at him, unmoving. Then after a few breaths, gaze unwavering, the corners of his lips rose up.

The smile was absurdly amazing and, despite an alluring and irresistible body, the most entrancing part of Kris. Thorne did not take such a gift lightly.

"Thank you for everything you've done for me," Kris said.

"No thanks are necessary. You know I like you, don't you?" Thorne asked. "A lot."

"I'd be horribly embarrassed if you didn't."

Thorne laughed.

"I like you, too," Kris added in a whisper. His dark eyes sparkled. "A lot."

Thorne warmed to hear him say it, though he wished for more. Love might be too much to ask so quickly, but every time he looked at Kris he wanted to be closer to him. He had great urges to care for him and protect him. And he had adored all physical contact with him. Kris might not realize it yet, but last night and now again Thorne could not deny a bond was forming between them.

After some silence, Kris clasped his hands in his lap and stared at them. "I have so many questions, though."

"It's all right. You can ask me anything."

"Well, I just feel so different."

"You mean after the Burn? You're fully matured now. A full adult Alpha."

"Yes, I guess that's it."

Thorne frowned. "Describe what you mean by different."

"I guess it's just me. After everything. It's why I came to you last night. I feel wrong to not be near you. Is it still the pheromones?"

Was Kris feeling the bond, too? Thorne wondered. "It starts with pheromones but doesn't lead to more unless there is compatibility."

Kris chewed his lower lip. "I guess that's what it is, then. But it's not what I was taught."

"What were you taught?"

Kris took a deep breath. "Father never took a real mate. He always used the farms. When he wanted a litter, he picked the Omega with qualities he wanted for his children. Like ordering off a menu or something."

"That's how it works for many Alphas. But not all."

"Well, I was taught that's how it would be for me and my brothers. Taking a mate was a rare thing that might never happen. Like feeling that compatibility you mention. He never ever talked about that. But I feel it with you after only one Burn."

Thorne's heart soared. "I'm glad."

"I can't imagine Father going his whole life not feeling that."

Thorne shut his eyes, letting Kris's sweet words sink into him. "Some people are not receptive to each other in ways necessary to form a bond. But it doesn't mean they can't perform a sexual act with another to make babies, or to assist an Alpha through his Burn."

"It seems so cold. You were warm and tender and I can't forget that. It's why I had to come upstairs. I couldn't sleep at all with you gone from the bed. I feel like some stupid kid saying that, though."

"You're not stupid. I'm glad you said it. I feel the same."

Kris looked up, eyes shining. "You do?"

Thorne grinned at him. "I do."

"I wish I was full Omega."

"Why?"

"Because then I could form the mate-bond with you." He flushed. "Is that too forward to say right now? Too soon?"

Thorne's entire body warmed. "You feel what you feel. And something is definitely there between us. If you were Omega, I would say we were bonding."

Kris smiled again. So beautiful!

"Well, whatever it is, I hope it never goes away!"

Thorne reached up and touched Kris's cheek. "Me, either," he said softly.

"Then when it comes time for your Burn, you'll allow me to help you, right? That's how it works." His gaze was both shy and tender.

All Thorne's pleasure at Kris's words plummeted. His heart started racing for another reason now. His mind spun. He had to think. To buy time, he picked up his bottle of water from the night stand and took long swallows.

"You would want that, right?" Kris asked, a slight waver to his voice as he became impatient for an answer.

"It's a little different for me, though. I'm not labeled dangerous for no reason."

"Oh."

"My Burns come on hard. And they're different for me than for others."

"You've never told me why, though."

Thorne took a deep breath. "I've never told anyone."

"And you don't want to tell me?"

Thorne started to shake his head.

"But I want to be there for you. And if I can't, shouldn't I know why if we are forming a bond? Shouldn't I understand the entire situation? So I can understand you and do whatever it is you need even if it means staying away from you during your Burns?"

Thorne thought of Ian and pain sliced through his solar plexus. He would never allow anything like that to ever happen to Kris. The mere thought of it was overwhelming. He blinked and stared forward, feeling himself close in as he had in near total isolation for twenty-five years.

"Why did they label you dangerous?"

Kris deserved to know the truth.

"*They* didn't. I did. After I knot, I black out at least fifty percent of the time."

"You actually pass out?"

"I didn't say that. I say I black out, and it happens sometimes during the sex act. That means I have no memory or conscious awareness of what I am doing during that time. And if I can't control any part of myself, the Burn flushing through my body offers no guarantee to the safety of my partner during that time."

"Did you get violent with Ian?"

"You're bold and to the point." Thorne didn't mean his voice to come out gruff, but the conversation was too difficult. He'd never talked about this to anyone.

"I'm sorry," Kris said, hanging his head. "But I feel a strong urge that I should know, but if you can't tell me, I will understand. I'll respect that."

How did Thorne deserve such a treasure in Kris?

He leaned his face into his hands. After a few deep breaths to calm himself, he began to speak. "You see, there's something called aftercare after sex with a mate. The farms are not set up that way. Alphas at the farms can of course choose to give aftercare to their Omega partners, but they don't need to. There are others there to see to their health and welfare after serving an Alpha."

"Aftercare." Kris seemed to mull the word over.

"Yes. Your first Burn was mild. But the Burn can be rough on Omegas. It can go on for too long."

"The sex part, you mean?" Kris asked, again being bold.

"Yes. Alphas have more constitution to withstand it, but Omegas need breaks. They need care. They need to remember to eat and drink or their bodies can become depleted."

"I see. So Ian was depleted."

Thorne shut his eyes tight again. "They say his heart had a weakness that had gone undetected. And I blacked out. I don't know what happened. I only know that when I woke he was dead. I failed to care for him. I failed to see he needed help and if I had been aware and conscious I could easily have called for paramedics."

Thorne opened his eyes.

Kris sat very still for a few seconds. He sniffed. Then he lifted his hand and put it over Thorne's, grasping gently.

"Did he say anything to you before you blacked out?"

"No. He wouldn't have said a thing if he felt distress. He gave his all to me."

"I'm so sorry." Kris squeezed Thorne's hand again.

"It might have been different if I could have called for emergency help."

"But you couldn't. And that's not your fault."

Thorne wanted to argue. "The cause of death doesn't matter. His heart failed and I was not conscious so I couldn't call for help. He died in my arms but I—I--" He couldn't speak further.

Kris moved closer to him and Thorne felt the wonderful warmth of him flow around him. Softly, "Tell me again. How long were you together?"

"Four years."

"I'm so sorry." Kris leaned his head against Thorne's shoulder.

They sat that way for a few minutes.

Kris spoke again. "So you put the label on yourself as dangerous. But you're not violent."

"He died from neglect. That's dangerous!" Thorne insisted.

"But Father neglects his Omega servitors all the time on the farms. And he's not labeled that way."

"I insisted on the label. So it would be on the public record for all to see. So it would never happen again."

"You insisted?" Kris sounded surprised.

"Of course I did."

"Your grief is great. Ian was very lucky."

Thorne tilted his head to look at Kris leaning against him, his golden hair twisted to one side. "Why would you say that? He's dead."

"I meant lucky to have someone who loved him so much that he would go to such lengths to ensure he would never have another mate." Kris's chin nearly touched his chest and his lovely brown eyes closed. "To be loved that much—wow."

The discomfort in Thorne's chest spread to his stomach and he felt a sudden urge to be sick. If he had loved Ian enough, he wouldn't have put him through such uncontrolled Burns. He had been self-serving. Cocky. And Ian had insisted he'd grown used to Thorne's routines but Thorne should have ordered him to see a doctor after each one. He should have known better. It made him sick to think he'd been so selfish. What happened wasn't right. He was indeed a dangerous Alpha.

"Father taught me a lot of things. But in the short time I've known you, I think you've taught me more," Kris said.

Disbelief flooded Thorne's system. He could take no more. "I have to get up."

Kris leaned away. "All right."

Thorne stood and headed for the bathroom without looking back. Once inside he shut the door and ran cold water into the sink, splashing it onto his face. He still thought he might be sick, but as he stared into the mirror over the sink the moment passed. What he saw there was a frazzled and rumpled looking dark-haired Alpha still in his prime at fifty, and facing a future of more loneliness if he pushed Kris away. The corners of his eyes were down-turned. He had not noticed this look on him of weariness and mistrust but it must have been there for a long time, much like the look on Kris's face when he'd first brought him in from the cold.

Kris had said his father taught him to trust no Alpha. It seemed Thorne had applied that lesson in his own life. He did not trust Alphas, most especially himself.

Chapter Twenty-Two

Kris

I stood in the doorway of Thorne's bedroom.

"You know you are welcome here," Thorne said to me, the lamplight falling over him like a transparent, pale cloak. He held up the covers of his bed in invitation.

It was the second night after my Burn. I'd gone to bed early, so I went to my own room again. And again I couldn't sleep.

In truth I couldn't stop thinking about our kisses on the couch. And I'd also been thinking of Ian. I was worried Thorne was still upset about that talk we'd had that morning.

"Well, I can't seem to stay away from you. My bed was just too empty. I can't sleep. I want to sleep here again if that's okay."

Thorne held up the edge of his blanket higher.

I came forward on bare feet and discarded my robe, letting it fall about my feet.

One eyebrow rose, slender and surprised.

My nakedness didn't shame me anymore. I wanted him to see me again. And again.

"Don't look shocked. You know I sleep in the nude." I shrugged at him, then slipped into the bed against the cool sheets and his warm, also very naked, body. My half-hard cock slid against his taut thigh.

"I'm not shocked."

"You are," I countered, skimming my chin along his shoulder.

"Hmm."

Were we lovers? I wanted to be. Did the Burn count?

I had never given him pleasure yet. It had all been for me, for my need during the Burn. Of course I had noticed his arousals during that time, but he always remained covered, even when he held me up in the shower between my bouts of knotting. I still had never seen him nakedly hard for me. I had never seen him come.

Tonight he had been adamant about me staying away from him during his Burns, so I would have to take this pleasure I craved before his time. And after. The question was, would he let me?

I intended to use my Alpha education—the identity I'd always been comfortable in—and boldly make my demands. The fact that he was Alpha, too, didn't matter to me. It didn't seem to matter to him, either.

I wanted him.

When Thorne reached up to turn off the lamp, his chest pressed against my nose and forehead, filling me up with his clean, autumn scent.

I gripped him under the arm, hugging him to me, and when he fell back I rolled on top of him.

His hands went to my shoulders. "Kris, you don't have to."

I rocked my pelvis into him. Obviously, he could feel my interest. "Have to what?"

"This," he said as if helpless to explain any further.

"Then that kiss on the couch was just to tease me?" To take the sting out of my words, I smiled, hoping he could see it through the shadows. Probably not.

"I went too far. Got caught up."

"So?" I asked, letting my voice rise.

"I'm not good for you."

"That doesn't make sense. Everything you've done has been good for me. Everything!" I wasn't going to let him close himself off to me now.

"You won't be complete, Kris. Not with me. Not if I can't share the Burn with you. You'll want to search for more, and you should. You should have whatever you want."

"What you just said is hilarious, since all I want is you." But I wasn't laughing.

Thorne thumped his head on the pillow, sighing.

I started to kiss him on the center of his chest, my lips moving gently over his firm skin, my long hair trailing along his side.

"Kris." He said my name with the conviction of a lover, not someone who wanted to throw me out and away.

I lifted my head. "I want to taste you. Suck you like you did for me. Please?" Did I sound pathetic or sexy? I didn't care. I wanted him and that was that.

Thorne made a small sound in the back of this throat that I took for consent.

I lifted myself to my knees and worked my way down his body. How I wished for more light so I could see him. All of him. Naked and erect.

I kissed over his ribs and around his belly button. His skin quivered for me. His cock pressed against my chest. I couldn't wait. I nuzzled it. The hard shaft bobbed against me and I pressed my mouth to the side of it, moving up to the tip and parting my lips.

I breathed on it and felt his entire body tense.

"I've never done this before," I said. "You don't mind if I practice until I get this right, do you?"

One of his hands came up and landed on my shoulder. He half sat up, his stomach muscles tensing where I lay my cheek. "Kris!"

"All right then." I was grinning as I used my tongue to lick him all over the head of his cock. I slid my tongue down the sides and over his drawn up balls until I could feel he was wet all over.

He was big. Magnificent just as I thought he would be. Alphas had big cocks. It wasn't legend, it was a fact.

If Thorne had had reservations, he didn't seem resistant at all now. I took heart from this and sucked the head of his cock into my mouth.

His body thrashed.

It was good. Salty and slightly sweet, and my mouth watered all around his thickness. I sucked hard, letting my tongue flutter underneath the head as he had done for me when I had been ready to burst, to knot.

I wasn't sure how much of him I'd be able to fit into my mouth, but I was going to try for at least half and milk him at the base when his knot grew as he had done for me.

It had felt so good for me when he had sucked me. I wanted it even now outside the Burn, but more, right now, I wanted his cock just where it was, slick and hard in my mouth.

My own cock burned between my legs, fully hard now. I had swept the covers off my back and now my ass was up in the air, presented to the cold and the dark. But I didn't feel cold. All my focus was on Thorne as I bowed between his spread thighs and pushed my mouth down on his cock as far as I could take it.

His pre-cum was pouring out of the tip and I gulped automatically. The slickness helped and his cock slid further in, giving a few pleasured throbs.

"Ah, Kris!" He yelled.

I held my breath and pushed harder until I felt the gag reflex, then pulled up. My hand wrapped around the base and I felt the knot, hard and pulsing, needing release. I milked him and sucked the tip, tonguing the slit where more pre-cum dripped out of him.

He was slippery down there where I'd dribbled my spit, unable to swallow. When I took my mouth off him, it dripped and I used it to slick the shaft up along the sides even more.

"I love this," I said breathily.

I took him in my mouth again and swallowed. I had Alpha stamina for this Alpha cock. I could do this.

I could hear the sounds of Thorne's desire fill the room. Groans. Hisses. Long breaths let out slowly through gritted teeth.

I milked his knot and sucked up and down as much of the shaft as I could take.

The knot firmed up even more. The tip of his cock swelled against the back of my mouth and I held my breath again as I felt the spurts of fluid begin to shoot from it.

Thorne yelled my name.

I sucked harder and rubbed the knot, grasping it hard.

Again, he half-sat up. With my free hand I pushed against my chest so he would lie back and let me finish him.

"Oh God, Kris!"

I grinned around his girth, pulling up a little. The knot in my grasp moved and more semen filled my mouth. I didn't hate the taste, simply I couldn't swallow it all.

The knot pulsed, pushing more and more out of him. I lifted off the tip and felt the sprays on my face, hot and liquid, and my own cock pulsed in eager response to his pleasure.

Catching my breath, I continued to milk him and lick all over the head as he spurted. I found a rhythm, finally, taking him into my mouth and sucking more of his juices, then pulling up and continuing to milk him as I caught my breath.

He groaned. His chest heaved.

Finally, the knot rose to just below the head of his cock and huge fountains of liquid burst forth, catching my lips and chin, running down over my hand and his shaft. I sucked the head, hoping to give him even more pleasure down this final stretch.

The knot deflated. I held his cock and rubbed it all over my face, spreading his emissions all over me.

It was messy and I loved it. I loved it more than I ever thought I would. Knotting was incredible. Our orgasms were minutes long, the pleasure continuing to build and build because of the knot. It didn't happen every time, but when it did it was overwhelming.

Omegas couldn't do it and hell, they were missing out, I thought. But then they had other areas of their bodies that gave them more pleasure. Their assholes made their own slick. We Alphas could not produce that. Plus, Omegas had pleasure points inside themselves we could never know. We had prostates, but they had even more sensitivity in every area of their hole.

I caressed Thorne's balls as his erection decreased, and moved up his body.

He cupped my face, getting his fingers sticky. " Kris, you—you—my God!"

"When you're ready," I said, "I want to do it again."

Thorne made a strangled sound and reached into a drawer at the bedside table. I heard a sound like paper tearing. Then felt a soft cloth on my face. The thought that he kept wipes by his bedside endeared him to me even more. I bent low so he could wash me. He didn't forget my hands, attending to each finger with care and a soft touch.

I was straddling him now and my cock throbbed where it rested against his belly.

"Next time, can we have just a tiny bit of light?"

Thorne burst out laughing and drew me down to him, kissing alongside my jaw until he reached my lips.

Our kisses exploded against each other as our mouths opened and our tongues dueled. My body vibrated with the intensity, my balls quivering.

I wanted everything with this man. I would not allow him to deter me no matter what.

His hands wrapped around my hips, pulling up and up until I grabbed the headboard for balance. Instinctively, I rocked my hips upward and his mouth closed over my cock.

I rocked back and forth as he milked me.

No knot formed this time but I didn't care. It was intense and beautiful. I threw my head back and came hard down his throat as his hand kneaded my buttocks, pulling me ever closer to him.

Later, with Thorne wrapped about my body, I fell into a deep and restful sleep.

*

As I came around the side of the house, my boots crunching through leftover snow, the top story of my old home came into view.

The side of the top story that faced Thorne's property had few windows and those were above eye level in the halls there, not bedrooms or offices. Thorne's front yard had a rise that kept me hidden from the road, and from all view of the outside world. I felt free here to walk about. Safe.

I stood in the cold air, the sunlight blinding on the white mountaintops, and stared for awhile.

Somewhere inside that giant house my four brothers went about their daily tasks. I missed them, even Mathias who pissed me off more than anyone in my last days living there.

It had been weeks now. I wondered if they missed me. None of their messages I'd read talked much about me anymore.

Father's messages that I could see were all business related. Over the past weeks, Trigg had sent a few messages to Mathias, who was at school now, asking if he still monitored my accounts. If he'd heard anything. Mathias would write back single word responses. "No."

For the most part, it seemed they kept living on without much concern for me or my welfare. Not that I expected more. I was only an Omega to them, now. Irrelevant.

I heard the crunch of footsteps approaching.

Thorne walked up alongside me and gazed toward the mountains and my old home.

"What are you thinking about?" he asked.

"That they barely looked for me."

"Did you want them to look?"

I turned to face him. "No. If they found me, I'm sure Father would force me home again, back behind his closed, locked doors. I was his. Like one more item he owned. He would not give me up."

"He wanted to mate you."

I winced at the memory. "He didn't know it, though. He was delirious. And I'm the strongest of all my brothers. I could fight him off again and again if I had to. He knows that. He wanted to keep me simply because I am his. His to control. Like an object. A pet. Father controls everything around him. Even his Alpha sons. He had our lives all planned out for us."

"You were happy, though. As a child, I mean."

I thought about that statement for a long time. Thorne was right. I had been happy. I excelled at everything I did. I looked forward to design school. I'd even looked forward to my first Burn and experiencing the Omega farms for the first time.

That thought shamed me now that I'd woken to reality. My own condition forced that waking, and Thorne showed me a different way of looking at life than I had ever known.

Thorne had his shame and I had mine. But together we gave each other such pleasure.

"I thought I was happy. But I am happier here." I snaked my arm around Thorne's waist and leaned my head into his shoulder.

Thorne took my face in both palms and tilted my face up to his. He kissed me long and deep, his lips warm and pliant, moving his hands until his fingers carded through my hair.

My heart pounded and I knew I was where I was meant to be. How it happened, or why, I couldn't know, but this was right.

We had not talked of his impending Burn since those first few days after my own. But I had plans.

Whenever Thorne went to town for supplies, I sneaked out his bag of toys. I turned on the shower and experimented with things. Lots of things. Including anal stimulation.

Though I never spoke of it, or had fantasies of bottoming before my diagnosis by Doctor Pokeme, now I dreamed of Thorne taking me. Thorne penetrating me. Thorne inside me.

I was legally an Omega, but I still didn't have the right body chemistry to be fully Omega. I used toys on my ass, trying to stimulate it, but never made my own slick. I had to get myself hard first, then play with a vibrating dildo to open myself. I didn't like it too much at first, but my new fantasies to please Thorne in this way spurred me on.

One day I found the prostate gland deep inside that shot my pleasure center off the charts. My cock jerked and when I slid the dildo in again to rub that spot and turned on the vibrator, I came so fast I saw stars.

With the right amount of lube and foreplay and stretching, I knew I could take Thorne. And I knew I could handle myself, too. I was still an Alpha through and through with an Alpha's strength and constitution. I would never really be dominated by him. And I didn't have a weak heart. I didn't need him to be perfect in his Burns, or to control himself or his black outs, because I could control the situation. I knew I could.

There was only one thing left to do. Convince Thorne I could handle myself. That I would be strong enough to not only handle his Burns, but to take charge of them and give him everything he might need.

Chapter Twenty-Three

Thorne

Thorne heard the car before he saw it come up the dirt drive. A sleek dark blue sedan with black tinted windows and a quiet hum.

One man got out, tall and muscle-bound, thick at the shoulders and neck.

He knew it was about Kris. There would be no other reason for a stranger to come on the property.

Weeks ago he'd gotten an email from a private detective employed by Varian Vandergale. Maybe this was the same guy.

Kris sat in the living room watching a movie.

As Thorne came out of the kitchen to open the front door, he said, "Kris! Take your tablet and anything else you have lying around. That drink, too! Go in your room and lock the door. Don't do or say anything until I come get you."

Kris's eyes widened, but without a word he did as he was told. Thorne saw him stand and glance about, straightening the pillows, grabbing his coffee and his tablet, and jogging from the room.

Thorne went to the door and peered out the little window at the top, watching as the man looked about, taking assessment of the property as he walked swiftly up to the porch.

Thorne moved back from the door and waited for the knock which came in seconds.

Slowly he approached. He undid the upper lock and opened it, looking through the locked screen at the strange Alpha standing before him.

"Hello," said the stranger. "Would you, by chance, be Hawthorne Mauresset?" He smiled disarmingly, but his sheer girth was intimidating.

"Yes."

"Hello. My name is Scard. Nice to meet you."

"Likewise, I'm sure."

"I'm sure you know by now that a search has been on for quite some time for a missing neighbor of yours. I sent you an email about it some weeks ago. Now I'm taking witness statements from the neighborhood and if you don't mind I would like to ask you some questions."

"Are you a detective?"

"Private," the man replied, shifting his massive shoulders.

"I do remember that email now. I'd almost forgotten. So the boy hasn't been found?"

"No trace, I'm afraid." The man came closer to the door as if to peer through the screen. "You are aware your land is the neighboring property of Varian Vandergale." The man turned toward the northwest. "In fact, you can see from here the top of his house. Over there." He nodded off toward the mountain range.

"Yes. I'm aware." Thorne kept his voice flat.

"I was just thinking perhaps you saw something. Anything, even the smallest detail, might be helpful. Kris Vandergale has been missing for some weeks now."

"Sorry to hear it."

"Well, you see, all Mister Vandergale's sons are Alphas, except Kris. He's an Omega, and he could be in danger. So you understand it is in Mister Vandergale's best interests to find the poor boy."

"The Vandergales keep to themselves," Thorne said. "We are not neighborly. I've never seen his sons outside much at all. And never face to face. I've never even been introduced to Mister Vandergale himself."

The man took a deep breath and let out a white exhale. He shuddered a little. "It's just that, well," he paused. "Do you think I could come inside while I ask you a few questions? It's awfully cold out here."

How to answer? What-if scenarios swarmed Thorne's mind. If he said no, maybe the man would think he was hiding something. If he said yes, would Scard sense Kris?

Even Thorne had scented Kris's delicious, heady fragrance when he'd first met him in stark cold temperatures in the middle of the night.

"How about I come out onto the porch instead." Thorne did not ask it as a question.

Scard gave a small sigh of disappointment but backed up a step as Thorne opened the screen door and stepped out.

"I have a picture of him here if that might help you," Scard said.

"Like I said, I've never met any of the Vandergales."

"Yes, but maybe you saw him about, or in town." Scard held up his phone and Kris's image stared back at him from the screen.

Thorne's heart was frenzy in his chest, but he maintained his calm.

"He does not look familiar."

"Are you sure? Because people say you take long walks on this road. I was thinking that you might have noticed if anything was out of the ordinary."

"No. I can't think of anything out of the ordinary. Except that the Vandergale house is usually ominously silent. If he has young sons, they sure are quiet." Thorne forced a smile.

"Yes, well they are well-managed. Alphas all, except for Kris. His father is concerned he could be in danger, hurt or worse. He's very worried."

"I can well understand that. He must be frantic."

"Yes. Kris is only an Omega, but he's Mister Vandergale's son nonetheless."

"I'm sorry I can't be of more help."

Scard glanced about. "I see there are lots of trails of footsteps about the property in the snow. Do you live with a mate?"

"No. I'm single. My mate died years ago. The footprints are all mine. I have gardens I tend to myself every day. Including a winter garden. It's my passion. I'm outside a lot."

"I see." Scard turned so he faced the road which was invisible just over the rise. "I guess you can't really see much of the road from here. So you wouldn't notice if anyone went by."

"No, probably not."

"Think again, Mister Mauresset. You're sure during your morning walks or your work about your yard that you never saw anything that might help us?"

Thorne shook his head. "Nothing but an occasional deer. And there's an old coyote who lives in the woods behind my house. That's it."

"Well, please take my card if you do see or hear anything about Kris. Anything at all, even the tiniest detail might help us locate him."

Scard handed Thorne a business card.

Thorne took it, pretending to stare at it but knowing he'd tear it up and throw it away as soon as he got back indoors. He said, "I hope you find him. For the kid's sake. It's a cold winter this year."

"And for his father's sake as well."

"Yes," Thorne echoed. "For the father's sake." He tilted his lips up in another fake smile.

"It was a pleasure to meet you." Scard lifted his hand.

Thorne said, "Yes. And you." He met the outstretched palm with his own, a quick, polite handshake with the very hand that had been wrapped around Kris's erect cock that morning not two hours ago.

Could this Alpha smell it? Thorne had showered, but still...

His breath caught a little in his throat as Scard turned away, heading back to his sleek car.

Thorne re-entered the house, sniffing the air to see if Kris's scent might be apparent to strangers. Thorne was used to it now, and didn't pay attention. Now he wondered, and not a little bit of fear curdled his veins to think Scard might have scented honey and summer and fresh cut grass.

He locked the screen behind him, then double locked the front door. Immediately, he headed to the guest room where Kris never slept anymore but still kept his things.

When he opened the door, Kris jumped up from the side of the bed where he'd been sitting and ran into Thorne's embrace.

"Who was it? What did he say? They're looking for me, right?"

"Shh. One question at a time. I'll tell you everything." Thorne ran a hand down the side of his beloved's face and led him to the bed where they sat side by side.

"Yes, they're looking for you."

"Who? Who was it?" Kris demanded.

"A private detective. Your father is keeping this under wraps so far, away from the media. That's why you thought they weren't looking or didn't care."

Kris frowned. "Care? He only cares about controlling what he owns!"

Thorne reached out and grabbed his hand. "I know. The man appeared not to know anything. He's combing the neighborhood. That's all."

"He could be watching your—our house even now."

"I don't think so. He didn't seem suspicious, just curious. My biggest worry was if he could smell you here. But I didn't let him inside, and it's cold out. Your scent would not be apparent unless you were standing on the porch with us."

"Fuck! I didn't think of that."

"I think we're okay. But Kris, I'm also thinking you can't just stay hidden like a prisoner forever."

"I don't feel like a prisoner with you." Kris leaned into him. "I'm fine. I feel safe with you."

"Yes, but eventually, well, I think we should move. Out of the state if possible."

"But this is your home," Kris said. He glanced about. "Your gardens you've worked so hard grow are here. And Ian. I think it's a terrible idea."

"To keep you safe?"

Kris's eyes filled. "I wouldn't want you to have to move because of me."

Thorne pulled him close. "I would do anything for you." He kissed the side of his head. "Anything."

Kris's arms came around him and hugged him tight.

Thorne's cock thickened in his trousers. He ran his hands up the back of Kris's sweater.

Kris said, "I have this terrible urge to just turn off all the lights and climb into bed with you and stay there all day."

"All day?"

"Yes. Making love all day."

Shutting out the world. Why did that sound so good?

"Ah! You!" With a sharp laugh, Thorne pushed Kris to the center of the bed, covering him with his body. He kissed him, then leaned back and caught the hem of his sweater, lifting it.

Kris's arms rose in compliance.

Soon they were both naked, scattering pillows and covers, bodies meeting in a private dance.

Chapter Twenty-Four

Kris

I woke with a start. I must have been dreaming, but I couldn't remember it.

Thorne lay beside me on his side, his face pushed half-way into the pillow, his dark hair falling against his exposed cheek.

The late afternoon sun through the half-drawn shade bathed the guest room in bronze shadows. We never slept here anymore. We'd gotten carried away in here and fallen asleep.

I stretched my arms up and was just about to slide my legs over the side of the bed when I heard it.

Banging. Downstairs.

My body jerked in surprise.

"Thorne!"

Thorne gave a little groan beside me and his weight shifted as he slowly woke.

"Thorne!" I punched him on the shoulder. "Someone's at your door!"

Thorne sat up wide awake now, pushing his hair from his eyes. He tossed the covers back hard and sprang up, already shuffling into his jeans before I could even blink.

"This isn't good. After that guy Scard came here this morning, this can't be--"

"Hush," he interrupted. He put his hand gently on my mouth and whispered, "Get dressed but stay here. Do not come out of this room!"

My blood rushed so fast I could hear it like a roar in my ears. I jumped from the bed and put on my clothes. Before I could say another word, Thorne had bolted from the room, shutting the door behind him.

I'd gotten dressed in record time, and now ran my hands through the tangles of my hair. It was loose and I gathered it up and pulled it over my right shoulder. Not knowing what else to do, I sat on the edge of the bed and waited.

My pulse thrummed. I took shallow breaths trying to listen for any sound, any sign of Thorne and whoever had been pounding on the front door.

I thought I heard voices but I couldn't be sure. Were they inside the house or still on the porch?

I didn't dare move. I had the bizarre thought of getting down on the floor and crawling under the bed. For weeks I'd hidden away here and felt safe. But how could I be so naïve? My father had ways like no other Alpha to accomplish whatever he wanted. Even though Thorne's house was fairly isolated, someone still could have seen me walking about the backyard or side yards of the house. I'd been a fool to relax my defenses.

Shoulders hunched, hands clasped tight in my lap, I stayed as still as I could.

I thought I heard more talking. Then I heard what sounded like Thorne's raised voice.

I couldn't take it anymore. I stood and walked as quietly as I could to the bedroom door and put my ear to the wood.

I heard at least three distinct tones. Thorne said, "Show me."

Another voice, "It's all in order."

Silence.

After what seemed like far too long where I heard nothing, a voice said, "Search the house."

I jolted back from the door like a trapped animal, turning. Immediately, I went to the window and pushed back the shades. As quick as I could make my fingers work, I undid the window latch and opened it.

The roof jutted out before me. Just as I straddled the sill and started to pull myself onto the roof, the bedroom door slammed open.

My heart leaped into my throat.

Men rushed into the room. I heard one say, "I knew I smelled him in here!"

One of them grabbed my leg, tugging hard. I kicked out, catching him hard in the chin.

But another was on me, and then another.

I yelled and struggled.

They dragged me, kicking and yelling, out of the room and down the stairs.

Thorne was nowhere about. Even as I pushed and pulled to get these men to release me, I kept looking for him.

The men half-carried me out the front door and that was when I saw him standing on the front porch. His face looked wild, his hair still a mess. He came toward us, reaching out for me.

"You cannot take my Omega! I've staked a legal claim!"

"Varian Vandergale has legal claim!" someone replied starkly.

"A father cannot make a mate-claim. He is here of his free will. We are bondmates," Thorne argued.

"Produce the proof."

I stopped struggling for a moment and met Thorne's gaze. We both knew he had no proof.

"We aren't fully mated yet, but the paperwork is in process!"

It was a good try and a good lie, but if he couldn't prove it, what were my rights?

"He's telling the truth," I said, struggling again. "You can't take me away from my bondmate!"

I wasn't even sure if I was allowed to choose without permission of Father in this matter.

"Tell that to your father," snarled the guy to my left.

They dragged me toward a white van.

Thorne tried to follow but another man held him back. Thorne could have taken him, I knew he could, but the man wore police blues and carried a gun.

"Thorne!" I called over my shoulder. "I'll come back. I swear I'll come back. I'll make Father listen!"

I was of age and an Alpha had chosen me. Father was going to get an earful when I saw him.

The two men on either side of me pushed me into the back seat of the van, strapping me in. One of them got in by my side as the other shoved the door closed.

"No sudden moves," he warned me. "Or I'll have to handcuff you."

"Fuck you," I snarled. I could have continued to fight, but it would get me nowhere. There were too many of them.

When the other men got into the van, I noticed there were four in all. Four men to come take a lowly Omega into custody? What a joke.

The drive to the mansion was short, of course, down Thorne's long, curving drive and about half a block up the road to the entrance to Father's property. A minute at most, and that was because the driver took it slow.

They pulled me from the van and escorted me up the flower-lined path, for even in winter Father had flowers imported and planted every time any batch died. I pushed away from the men and stood, then walked so they no longer had to carry me.

I wasn't going to let these men or Father take my pride. I had Alpha genes and Father's bloodline. I looked up when the front door opened.

Reilly, Father's butler, stood in his usual formal suit looking down his nose at me.

"Reilly," I said as if nothing were out of the ordinary. I shook the men off me and waltzed inside. "Nice to see you."

"Hmph," he replied.

I faced him. He was a smallish Alpha, never nice to me. "Was that a word?" I asked.

He did not reply.

"Where's Father?" I asked.

"Here."

I looked up to see him descending the palatial, curved staircase that dominated the front room.

He looked the same as he had before I left. The wounds I'd given him were healed. He held himself straight and tall, shoulders back, chin lifted.

I emulated that posture not only because he challenged me, but because I'd learned to stand and walk that way since early childhood.

"Father. Took you long enough to find me." I glared at him.

He moved toward me, looking me up and down. "You are unharmed, then?"

"You know I am. You know I've been with our neighbor."

"I didn't know until this morning when Scard told me he smelled you all over that property! Hawthorne Mauresett! How could you? He is a dangerous Alpha. I didn't know if you were dead or alive."

"He's my bondmate and you will let me go back to him at once!"

"Bondmate? You can't form a mate-bond."

I heard more footsteps on the stairs. I saw Trigg round the bend, his hand on the rail. He stopped when he saw me, eyes wide, but said nothing. I nodded at him but he did not respond.

Turning back to Father, I said, "Whether I can or not, he's legally claimed me." I was hot all over. I'd never been more enraged in my life.

"I have yet to see any legal paperwork. Believe me, I've checked," Father said.

Of course he would have checked. Father was nothing if not thorough.

"But it doesn't matter. I'm eighteen and I've chosen him."

"You've chosen him?" Father let out a laugh, but he was not smiling. "You ignorant, stupid Omega. I choose here! I choose everything for you, what you eat, when you sleep and everything else."

"You raised me to be strong, Father. To be an Alpha, so excuse me if I don't instantly submit to your authority!"

"You're my son. I am your authority! You're an ungrateful, sniveling whore, fucking about the neighborhood, aren't you? You haven't even asked after my health. After what you did!"

I had never heard Father so angry unless it was pertaining to business. He disciplined his children hard, but he rarely raised his voice. He was stern and unbending, with a pervading aura of dominance. He didn't have to yell.

My younger self might have been intimidated. Not now.

"After what I did? What about you, Father? What about what you did!"

He came toward me so fast I almost couldn't deflect him in time. As he reached out to smack my face I ducked.

I heard Trigg gasp. The men stood with Reilly by the door, all silent, all on Father's payroll and no doubt instructed to not interfere except by his order.

I stood up straight and faced him. "Do you really want to do this? With these men here? With what I could say about you?"

"You would tell Omega lies to subvert Alpha dominance."

He was right, not about the lies but that no one would believe me. They would all believe I lied to save myself. Only he, Trigg and Mathias knew the truth. I couldn't count on any of them. Thorne knew the truth as well, but Thorne wasn't here.

Father was the first to break our stare. It wasn't much of a victory because right after that, he said, "You will go to your rooms and stay there."

"I won't be locked away!"

"Would you rather I order my men to escort you?"

Continuing to defy him felt good, but it wasn't getting me anywhere. Pleading my case when he had calmed down might help. If he would listen to me.

I had had no time to think about Thorne and what he might be going through. Knowing him quite well now, he'd be making plans to win me. To confront Father.

"I would ask you to ask them to keep their filthy hands off me," I said. I turned and headed for the stairs.

Trigg, mouth still open, seemed to wake from his shock. "I'll go with him, Father."

When I passed by him on the stairs, he came by my side, keeping pace, and took my hand. I started to pull away before I realized his gesture was not one of force, but of comfort. His fingers touched mine with gentle reassurance.

When we were out of ear-shot of Father and his men, Trigg said, "I missed you."

I bit hard on my lower lip, the pain helping me focus. "I missed you, too, Trigg. But being forced back here against my will is--"

"Wrong," he finished for me. "It's wrong in every way." He sighed. "Is it true you found a bondmate?"

I glanced at his face to see if he was teasing, but saw instead only curiosity and affection. "It is. And Father won't let me go to him."

"But how can that happen? You're not really an Omega. You can't form the mate-bond, can you?"

"I don't know, brother. I never had the chance to try."

Chapter Twenty-Five

Thorne

Within minutes of Varian Vandergale's men taking Kris away from him, Thorne was on his computer researching everything he could about Alpha claims, Omega rights (or lack thereof), and what the actual legal definition of bondmate was. He'd been mated before, but he'd never had to research the subject. Everything fell into place easily for him and for Ian. They hadn't had to fight for their rights.

He thought he knew most of it but was surprised by some things. There was no law against Alpha and Omega marriage without the bondmate status being verified by a certified M.D. He had not known that. But the Omega had to have permission to enter into the marriage from his parent, guardian or the warden of the farm where he resided.

However, if a mate-bond had been formed, no parent, guardian or warden could defy it. It was above all law, a sacred pact.

Thorne took no time getting an appointment with a law firm for early the next day to make his marriage claim.

Whether or not Varian Vandergale would listen to him, or to the will of his own son, remained to be seen.

Thorne searched for and read stories about unusual pairings and how they came to be. He read up on every possible combination and the stories that told about how those pairings worked or failed to work.

He researched long into the night. It was the only way he could keep control of his agony, his hurt, and his rage.

When he finally climbed into bed, the room felt far too empty and the bed was cold.

He lay awake fantasizing about storming the Vandergale mansion and taking Kris by force. That scenario was the only comfort he found that night.

*

"If you sign this form, you are stating the Omega in question, Kristofer Vandergale, gives consent."

"Will my status as dangerous hinder this process?"

"It shouldn't if the Omega has given consent. Your signature verifies this. If it is to be discovered fraudulent and the Omega is being forced, you could do a month in jail for it."

"A month?"

"I know. It's a bit harsh I think."

"Hand it over," Thorne said through gritted teeth.

The form was ten pages long. Luckily, Kris had left his belongings behind, including ID, and Thorne was able to provide the numbers the form required. But he did not have identification information on Varian Vandergale, the parent. For the time being, those spaces were left blank.

It worried him to leave some of the form's questions unanswered. It was even worse when the attorney said, "Processing takes two to five days."

"That long? I thought I could get a formal claim by later today."

"Sorry."

Thorne wanted to kick something. "I'll pay extra if you can put a rush on it."

"That can be done if an Alpha is about to go into the Burn."

"If I say my cycle is due in two days, will that help?"

The man sighed. "I can put that in the letter. Usually a doctor's note accompanies such a request."

"I don't have it but I'll see if I can get one."

"Why the rush? Is the Omega in danger?"

Thorne shook his head. "Maybe. I don't know."

"They may be less busy in the department today and not require the doctor's note. I'll put a rush on it. If they push it through, you might have it by tomorrow or early the following morning. I'll keep you informed."

Disappointed, Thorne left the office building and went to his truck and sat staring at nothing for a long time.

He missed Kris more than he could comprehend. The pain of it was wrenching. His stomach was in knots and he hadn't eaten all day.

He thought again and again about going up to the Vandergale front door and demanding to speak to Varian. But all the rational voices in his head warned him not to do it too soon. When he did confront the man, he'd have a legal claim in hand. Without that, any confrontation might make matters worse than they already were and ruin his chances of winning Kris forever.

If only he could contact Kris, reassure himself the boy was okay. But Kris had left behind his tablet, the one Thorne had tinkered with so Kris could spy on his family.

He knew of no way to connect to Kris. If Kris even had access to any type of computer, it was a safe bet to assume Varian had restricted his usage again.

All he could do was reassure himself things would work out. He'd get the claim. Then he'd go to the Vandergale house and legally ask for Kris's hand in marriage.

It had to work.

In the meantime, two days seemed like an eternity to wait.

Chapter Twenty-Six

Kris

"I'm not allowed to visit you." Trigg stood in the open doorway to my room. "But I don't care. I'll take whatever punishment Father throws at me."

My brother entered the room and closed the door behind him. He looked good, taller than when I'd last seen him, his short hair trimmed perfectly, the bangs upswept.

"Mathias is at school, or I'm sure he'd be barging in, too."

I sat in the center of my bed, my legs crossed, my elbows digging into my thighs. I didn't want to talk to Trigg or anyone. I just wanted to get out and go back to Thorne. I could not understand why Father would prevent it. Certainly, if he had to keep me locked away, he didn't want me around. I was a burden. His burden. Why not let me go to the only Alpha who really wanted me?

But Father was all about control. Of his business *and* his family. I sullied the Vandergale name and he would not stand for that. Better to keep me hidden. Better to make my existence a non-existence, and never publicly speak of me.

Trigg came to my bed and sat on the edge. I swayed away from him.

He bent his knee and lifted it onto the bed, turning to face me. "You don't have to be afraid of me. I'm not Mathias."

"I know."

He smiled. "So do you really have a bondmate now? What's it like?"

"We're not truly that. Yet. But as I said before, we want to be together."

"Do you love him?"

I appreciated the question, something Father would probably never think to ask. "Yes. Very much."

"And did he—well, you know, did he actually kill his first Omega mate?"

"You would ask me that."

"Well, I'm worried about your safety, Kris. Anyone would be. So?"

I tilted my head to look at him. "No. He took the blame, but his mate died of natural causes if you want to know the truth. And Thorne is the most generous, good man I could ever meet."

"I'm glad."

"He rescued me, you know. After I ran away."

"Well, that's kind of romantic, right?" Trigg asked.

It was then I knew for sure that Trigg, too, was one of the good ones, an Alpha with a heart and a conscience no matter what Father had taught us about our supreme privilege.

I gave him a little smile. "It is."

"I had my first Burn," Trigg said softly.

"Was it good, I hope?" I asked.

"Yeah. I liked the Omega I paired with. He was nice and it wasn't his first time so he was very patient. I might see him again."

"Really?"

He nodded and his cheeks flushed. "So will you ever have a Burn? Or… well…"

His questions were personal, but fair. He was my brother after all.

"Yes. I already did. It lasted two days and Thorne saw me through it."

"But—but…" He sputtered. "He's an Alpha!"

"I know. It was wonderful."

"I'm happy for you, Kris."

I could feel the old kinship—our sibling bond—and I was truly grateful for Trigg's company and loyalty. He was the only one who didn't think differently of me, and it felt like the greatest of gifts.

"Will you tell Father? About your Burn, I mean, and how much Thorne means to you."

"I will if he'll talk to me. If he'll listen."

"Maybe I can help you."

"You're already are helping me by supporting me. Thank you, Trigg."

He slid off the bed to stand. "I want to stay longer, but I can't. If Father catches me--"

"I know."

"Maybe Thorne will come for you and talk to Father himself."

It was what I was hoping for, but I wasn't sure if Father would even receive him.

After Trigg left, I watched the sun go down and stared into the dark out my window for a long time.

That first night, Father never came to see me.

*

I slept curled in a tight ball and did not get up until the sun was high in the sky.

No one visited me.

I rummaged through my kitchen to see if any food had been left there that wasn't spoiled or thrown away. I found sodas and water still in the fridge. I found unopened snacks, as well as canned fruits and veggies. The freezer held ice cream and frozen goods. I was used to fresh meals all my life, and Thorne was also an excellent cook, but I couldn't be picky now. I heated up a frozen breakfast burrito.

When I turned on my computer and tried to go online, the service didn't work, of course. I'd been cut off entirely.

Not once since being taken from Thorne had I cried. But my heart felt dead in my chest. Broken. All I could think about was Thorne, how he'd taken me in and treated me with respect even after finding out I wasn't a true Alpha. How he'd held me and brought me pleasure during my first Burn. How I'd fallen so deeply in love with him. If I couldn't be near him I didn't feel whole.

Whenever I thought I heard footsteps outside my door, I would stand and wait, hoping it was Father. I waited and waited for him to come to me. To ask me about my feelings. About what I wanted.

At some point, unless he intended to starve me, he would have to let someone bring me groceries. I didn't expect to stay here but I didn't know how soon I would find my way out of this, either.

Trigg had said he would try to help me, but I wasn't sure what he meant by that. How could he help? Even though he was technically an adult Alpha now, he was not in charge in this house. In the spring, he would go away to school himself.

All day my thoughts wandered.

I played some games on the computer since I wasn't able to go online, but I couldn't concentrate.

I wondered what Thorne was doing right now. He had to be going crazy trying to figure out ways to get me out of here.

All I could hope was for Father to see reason after he calmed down from our confrontation yesterday. How long would that take? A day? A week? I had no idea. Father could hold a grudge for a long time in business. Would he be as harsh with me?

All afternoon I waited, growing more and more angry and frustrated. How could he ignore me like this?

I fixed myself a frozen dinner and ate only half.

I stared out the window, wishing my wing faced Thorne's house. I saw nothing but a few cars drive up the road, none of them belonging to him.

I paced and did laps about my extended room, bypassing the gym equipment and the hot tub.

Father could not ignore me forever.

Finally, as the evening deepened, I heard footsteps at my door and the handle rattling.

I stood about ten feet away, facing it, my hands fists at my sides.

Father entered, looking a bit startled to see me already glaring.

He raised an eyebrow and said, "You are settling back in, then?"

I swallowed hard. "No."

"I have given you plenty of time to calm yourself. Do you want a rational discussion now? Or--" He turned slightly toward the door. "I can leave and come back another time."

"I'm not calm, Father, and I never will be. Your men took me away from my husband!"

"I see. You're not being rational, then." He let out a heavy sigh. "He's not your husband and you know it."

"My fiancée, then. It's what's between us that matters."

"No, Kris. It matters what is legal and binding. And this man is dangerous. He killed one Omega already. He's obviously unpredictable. You can't trust Alphas. I've taught you this. If you have nothing in writing, you could be abandoned without notice and there would be nothing you could do."

I couldn't imagine Thorne ever abandoning me. But the more I tried to plead my case with Father, the more he seemed to deflect me.

"How could this work then? What do I have to do?"

"Nothing. I think I've made myself very plain. I do not sanction this—whatever is going on, this cohabitation with that Alpha. It's a very very bad choice, son."

"You can't know that. You've never met the man!"

"I see you have not grown up much since you ran away."

"Since you attacked me?"

Father turned away, ignoring my statement. "I'm looking out for your welfare, Kris, whether you believe me or not."

"I don't believe you. I'm not even safe from you!"

Father took a deep breath. I saw his chest puff out. He would not look at me.

"Which is why I am making other arrangements for you."

"What arrangements?"

"I'm sorry, Kris. But you can't stay here. You ran away once. You need to be in a safer place." When he spoke, it was with authority, his tone edged with something like sorrow.

But for me? I didn't think so. It was for himself and his pride. He was ashamed of me. And he needed me out of his sight and mind.

Sending me away meant a farm, or worse, an institution. This was the coldest sort of betrayal I could have imagined.

Rage swept over me. "You can't do this!"

"It's for your own good."

"Don't tell me that. I have a perfectly safe place to be and you won't allow it! That doesn't make sense."

"With that wild man down the road? Kris, this is why--"

"I don't want to hear any more!" I interrupted. "I was with him this whole time and nothing bad happened to me. In fact, we were starting to bond."

"You technically cannot bond to him if you're not an Omega."

"Do you know that for a fact?"

"I won't discuss this further, Kris. I've made my decision." He moved to the door.

"Father!"

He turned.

"Don't send me away."

"It's for your own good, Kris."

"Please!" I ran to him then like when I was little and needed his guidance. I reached out and took his hand, bowing my head in submission. "Please!"

"Don't demean yourself more." He snatched his hand from mine and just that much of a yank pulled me to my knees.

I peered up at him. "Thorne will have me. Why don't you believe me?"

Father shook his head. "Then why isn't he here? No claims have been filed. I checked. Why hasn't he come for you? He has not even tried to contact me. No, Kris. This fantasy of yours must stop. Tomorrow you'll be transferred."

Was this really happening? Had Thorne not even tried to speak for me? Tears sprang to my eyes. "Where will I go?"

"It's a very nice place. The best money can buy with gardens and things for you to do. It's pleasant. You won't have desperate Alphas coming to win you over. You won't be required to service them."

"An institution then. You're sending me to an institution." My voice got lost in my throat. I couldn't believe what he was saying.

"You broke the law. You ran away. An un-mated Omega without any chaperone—it's illegal."

"You can't--" I realized I was openly crying now.

"I can. It's what's best for you. You'll see in time that I'm doing you a favor. This is a gift, Kris. You will suffer for nothing."

But I was already suffering for lack of my mate. My true mate. Thorne.

Had he truly abandoned me? It had only been a little over a day since Father's men had taken me. He would come for me. I knew he would.

*

The next morning Father wasted no time. He sent servants in to pack things up for me.

I wanted nothing and would not help them or even look at them as they worked.

When Father appeared in the doorway, I ran to him. "Did Thorne contact you yet?"

"No. I have heard nothing from him."

I wasn't sure I believed him. But maybe it could be true. Thorne was paranoid about his upcoming Burn. He had told me I would not be able to stay with him during it. Was this his way out, then? Did he, like Father, think he was protecting me by staying away?

"The van has arrived and your things are being loaded in."

"I won't go!"

"You will come peacefully, Kris, or should I call my men?"

His "men" meant the bullies who'd taken me from Thorne's house.

I crossed my arms in front of my chest. "I'm not going!"

He took out his phone and I watched him make a call as if he were calmly ordering a reservation for dinner.

When two large Alphas arrived, I decided I would make it as difficult as possible for them. It was either that, or break down and weep in a puddle at Father's feet. Since I knew Father had no heart anymore where I was concerned, it would do no good to succumb to the latter.

Maybe it was the Alpha still inside me, strong and tough the way Father raised us. Maybe it was my own pride I did not want to lose. Or maybe I just needed to feel my rage in its full on power.

I chose to fight.

I slammed my body into the first man who tried to touch me. As the other made a grab for me, I kicked out and knocked him hard in the stomach, though I had been aiming for lower.

My braid whipped about my head as I fought. I kicked and punched and dodged, but two against one meant I couldn't win.

Still, I delayed them. I made blood run from the nose of one. The other let out a yelp of pain. I had to admit it was satisfying at the very least.

But too soon they had me in a strong hold, both my arms twisted behind my back, their bodies close to my sides. My bucking and kicking only served to annoy them now.

I couldn't escape.

They dragged me yelling down the stairs.

I saw Trigg come running, but there was nothing he could do. He hung back in the shadows, which was the right decision. He should not have to get himself into trouble over me. His eyes were big; his mouth opened in a look I hoped never to see again on someone I cared for.

As the men shoved and dragged me down the stairs, I tried to get them off balance at the curve. I didn't care if we all fell. But they were prepared for me now. They didn't budge.

Father led the way to the front door, seemingly calm, though I could tell by his taut shoulders he was affected. Father never liked when we kids made a scene. When we were little we were spanked for misbehaving, but later he punished us by forcing us into isolation, or making us skip meals. Mostly, though, he shamed us, which worked horribly well on impressionable young boys who only looked up to him, only wanted his approval.

As the men swung me off the bottom step of the staircase, Father turned, watching. His face remained slack, his eyes dark and unreadable.

I thought he might say a word to me. Or tell them not to hurt me. Instead, he opened the door for them and they propelled me through the front door.

I saw down the winding, flower-lined path, the black van waiting, its engine running.

This was the end of my life as I knew it.

"Father! Please!" I put all my heart into my voice. "Don't do this! Don't."

Father stood in the doorway. I saw Trigg come up alongside him and say something to him, but I couldn't hear him.

Father merely shook his head and moved his hand up as if to shoo Trigg away.

"Father!" I kept calling out as I was pushed toward the van. The side door opened. A large Alpha man got out, starting to give orders to the other two.

"Put him on the couch in back. Strap him in tight."

"Father! Please!" I turned, trying to fight my way out of the men's grips. I saw Trigg start to run out the door toward me.

"Trigg!" Father's voice carried over the front yard. "You will go to your room now!"

Trigg stood, face darkened, eyes gleaming. He did not move.

Father ignored his disobedience but I knew Trigg would pay for this later.

All I could see now was red. I heard myself rage, my voice a scratchy cry howling my pain. I had no more words, just sounds that fell from my mouth and broke through the air.

Nothing could stop my pain and my screaming. Nothing ever would.

Until I heard a different sort of roar, churning, revving, mechanical.

For a moment, I didn't know what to make of it, but it broke my cycle of fury and I looked up, vision clearing, and saw Thorne's truck speeding up the driveway.

The black four by four screeched to a stop and everything seemed to still as I heard the driver's door open.

Thorne got out, anger marring his beautiful features. If I didn't know him, I'd have been afraid. But now I only started laughing, loud and clear like a maniac.

"What's going on here?" he demanded, shouting toward Father.

"You, Alpha, are not welcome here," Father yelled back.

Thorne held up his hand. In it was some sort of folder. "I have papers. Legal papers for my legal claim on this Omega." He strode toward me and said to the men on either side of me. "Let go of him at once!"

They actually shrank back.

Father came down the path. "Those papers will never stand over time. You need to bond an Omega for them to be binding. And legally, you only have a year to do so! You'll never manage it no matter how much you try. He's not fully Omega!"

"I intend to bond him. He's mine!" Thorne roared.

Father let out a sharp, single laugh. "It can't happen."

"But he can take me from you now." I spoke sharp, though my throat still ached from my rage.

"You cannot stop me," Thorne said. "I have the police on speed-dial if you'd like to talk with them about my own Alpha rights!" He shoved aside the Alphas who'd been holding me, and put his arm around me.

I had to be dreaming.

My heart started to beat again. My lungs filled with air.

This was Thorne. Staking his claim.

"What took you so long?" I asked in a raspy whisper.

"How was I to know the registration for a marriage and bondmate claim took so long? This one was put on rush," he whispered back.

"Oh." I was grinning now. I should never have doubted. Thorne had been working to get me back from the moment Father's men had taken me.

I turned and put my arms around him, squeezing him in a tight hug. I thought I heard Father trying to argue. I leaned my head against Thorne's shoulder and closed my eyes.

When I stepped back, I saw the van pulling away. Father's men were gone.

Father stood on the pathway. Trigg still lingered at the open front door.

"Unless you show valid bondmate cards before a year is up, I will be forced to take him," Father said. "You'll never do it. You'll never mate-bond Kris. He's a freak. Neither fully Alpha nor Omega. Mark my words! He'll be mine once again and there will be nothing you can do about it!"

Father turned and walked back inside the house. He shoved Trigg aside, then disappeared into the mansion's interior shadows. Reilly shut the door with Trigg inside. I hoped it wasn't the last time I'd ever see my brother.

I turned to Thorne. "I would have introduced you to Father sooner, but apparently he needs no introduction."

Thorne grabbed me again and hugged me. "Kris," he said. "Fuck!"

"Fuck," I replied.

"Was he sending you away?"

I nodded. "You got here just in time."

Thorne could only shake his head in amazement.

"Get me the fuck out of here. Please. Please."

"It will be my finest pleasure."

Those words, though true in the moment, proved to be wrong, for our finest pleasure was still to come.

Chapter Twenty-Seven

Kris

I had never really paid attention to my tutors when it came to Omega biology. What did I care? I was a privileged Alpha back then. I had the whole world in front of me to dominate. As long as Omegas were available for my use, that was all I needed.

But now I studied. I read everything I could about it. Thorne didn't know. He thought I was just reading novels or following the news on my tablet.

I couldn't talk to him about my research yet because it would lead to further arguments about his upcoming Burn. Even though we had an agenda—to bond within one year—he was not ready to try anything yet. If I brought up the subject, he would start to fidget and withdraw. He was stubbornly adamant about handling his Burn alone.

But there were many things I wanted to know so I could understand what future might be in store for us, for I vowed never to return to Father's house as mere chattel to him to be sent away on his whim.

Alpha to Alpha marriages were not unheard of. Some people fell in love with a person, not a gender, and Alphas recognized that among themselves.

But when it came to Omegas, Omega to Omega pairings were considered disgusting and were illegal. Alphas recognized only their dominance of them as correct and right behavior. Omegas must be ready for Alphas to pursue at all times, whether they lived on farms or unmated in private homes. Only the asylums were off-limits, like the one Father had intended for me.

But there was another perhaps more sinister reason for the illegality of Omega to Omega pairings. They produced Sylphs.

All this information was stuff I had never heard of before. But my main reason for researching was to find out about myself and how my body chemistry might relate to Thorne's.

I already knew I smelled different to Alphas, but not like an Omega. I wondered if I was more like a Sylph but without the altered brain chemistry. I had entered my first Burn right on schedule after my eighteenth birthday. Only Alphas experienced the Burn, not Omegas, and Sylphs experienced the Burn almost constantly.

I decided I wasn't one of them, either. Besides, my fathers were an Alpha and an Omega, not two Omegas. Though labeled an Omega, I was technically unclassified. The percentage of people like me was about point one percent of the population and there was little written about it.

What I wanted was a true mating with Thorne so Father would have no legal right to take me away from him.

Technically, we could be married either as an Alpha/Alpha couple, since it was legal, or an Alpha/Omega couple since I was legally an Omega. But I wanted more not just because my father would press the issue. I wanted it for me and Thorne. I wanted to know if our chemistry could mix to bring us together in more than just paperwork.

Could I actually become Thorne's bondmate?

Our minds had already bonded, no question. We'd fallen in love.

If Thorne mated me, which could only be done through anal intercourse during the Burn of the Alpha top, and our scents became one, no one could ever touch us. The mate-bond was considered one of the most sacred pacts of our country.

But for Thorne, who was labeled as dangerous, and for me classified as Omega but with dominant Alpha traits, this was not straight-forward.

The bigger problem was we could not even try to become fully bonded mates if he made me stay away from him during his Burn.

Damn it, we needed to talk.

It had been two days since Thorne had made his claim on me in front of Father, Trigg, and everyone else who was there that day. We'd spent a good deal of that time in bed and it was wonderful. But whenever I brought up the subject of Thorne's burn, he would shut me out.

It was right for us. I could feel it in my heart. It was the only way we could stay on here legally and safe from Father's reach.

The second night I was back with Thorne, we sat at the table having finished a wonderful dinner of steak and baked potatoes.

I brought the subject up one more time.

"I'm not fully Alpha. I'm not fully Omega. I'm not a Sylph. There is no word for my kind."

Thorne raised an eyebrow.

"I've been thinking a lot about it. Reading."

Gently, Thorne said, "I can understand why. Your identity--"

I interrupted. "No. That's not why. I don't care about that stuff. I'm still me deep inside. Father locking me away didn't change who I am, just how I perceive the world now."

"Wise before your time?" he asked with a sweet smile.

I shrugged. "I have another reason and you know what it is."

He frowned.

"Please don't get mad and walk away. I want to talk about us. About the mate-bond."

"I know you do. But another time. We have time."

"No. Now. Do you not even want to try with me?"

He took in a slow, deep breath. "It has nothing to do with you…" He trailed off.

"How can you say that? It has everything to do with me. It has to do with me wanting more."

I stopped, letting the words soak into the air around us.

Thorne said nothing.

"I know what you're thinking. You said it a million times. You won't let anyone near you during the Burn. I understand that. Also, maybe we're incompatible to that bond. But what if we're not? What if we could try? Just once. I mean we could put some safety features in place first."

Thorne stood abruptly.

"You walk away every time I bring it up."

"It's impossible right now."

"Why?"

No answer.

"I can't talk to you?" I took a couple of fast breaths. "I know you're not rejecting me. I feel your acceptance of me every night we make love. But you have to talk to me about this."

Still no response as Thorne went into the kitchen.

I got up and followed him.

"I want it and if you weren't labeled dangerous, if you didn't suffer blackouts, I know you would admit you want it, too! You didn't make the legal claim on me in front of my family for no reason!"

Thorne stood a few feet away from me, shoulders pushed up tight, his entire body taut. The kitchen light made white lines in his glossy hair.

I went to him. Facing his back, I put my arms around his waist and held him to my chest. I pressed my cheek to his left shoulder and hugged him tight.

After a few seconds, I felt his hands cover mine at his belly.

Finally, he turned and cupped my face in his palms. "I want the mate bond with you more than anything. You are very dear. I love you so much."

"I love you, too." I pressed my forehead to his.

"That's why we can't. Not right away."

"I won't accept that. I've been experimenting. I found I can take pleasure from penetration."

"What?" He tilted his head back, staring into my eyes. "When? With who?"

"What?" Then I realized what he was asking. "Oh, not that! It was no one. No one but myself." I flushed all over to say aloud what I had done. But he'd seen me through the Burn and after, all of me, and in almost every naked position imaginable.

I tugged my lower lip into my mouth and lowered my voice. "I might have borrowed one or two of your things from—ah—from your bag of toys."

"I don't remember loaning them to you," he replied, voice flat.

I flushed again. "You did. You offered them to me during my Burn and I shoved them all onto the floor." I leaned back, changing my tone. "I remember rejecting them then, but I don't remember you rescinding the offer altogether."

"You little shit." But his voice was affectionate, and he planted a kiss full on my lips.

"Please. I want to try it."

"Try it?"

"Yes. Full penetration with you. During the Burn. I want you to knot me and see if the mate-bond will form. I already feel like I can't be away from you for even one minute. Our minds seem attuned. And our bodies, well, I don't even need to say it."

"Are you insinuating we fuck all the time?"

"I am." We did spend a lot of time in bed. "So what do you think?"

"About penetration?"

I nodded.

"Sweetheart, I'm sorry. I will say this one more time. I can't do it during the Burn. I won't and you damn well know why!"

"Not ever? Is that what you're saying? Because that's the only time the mate-bond can happen."

"You are correct. Which is why I am looking for a place to move us far away from your father's clutches."

"But I didn't know that meant you would never try with me. You kept saying we'd discuss it later!"

"That's because you're still so vulnerable about all this. I didn't want to get into it so soon after your return. But I guess now we're having that discussion."

"Yes. We are."

"And my final word on the matter is I will not risk you."

I stood back a step and spread my arms. "Me? Risk? Look at me! I'm not a tiny Omega. I don't need protection. I fought off Father and won. I put *him* in the hospital. I fought Mathias. I'm big. I can take care of myself. And I have an Alpha constitution, not an Omega's. If you black out and start going crazy on me, I can fucking take you!"

"Oh you think so?"

"I know so."

In that moment, Thorne reached out and grabbed my arms hard. With a swift kick, he swept his leg across mine. Hooking it and taking me off balance, he threw me to the floor.

I landed ungracefully on my ass, looking up at him with part fury and part amusement that he had just done that.

"Fuck!" I sat on the cold tile staring up at him.

"So there you have your answer."

But I wasn't done. I was eighteen and strong from years of Father's harsh conditioning. He was fifty and had been alone far too long.

As he turned from me, I jumped up in one fast motion and tackled him. Part of me was holding back because I didn't really want to best him, or hurt him. My fury was, at worst, affectionate.

Thorne fell back against the kitchen island, his upper body hitting a glass that went skittering off the edge. The crash sent pieces of crystal flying.

Struggling, Thorne pushed me back. We were both almost the same height, but though I was slightly slimmer, my muscles were younger. Bigger.

I did not allow him to budge me this time, and when I pushed him to the floor he went back hard. I landed on top of him and he let out a loud, "Omph!" sound.

Quickly, I pinned his arms above his head and straddled him with my thighs. His eyebrows shot up and he kicked uselessly as I held him down.

"This is me holding back," I said, looking down at him.

"What makes you think I'm not holding back?"

"Are you?"

He squirmed again but failed to topple me.

"Father trained us every day. Plus, I'm thirty-two years younger than you."

He grimaced. "Are you calling me an old man?"

"Are you an old man?" I teased. I knew his age, but Alphas retained their youth for decades.

"Let me up," he said with a sigh.

I backed off, standing and reaching down to offer him a hand up.

When we were both standing, Thorne shot me a disapproving look, his gaze roaming up and down my body. My skin heated under that gaze.

Saying nothing, Thorne went to the kitchen closet and got out the broom and dust pan.

I held out my hand. "Give those to me. I'll clean it up."

He did not argue as I swept, but watched me warily. I loved the attention, but I wished he'd use his words and talk to me.

I knew I'd made an impression on him and he was thinking about my offer. Impatience revved me up but I didn't want to push him further. I loved him and knew he'd talk to me when he was ready.

When we were done cleaning the kitchen, Thorne continued his silent treatment.

I put on a movie and we watched in silence. I leaned against him, my hand on his thigh, but he didn't move to touch me in return, which smarted.

As we got ready for bed, I had an idea.

I turned to him as he pulled off his sweater. "I'm taking a quick shower."

He stared at me, unblinking, before turning away. His behavior was very unlike him, which meant I was probably winning him over to my way of thinking.

Suppressing a smile, I entered the warm fall of water and cleaned myself thoroughly. After I stepped out, I made some more bodily preparations. A little awkward, yes, but more to the point I wanted to do this not only for him, but for myself. Even if we could never achieve the mate-bond, I wanted to experience him inside me. As an Alpha, I never imagined bottoming for anyone, but life is funny in ways we can never predict.

I lubed and stretched my hole and when I was satisfied, I entered the bedroom naked, my hair still damp down the center of my back.

The lamp glowed by the bed and Thorne looked wrapped in shades of bronze light and shadow. His dark head bent and I saw he was reading.

Wanting him to look at me, I cleared my throat.

Thorne glanced up. He had a look about him that was almost nervous. I'd never seen him nervous since the day I'd met him. Thorne might be a loner and the silent type, but he was never unsure.

"Are you coming to bed?" he asked.

Usually he opened his arms to me and invited me under his covers with a smile.

Disappointed, I strode to the bed and looked down at him, my hair falling forward in messy tangles. "Yeah."

I jumped into the bed and he moved back to make room for me. Or at least that's what I told myself. But actually, it felt awkward as if he had moved away because he didn't want to touch me.

My ass felt slick and ready, making my cock lengthen in anticipation. I reached for him, still on my knees, and drew his head to my chest. "Are you still mad at me?"

"No."

He was stiff in my arms. And hot. His hair glistened, damp with sweat at the temples. I petted it, so soft.

He drew his head back and looked at me, eyes dark but with an edge of sharpness I'd never seen before.

"You still think you won that bit after dinner, don't you?"

"Didn't I?" I asked.

Suddenly, he flipped me over onto my back and pushed my legs apart, hooking his arms under my knees and bending them back toward me. He was naked and instantly I felt his erection press at my balls.

"I can smell you," he said. "Honey and summer. Ripe and ready for me. And you think you're playing. You think you're so clever and smart, don't you." It wasn't a question.

His body hovered over me like a furnace of raging heat and that was when I knew. Thorne had entered the Burn and I hadn't noticed. Apparently, neither had he until just this moment.

When had it happened?

I thought back on the day. Of course some of the signs were there. I could list them now. The sly hardness of the muscles around his gleaming eyes. The dry heat of his skin. The tone of his voice down a notch from his usual range, and gravelly. A faint scent of fire.

It had started some time in the afternoon. Maybe our little skirmish had caused it to progress faster.

His hands, where they held my legs back and spread, gave off a faint tremor. His breaths were quick and short. And oh the fragrance he emitted now as he went into full fever. Like cedar chips burning on a dusk wind. Like salt from the edges of a dry sea.

My mouth watered for him. A surge of lust overcame me and my body arched in his arms.

Yes, I did think I had won. I won him. And now he was in the Burn.

I had only one more thought after that. *Good thing I'm ready.*

I reached up between us and touched his fevered face.

Thorne let go of my leg and pushed my hand away. "All this time and you never listened." His teeth clenched. "This is cruel, you know."

My heart fell. "What?"

Thorne pushed himself up and let my legs drop as he climbed out of bed. Moving quickly through the room's shadows, he put on his robe and began opening and closing drawers as if he were looking for something.

"Thorne. I'm not trying to be cruel. I only want to do for you what you did for me during my Burn."

Without looking up from his search, he replied, "It's not the same and I've told you that. You need to leave. Go to your room and lock the door. I can't control myself around you. Your smell alone is driving me mad!"

He said that last word with no small amount of disgust, much how Mathias and Father had spoken of my scent, as if it both pleasured and disturbed him.

Grabbing a blanket and the bag of toys I myself had explored, Thorne stomped from the room and slammed the door after him.

But I was not going to be so easily deterred. I'd proven myself to him. I was stronger than any Omega mate would be and he knew it.

I jumped up and followed him, naked, into the hall. He was already halfway down the stairs, behaving as if he didn't hear me. Or smell me.

When he got to the basement door, he forced it open so hard it banged against the wall.

Abruptly, he turned.

"Do not follow me down here!"

I had never been in the basement before. I'd never had any need to go down there.

Now I wondered how I could not have been somewhat curious. What was down there? An Alpha Burn lair? A nest full of scorpions upon which he tortured himself during his Burns to stave off his precious guilt?

I had to see.

Of course I didn't obey his command to go to my room.

He tried to slam the door in my face, but I caught it hard and yanked it back. He stumbled.

Ignoring me, he flew down the stairs two at a time.

I followed.

When I reached the bottom step, I saw only blackness. Fumbling my hand about the edges of the wall, I found a light switch and turned it on.

A haze of dim orange filled the room.

I saw a neatly made bed on the floor. It wasn't dirty, but it looked cold and uninviting and it wasn't on a frame. Beside it lay ribbons of sparkling silver and as I peered closer I saw they were chains with cuffs. The chains themselves were attached to an o-ring imbedded in the hardwood floor.

"Thorne." I choked out his name. "Do you chain yourself down here every two months?"

No answer.

"Thorne!"

"I have to be sure I don't wander during my blackouts and do something I can't control. This is the only way to be sure."

My mouth gaped open. "You think you'd hunt Omegas in your fever and not remember? That you'd actually take victims and rape them?"

"It's been known to happen with the wilder, less controlled dangerous Alphas. It's why we're marked. Why there are special farms for us go to. But I refuse to use them."

"Oh, Thorne."

"Get out! Before I do something to you I'll regret for the rest of my life."

Thorne stood alone in just his robe in the center of the room and threw the blanket and the bag of toys on his mattress. He tore the robe from his body as if the material were burning his skin and threw it at the foot of the bed.

I saw a small fridge by one wall. I realized he probably stocked it with food and water for his days spent alone down here in the dark, raging and hot and hard with no one for company, no one to comfort him.

Tears sprang to my eyes.

"Did you not hear me?" He was turned away from me, naked and beautiful, his back flexing and gleaming with muscle, his hands fists at his sides. "Get out! Go lock yourself in your room now!"

"I won't."

He turned with a feral look. "You will!"

"You knew I wouldn't leave you if it got this far from the first moment you decided to bring me back into your home. You brought me to stay, Thorne."

"I was helping you!" His voice rose.

"You saw me through my Burn. You did things for me I never imagined another could do for me. You brought me awake. You made my heart full. You made me feel like I wasn't the oddest misfit burden to ever walk this planet."

"And now it's done. I've done all I can for you. Time to leave!"

I stepped toward him. "It's *not* done."

"You will obey…"

"*I'm* Alpha. *You* will obey!" I used all my strength to get those words out. They echoed off the basement's stone walls.

Thorne stood before me now, erect and trembling, teeth bared, sweat rolling into his eyes. But I wasn't afraid. I knew him and I knew myself. I wanted this. *He* wanted this. It could never be wrong or bad. And if he lost control, I was the right partner to meet that head-on.

I ran toward him, and before he knew what hit him I tackled him down to the bare mattress. It was cold down here, but it didn't matter. Neither of us would feel it in a minute. In fact, right now I was sure he couldn't feel it at all.

Thorne made a lot of protesting noises, but I kept softly talking to him. "Shh. You're okay. I'm in control now."

Our thighs slipped together. Our erections met and dueled. He was already leaking from the tip.

He raged for a minute or so, yelling, trying to break free, but I easily held him. Had he not believed me when I said I was strong? Did he not see me as equally Alpha to him in every way?

Well, I'd make him see.

"Look at me," I stated over and over. "I'm on top. You'll be in me soon, but I'm on top. I'm in charge. I'm not submitting to you. I'm not going to let you take me past what I can handle."

He kept squirming, his head twisting back and forth.

"You'll be inside me where it's warm and safe." I reassured him. "You'll like it so much. It will feel so good for you and for me. I know it. I may not be fully Omega, but I've prepared myself. I can make it pleasurable for us both."

A lot of what I said was in whispers, my breath on his face, in his hair.

His yells quieted to soft whimpers. "No. No. No."

I knew his words were not about consent. They were about me and my welfare. They were about love.

His cock was raging hard against my own as I rocked upon him. My own erection came forward to rest alongside his on his flat stomach.

I grabbed his wrists with one hand, easily holding him in place, my biceps bulging, and used my now free hand to touch him. Slowly, I lifted my hips as I gripped his cock and lifted it so it stood straight up from his body. I milked it and it slid easily over my palm, hot and hard. I lifted up and positioned him against my ass, arching my lower back to spread myself better.

Thorne moaned but stopped trying to push me away. He was already lost in his pleasure.

I hadn't done this before, but I'd seen videos. I'd only ever imagined what it would be like to be inside another. Never in this way, until I met him.

Now, I was ready. I did not allow my confidence to falter.

There was no time for foreplay, but I'd done a good job on myself after my shower.

As Thorne trembled and groaned, I gently lowered myself onto his slick shaft. I felt the head of his cock press against me, hot and wet, and my own hole was slick from my prep, but this feeling was new to me. Startling, even.

But I wanted this. I wanted everything with this man. I had already lost my virginity to him. Now I was ready to lose it again, in this way.

It hurt at first, even with the lube and his naturally flowing pre-cum. But I didn't mind because it felt good, too. Really good. Because this was Thorne, a man I had grown to love in only a few weeks, and he was inside me now as far as I could take him, our bodies melded in the most intimate of ways.

For an Alpha in the Burn, he showed amazing control. I would have been immediately thrusting, unable to contain myself. I knew that from what I'd experienced without penetrating anything but Thorne's mouth.

But Thorne held himself still, letting my body get used to him, letting my muscles accept this deep immersion of him into my body.

I kept my hand on his wrists, but he was straining less now. My other hand came up and rubbed up and down the center of his chest, calming him.

He responded beautifully. I kept him under my control until I was ready, and then I began to move.

Up and down, I slid more and more easily as I began a rhythm.

He let out moans and groans, his mouth stretching wide open at some points.

When I felt my own body fit to his own in a pace I was comfortable with, I leaned down and kissed that mouth, pushing into him with my tongue, doing a little penetrating of my own.

I rocked and rocked on him. I felt filled up to the brim, my cock slapping at his stomach as I undulated.

And it was wonderful!

Thorne gave a low growl and that was my only warning as hot liquid spilled into me deep, deeper. When I felt his knot form, I pushed down hard taking all of him into me and stilling my body as he continued to orgasm, hips bucking against my weight.

I held onto his hip with my free hand and it was amazing to feel him form inside me, the knot growing hard and thick at the base of his cock, stretching me almost beyond what I could take. Pain shot through me, but gradually vanished. I could feel every inch of him throb inside me and I squeezed my muscles around his shaft and his knot.

He gave a yell.

I did it again.

His cock continued to pulse and I knew he was lost in euphoria and would be for quite some time.

I leaned down and kissed him again and again, so happy that I could be doing this for him.

He tossed a little more, but I murmured sweet words into his ear because it had seemed to help before, and because I wanted to tell him everything I was feeling.

"It's wonderful. So wonderful, Thorne. I can feel your knot moving and it feels so good. It's pressing inside me in the sweetest way now. I'm so close to coming. Do you feel what you're doing to me? Do you know? Does it feel good? Keep coming, baby, keep coming and I'll take it all inside me. And then I'll come, too."

"You—you--" But those were the only words I could understand from him.

When I leaned back to look at his face, he was rapt. His eyes began to roll back. It was normal… until it wasn't. His body went lax. His muscles, once straining, now loosened.

Ah, so that was it. He was blacking out. Now I could see. I expected him to go crazy then, maybe shift me around and try to mount me in other, more dominant positions, but instead he stopped everything, though his knot continued to move and his cock still pulsed inside me.

I cupped his face. "Stay with me. Stay with me."

His sweet little Omega would never have died from this. Thorne wasn't aggressive at all, but actually fainting from pleasure.

No, Ian had died from a weakened heart that had gone undetected his whole life. Natural causes. Thorne had been unconscious when it happened, but he had not been a party to it. And even if he had been aware, there would have been nothing he could have done. Paramedics would not have been able to save Ian.

People died. Sometimes there was no rhyme or reason.

I could see now that none of what had happened to Ian was due to Thorne or his neglect. Maybe Ian had been enthusiastic and forgot to drink enough water or care for his needs, but he had died because it was his time and not because of anything Thorne had done or failed to do.

"Thorne! Stay with me!"

I continued to whisper to him. "I mean no disrespect to your beautiful love from the past, but he died of natural causes. You have blackouts, yes, but you didn't kill him! And you're not even close to killing me."

"My fault," he groaned softly.

"No. It wasn't! You need to realize that!"

His eyes rolled up.

"Come on." I gently slapped his cheek with one hand. "Look at me. Knot me properly while looking into my eyes. Thorne, mate me. Bond me. Take me with you over the edge."

How it worked was a mystery ensnared in love. The mate-bond. Alphas and Omegas were compatible or they were not. They fell in love and they mixed their scents and their essences, and opened their minds. A mate-bond could not be forced. It did not happen by accident. It was a natural extension of two people wanting each other with all their hearts.

I was so aroused I almost couldn't speak, let alone think. But the words poured from me as if they were meant to be.

"Take me. Take me with you over the edge. Thorne, I love you. I love you!"

Thorne tried one more time to pull back, but we were stuck together physically. There was nowhere to go until his knot fully expanded to just beneath the head of his cock and released.

I moved my body again to help him. I squeezed my muscles around the huge bulge. It pressed lovingly against the gland inside me and I saw white. I was tuned to him and he to me. The pleasure grew and grew.

Could this work? Would the mate-bond happen even if I wasn't fully Omega?

I had all the mental feelings for it: protectiveness, desire, love. My body raged with his making a furnace of heat on its own as if I, too, had entered the Burn. But my mind was clear through the ecstasy. Clear enough to see to him, care for him, pull the pleasure from him until he gave himself over to me completely.

Thorne's eyes opened and closed. The irises came back into view but he kept rolling them. I saw the abject pleasure there, and felt the intense need he had to pull back, to not allow himself to black out.

"Look at me. It's only me. You and me together. Please mate me. Hold on to me. Stay awake. Stay with me."

I let go of his wrists. Slowly his hands came up and over my shoulders. The fingers dug in, increasing my stimulation.

I was ready. So ready.

His knot bulged deep inside me. It began to throb at a fast pace. Everything was attuned to this moment, this time in our lives in the world. I couldn't breathe. I didn't want to. I wanted only to feel my body and my heart fill up and up until I could contain no more.

I climbed in my mind higher and higher. Awaiting the crescendo. When it seemed I could go no further I floated there, suspended in white heat and torrents of rushing pleasure.

It was forever.

It was only a second.

"Love you!" I cried out again.

When I finally fell, everything about me exploded into silver and glitter and an amazing lightness of being.

I felt my body collapse, still coming, onto Thorne's broad chest. Everything was wet but free and beautiful. And hot. So hot. Thorne gushed into me as his knot pressed everything inside him up and out, and began to deflate.

Whispers came from his mouth. "Kris, I love you. I love you."

Our lips met. His arms held me tight to him. He thrust up a few times, making me come again before he withdrew and we both collapsed in a heap of sweat and breathless moans.

Side by side, in the cold basement next to the glittering chains and Thorne's discarded bag of sex toys, we lay naked, wet and breathing hard. My hand moved to my lips, feeling the big grin on my face.

Something very magical had happened between us. I didn't care if it was the mate-bond or not. I only knew I wanted to do it again and again. Forever with him. If he'd let me.

No matter what, to my mind, we were mated.

And I would fight anyone tooth and nail if they ever came between us.

Chapter Twenty-Eight

Thorne

"Are you ready?" Thorne asked.

Kris nodded.

Thorne wasn't sure at all about this, but Kris seemed confident, if not downright happy. This was going to be hard for him, but the boy had a little spring to his step as he got out of the truck.

They'd come straight from the Administrator. Specifically, the Offices of Marriage and Mate-bonding. Blood had been drawn. Exams given. They had taken all the tests.

And passed.

Thorne had the certificate in his hand.

It had been unprecedented. Kris presented as Alpha, but his official Omega status made everything legal and binding. And because of his Omega hormones, their mate-bond had succeeded.

Kris was Thorne's now. One hundred percent. It would be illegal for anyone to take him away.

"Maybe you should have messaged first," Thorne said.

Kris shook his head. "He doesn't deserve it."

Together, they made their way up the ornate path lined with flowers and onyx sculptures of wolves, panthers and lions.

The mansion loomed over them, three stories of silent dark walls and square windows.

The air was cold but windless today. The only snow left was up in the hills.

"I have a key. But I think I'll knock," Kris said.

There was a slight tremor in his voice, but Thorne also heard profound determination, and an Alpha's strength he would never again second-guess for as long as he lived.

Kris wore a white sweater and gray trousers. His long hair was done in a neat braid that hung over one shoulder.

They walked up the steps side by side, but when they got to the porch, Kris led the way. He came to the tall, black door and reached up.

The knocker was shaped like a lion's head with the weight of the ring piercing its nose.

Kris took firm hold with his fist and pounded it three times against the door.

He stood back and waited. Once, he glanced up at Thorne, his eyes a little wider than usual, a little more open and vulnerable.

Thorne nodded with a smile, and the determination returned to Kris's gaze.

Footsteps from within sounded. Stopped. The door opened. A man in a white shirt, black vest and black trousers peered out at them.

"Hello, Reilly," Kris said. He turned to Thorne. "He's our butler."

"Sir. Kristofer! Uh, sir!" Reilly glanced over his shoulder a couple of times as if he didn't know what to do.

"May we come in?" Kris asked.

Reilly opened the ornate screen door and let them in. "The master is in his study. I'll inform him you are here."

"Thank you, Reilly." A small smile curved Kris's lips.

Reilly looked up at Thorne, meeting his eyes, brows narrowing in question. Then he hurried off to find the master of the house.

Thorne shrugged at Kris. "Well, I guess we wait."

"Yes."

Thorne had never been inside the mansion before. The living room was vast with high ceilings and velvet couches and more animal sculptures everywhere Thorne looked. The huge staircase curved up and out of sight right in the middle of it all. Tiny dust motes played in dusky light from the arched windows.

Thorne reached out and clasped Kris's hand in his own.

Soon they heard footsteps on the stairs. More than one person.

The first one to appear on the curving stairs was a young man with dark hair and a smug expression.

"That's Mathias," Kris whispered. "He must be on vacation from school."

Mathias practically ran to Kris. Varian Vandergale followed.

Another young man stayed back a way, looking uncomfortable. All had black hair. Kris had been the only blond of that litter, Thorne knew.

"That's Trigg," Kris continued.

Thorne had seen Trigg that day he'd come to make his claim on Kris. But never up close.

"And lastly, there's Father. My little brothers are probably with their tutors this time of day."

Mathias, the first to arrive, looked Kris up and down, nostrils flaring, and then turned to Thorne with an outright, freezing glare.

Thorne found it annoying that Mathias seemed to show no affection to his litter-mate, not even enough to embrace him after not seeing Kris for so long.

"Come to return the flawed merchandise?" Mathias asked, puffing out his chest and lifting his shoulders.

"He's not returning me," Kris answered. His clasp tightened on Thorne's hand.

Varian Vandergale came up alongside Mathias with Trigg trailing a little behind.

"Kris," he said.

Vandergale made no move to embrace his son, or show any form of affection.

Kris stiffened.

Thorne moved even closer to his side, their shoulders brushing.

"What are you doing here? Is your Alpha throwing you back on my doorstep?"

The words were cold, insulting, but Kris stood his ground.

"Father." Kris's voice came out strong and dominant. He tilted his head toward his other brother. "Hello, Trigg."

"Hi."

All gazes now went to Kris and Thorne's clasped hands.

"What is this?" Vandergale asked.

Thorne felt his own Alpha energy puff up in Vandergale's presence.

"We have come to tell you, as the official parent of an Omega, as stipulated in the rules on page five of the mate-bond document, that the mate-bond between has succeeded and been verified. You have no jurisdiction over me or my actions for the rest of my life."

"What?" Vandergale looked at once furious and stricken. "You can't do that. Kris, as an Alpha you can't mate-bond with another Alpha. It's a trick."

"An Alpha, Father? You are calling me that now?"

"You have the Alpha gene. You were raised Alpha. You're an Omega, too, but it's obvious you are both lying to me because you want my blessing after your legal year is up. Well, I won't give it!"

"Whatever I am, it worked for us, Father. You can have your lawyers double check all the documents themselves."

"I assure you, I will. This isn't over. It's impossible that you are mate-bonded. Impossible!"

Thorne let his eyes wander about the room as he listened to the sounds of a typical family. Broken, but typical. He wasn't surprised that an un-mated Alpha like Varian Vandergale who obviously held no value in Omegas except as holes to fill would continue to assert his authority.

"It's true," Kris said softly.

"I don't believe you," Vandergale said. "What you need to do is be a good son and come home and stay home."

"You had better believe it," Thorne interrupted calmly. With his free hand, he pulled a card from his pocket. It had the official hologram logo of certification that he was mate-bonded to Kristofer Vandergale, complete with magnetic strip.

Vandergale stared at the card in Thorne's hand. His face darkened.

"I will have my lawyers verify it. Any forgery will be detected."

"You are welcome to it," Kris said.

Mathias shifted back and forth as if ready to explode. "It's gotta be some trick you're playing yet again," he said to Kris with a sneer.

"Mathias, it's not," Kris said. "I don't care if you all think it's a trick or not. It's on record and legal." He turned to his father once more. "And Father, you can never touch me again. If you do, Thorne has the right to press charges now."

"I would never. Kris, you know that."

"But you did, Father."

"How dare you accuse me? I was impaired by the Burn!"

Mathias was frowning. Trigg just looked sad.

"Yeah, the Burn." Kris nodded. His smile was cold. "We Alphas use the Burn as an excuse for everything, don't we? To be assholes. To be abusive. Or to cut ourselves off from the real world." He turned to Thorne and his face softened.

Thorne nodded encouragingly. He loved to hear Kris refer to himself as an Alpha. To be honest, it was Kris's Alpha side that had awakened Thorne and saved him from more years of isolation.

It turned out, they had saved each other.

"You're not Alpha and you never will be no matter how many ways you say it," Mathias said. He crossed his arms.

"All right, then," Kris said, ignoring Mathias. "Father, I just wanted you to know. You can stop worrying, if you ever were worried about me. And you never have to see me again." He sighed.

"Good, because you're not welcome here. Ever."

Kris blinked hard, then lifted his chin. "I assumed I wouldn't be. But if you ever want to see me, I'll be living right across the road. I won't forbid you to visit, though I know you never will."

"Reilly," Vandergale barked. "See them out!"

With that, Vandergale turned, followed closely by Mathias, and went back up the stairs.

Thorne was used to Alpha arrogance but this was downright hateful. A spark of pain lanced through him, then receded.

Only Trigg remained, running an unsteady hand through his short, dark hair and making it ruffle.

"This way, sir," Reilly said, steering them to the door.

"I know my way out, Reilly," Kris replied. "I lived here for eighteen years."

The Alpha servant said nothing as he opened the front door and then the screen door.

At the last moment, Trigg ran to Kris, pressing a hand to his shoulder.

Kris turned at the threshold.

"Kris," he said softly. "I want you to know. I love you. I'm so glad you ran. And that you have found happiness. It's right for you, I can see that. Father and his pride..." His eyes glistened as he looked from Kris to Thorne, and then back to Kris. "You got away from Father and this place and everything. And you found love. I'm so glad."

Thorne watched the two brothers, litter-mates, and saw how their images reflected in each other's tears. They had shared a womb. Even if their other triplet turned away, these two still had something left of that caring sibling bond.

They embraced fully.

When they parted, Kris said, "Will you give my love to Mica and Bren?"

"I will." Trigg pulled back. "And we can keep in touch online. I'm eighteen now and Father can't rule everything I do anymore."

"I'd like to keep in contact."

"Thank you." Trigg glanced up at Thorne. "Thank you," he repeated. "For taking care of my brother. He's very precious to me."

"He's precious to me as well," Thorne replied.

Trigg nodded. "Congratulations on the mate-bond."

"Thank you," they both said in unison.

Together, Thorne and Kris descended the porch steps. The sun was blinding today, the sky a dome of flawless sapphire.

Thorne heard the front door close behind them with a loud clunk.

Hand in hand they walked to Thorne's truck.

Kris said softly, "I can't believe I was eager to be one of them. A Vandergale Alpha thinking myself superior to all, ready to take whatever I wanted without conscience."

"You could never be one of them. And neither is Trigg. For one thing, you do have a conscience."

"And I have you." When Kris looked up, his eyes were like golden light. His smile bloomed as he left all the shadows of his past behind.

"You're just lucky I guess," Thorne said, chuckling.

Joining in with his own sweet laugh, Kris said, "The luckiest Alpha-Omega on Earth."

THE END

Contact links for Wendy Rathbone:

Join my Facebook group Wendyland. I post updates, cover reveals, snippets, sales and other fun stuff every day:
https://www.facebook.com/groups/718074255203918/

Friend me on Facebook:
https://www.facebook.com/wendy.rathbone.3

Follow my Amazon author page:
https://www.amazon.com/Wendy-Rathbone/e/B00B0O9BMS/ref=dp_byline_cont_ebooks_1

Follow me on Bookbub:
https://www.bookbub.com/authors/wendy-rathbone

Dear Reader:

Thank you for reading *Trust No Alpha: The Omega Misfits Book 1*.

I so loved writing about these characters as well as making the cover. Every part of this book's process toward publishing was a joy!

Next on my agenda is book 2 in the Omega Misfits series: The Alpha's Fake Mate. I hope you come along with me on this journey of continuing my discovery of this wonderful trope.

Happy Reading!

Love,

Wendy Rathbone

About Wendy Rathbone

Read Wendy Rathbone… where imposters and outcasts, princes and lost boys always find their happily every after.

I have written in all genres: sci-fi, fantasy, horror, paranormal, contemporary, erotica, romance. But I keep coming back to romance as the main focus. Gay romance. Male/male romance. The idea of two men falling in love is irresistible to me. It's all I write now.

All my books are available on Amazon and most are in Kindle Unlimited. So if you have the urge, go take a look. See what's on the shelf.

Male/male romance books by Wendy:

The Kingdom of Slaves Series (contemporary fantasy mm romance)

The Slave Palace
The Slave Harem
Master of Halloween (short story)
The Secret Slave (coming some time 2020)

The Omega Misfits (Omegaverse mm romance)

Trust No Alpha
Alpha Role Play (coming March 2020)
The Alpha and the Sylph (coming April 2020)

The Imposter Series (fantasy mm romance)

The Imposter Prince
The Imposter King

The Moonling Prince Series (fantasy, sci fi mm romance)

The Moonling Prince
The Coming of the Light

The Foundling Series (contemporary billionaire mm romance trilogy)

Rescue Me
Sacrifice Me
Remember Me

The Fantastic Immortals Series (fantasy/myth mm romance)

Ganymede: Abducted by the Gods
Zeus: Conquering his Heart

Stand Alone Novels

Sci Fi MM Romance

Solstice Gift (holiday)
Not Another Hero
Cocky Virgin Prince
Prey
Scoundrel
The Android and the Thief (Second edition coming spring 2020)
Letters to an Android

Fantasy MM Romance

Lord Vampyre
Lace
Snow of the White Hills (mm fairy tale)
The Elves of Christmas (holiday fantasy mm romance)

Contemporary MM Romance

Romantically Incorrect
Snowfall and Romance (Christmas novel)
The Bodyguard's Valentine
Buying You

ROMANTICALLY INCORRECT
Wendy Rathbone

"If you were mine, I'd treat you like gold."

How to avoid being romantically incorrect:

When your eyes meet his across a crowded room and your heart jolts to a stop, don't mistake lust for love.

Never follow him to a public restroom to tell him how you feel.

Don't stalk him online or to a trendy gay bar in L.A.

And do not give him advice on breaking up with his billionaire fiancée who treats him like crap.

Finally, do not offer your house as a haven when the press hounds him, or your arms for comfort when the pressure all around him breaks him into a hundred little pieces.

And, whatever you are hoping for, DO NOT let him model nude for a new art series you are painting.

Artist and model. They hardly know each other. They've never dated. But neither can stop craving the other.

Rescue. Hurt/comfort. Nude modeling. Insta-love. L.A. scene. Dealing with fame. Angry billionaire ex. No cheating. HEA.

SNOWFALL AND ROMANCE
Wendy Rathbone

A blizzard. A Christmas rescue. A man with the heart of an angel.

Hayden

Hayden knows it was stupid to think he could walk home from the office and beat the blizzard. So what if he worked out all the time until he was big and strong. So what if he hated to ever ask for help. Loners who think they can do everything themselves are just as vulnerable as anyone. His only consolation is if he dies there will be very few people who will miss him.

Matthew

The half-frozen man falling through the door to Matthew's coffee shop is more than alarming, but it's a good thing he'd forgotten to lock that front entrance or the beautiful guy covered in snow might have died in the cold.

The man is gorgeous, soft-spoken, helpful, maybe even a bit old-fashioned in his manners. Just the type Matthew always wished for but never met. Sharing a fire and a snowed-in night with him will be no hardship.

When the storm lasts more than a day, attraction blooms. But when it is over, will Hayden and Matthew's feelings fade? Or will holiday charm and a heart-warming miracle draw them together again?

Rescue, forced proximity, overwhelming attraction, blizzards, and a heart-warming Christmas miracle.

Although this book is part of A Snow Globe Christmas series, it is a complete stand alone and it isn't a requirement that you read the previous books to follow along. We wish everyone a happy holiday season.

THE SLAVE HAREM
Wendy Rathbone

The slave harem is all. If you enter, you can never leave. Contact with the outside world is forbidden.

With a secret talent for seeing auras of physical and emotional arousal, Ren, a sought-after pleasure slave, is sold to a mysterious master in a foreign land where he will become part of a collection of beautiful men.

Though the men appear welcoming, there is competition and jealousy among the ranks. And their mysterious master who is heard but never seen elicits more questions than answers.

One friendly slave, Li Po, helps Ren settle in, but it is the voiceless man, Zanti, who draws Ren's attention. With his wicked beauty and bratty scowls, Zanti is the least welcoming of them all, and Ren's training and control are put to the test.

Gay harem, slow-burn, enemies to lovers. Extraordinary and strange. Hot and cold. This book explores the many levels of sex, lust, loneliness and belonging. And maybe, just maybe, there can be love.

THE SLAVE PALACE
Wulf and Locke
WENDY RATHBONE

Conquered. Captured. Sold as a pleasure slave.

After being taken as a prisoner of war, Wulf fights his captors and is sold as a One-Night Thrall to be used and abused, then put to death. He is purchased by a high ranking master of the famous Slave Palace. Why Locke buys him, Wulf has no clue, but something about this master is intriguing. Instead of abuse, Wulf is plied with luxuries he has never known by a man who actually seems to respect him.

Jaded. Looking for a challenge.

Eminent Master Locke takes on a bet with his best friend that he can't train and tame a dangerous One-Night Thrall in ten days. But something about this slave stirs him like no other before. All bets aside, Locke has the urge to keep Wulf, as well as save his life. But Wulf is fierce, unwilling, and his consent papers have been forged. If Wulf doesn't soon submit to his role as a slave, he will be sent to death as a prisoner of war.

A sweet, slow-burn love story taking place on an alternate contemporary Earth where owning pleasure slaves is legal.

LORD VAMPYRE
Wendy Rathbone

When Lord Neverelle becomes a guest at Cliffside Keep, Vanni watches helplessly as Damion, the young man he's grown up with and secretly loves, falls for the alluring and seductive stranger. Lord Neverelle is danger incarnate, and soon takes control of the household.

Not satisfied with Damion alone, Never uses a vampire trick called "the tempt" to compel Vanni, who is swept into a love triangle that includes fiery passion and nightly threesomes.

Now Vanni must ask himself, is any of this consensual? And what about Damion—does he really want to be with Vanni, or is it all a sensual play controlled by vampire compulsion?

M/M and M/M/M romance.

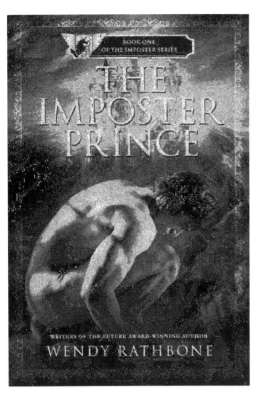

The Imposter Prince
Book 1 in The Imposter Series
Wendy Rathbone

His love for an enemy prince threatens his very life.

Dare does not mind serving the spoiled and cruel Prince Darius. Growing up with him, Dare does everything for Darius including homework, bed play demands, and even doubling for him as the prince grows too paranoid to face even the smallest of crowds.

But everything changes in a single moment when Dare, while posing as Darius, is abducted by the enemy.

A captive in a new and hostile land, Dare meets another prince who seems just as indulged and rotten as Darius—until Dare gets to know him, until they fall in love. Against his will, Dare must continue to play the role of Prince Darius for real, or risk everything: his love, his land, and his very life.

His only chance for survival is to keep a secret from the one he loves, a secret that is also killing him.

A male/male, enemies to lovers novel of mad kings, troubled princes, abduction, fevers, cold dungeons, warm hearths, comfort, wine, and true love.

THE IMPOSTER KING
(Book 2 of The Imposter Series)
Wendy Rathbone

*Their love made them close.
Their secret kept them closer.*

Dare and Prince Malory are happily married and in love, but the secret of Dare's true identity as a mere servant threatens their romantic bliss.

Messages to the king of Brookfall go unanswered, and rumors of war unsettle both kingdoms. Until one day heralds arrive with bags of gold to ransom Dare and demand his return to Brookfall.

King Millard, Prince Malory's father, orders Dare to make the journey to see his father. But Dare is not the true heir, and if they meet, the secret he and Mal have been guarding will be revealed. Also, impersonating a royal means a death penalty offense. Worse, it could mean all-out war between their countries.

Panic. Despair. Lovers torn asunder. Personal sacrifice. More dark secrets revealed. An ending that will leave you breathless.

Ganymede: Abducted by the Gods
Book 1 in "The Fantastic Immortals" Series (A standalone read)
Wendy Rathbone

My name is Ganymede, and I have been betrayed.

Every boy my age dreams of leaving home to embark on a noble adventure, but never does any boy imagine it happening as it did to me. On the evening of my 18th naming day, when I expected no more than a chalice of wine and a few drunken flirtations to tempt my innocence, I was instead sold by my father to the god, Zeus - not because of anything particular I had ever done or said, but solely because I am considered beautiful among mortals, and my father found more value in a few gold coins than in the well-being of his youngest son.

To be honest, I never believed in the gods, but my lack of belief held no power in Olympus or on Earth. Now under Zeus's influence, I am kept drunk on ambrosia in the sun-lit halls of the immortals, alternately amazed and horrified at the power these beings hold over others, and how darkly they influence the progress of humanity itself. How very much I want to hate Zeus for kidnapping me, and yet he shows me mostly kindness, even on that fateful night when we shared a bed for the first time. Kindness, yes, but also a godly and unyielding refusal to take no for an answer... probably because he could read my ambrosia-fevered curiosity as much as my naive, inexperienced terror. He owns me, after all, just as he owns everything else, so perhaps it never occurred to him that a captive and a slave might not make the best of lovers.

Throughout my time at Olympus - who's to say how long I've been here, for time on Olympus is not the same as that on Earth - the only thing that gives me hope comes to me in dreams and visions. His name is Sable and he is a magnificent shape-shifter in the form of a giant raven. When he first spoke to me in my mind it was with a resonance unlike any I had ever known - his mind and mine sounding a single note together, a song without words, a promise of freedom, a glimpse of some distant but very real possibility of this thing we humans call Love. But now he is silent. Perhaps I dreamed his voice. Perhaps I have finally lost my mind.

ZEUS (Conquering His Heart)
Book 2 in "The Fantastic Immortals" Series (A standalone read)
WENDY RATHBONE

When I throw the lightning and summon the thunder, it isn't always out of anger, but often from a love so all-consuming it could only be the effect of Eros himself. Yes, he is beautiful. Of course he is. How could he be otherwise, with hair the color of sunlight and white-feathered wings that drape to the floor? And he is as ancient as the myth of time itself, an immortal with powers and glamour beyond my ability to imagine. He struggles to teach me wisdom, control, strategy, yet I sit here babbling like a child, for all I can think of is how I might try - at least let me try! - to prove myself to him in some way that will cause him to crave my company and my touch, just as I crave his.

I do not yet know how to be a god, for I am only 18 and still just a silly boy who has fallen in love with Love himself, while my father Cronus plots and schemes to lock me in his dungeon and make me his slave forever.

A male/male romance.

BUYING YOU
Wendy Rathbone

It's one thing to be a beautiful cover model on billboards, buses and magazine covers. It's quite another to be sold as one.

Prized for his looks, Dane knows it's shallow, but he is on his way to having it all. It feels good to be gorgeous, smart and have top designers from around the world requesting him.

When he returns to his hometown to participate in a small Date-For-Charity auction, it seems harmless enough—until a hooded man walks in and bids higher on him than anyone else. Dane is intrigued but nervous when he finds out the guy has vanished after the winning bid, leaving only a limo behind to whisk Dane off into the night.

Enemies to lovers, opposites attract, and hot steamy nights that challenge two guys' trust issues along with their biggest fears.

The Foundling, Rescue Me (Book 1)
What do you do when you find an unconscious man floating on a raft in the middle of the Caribbean? Rescue and fall in love with him, of course!

Well, that's not me! I'm a businessman first and foremost with an underworld reach that stretches from my island all the way to Miami. I'm too busy to rescue strays. I have no time for lovers. And I don't fall in love.

But Alec is beautiful, vulnerable, and my heart won't stop pounding. My every waking thought is of him. I can't concentrate. The world is suddenly vibrant and colorful. Flowers assault me with their sweet fragrance. Food tastes fresher. And my body is hot, so hot all the time.

I have done some dark deeds in my life and cared little for their affects on others as long as they gained me everything I sought. But now... one good deed and I don't know who I am anymore.

Billionaire, organized crime, amnesia, hurt/comfort, tropical hot-hot, happy for now. Book one of the Foundling trilogy. (Previously published under the title "The Foundling," this book is a newly edited, updated edition.)

The Foundling, Sacrifice Me (Book 2)

What do you do when your beautiful new lover's life is in danger and he wants to be bait to catch the enemy? You protect him with all your might.

Alec is still trying to remember who he is and is haunted by terrible nightmares. Diego is being investigated for murder. Their chemistry grows hotter and stronger even as Diego's ex, Sasha, comes for a visit and looking for a job.

Who can they trust to help them? Enemies are everywhere and the jungle closes in.

The Foundling, Remember Me (Book 3)

What do you do when your memories return and the most horrific nightmare you can imagine is real?

You try to bury it. You try to run. But none of that works.

Your lover is rock solid. He is always there for you, but is it enough?

Diego and Alec now live under witsec in San Francisco, thousands of miles away from the Caribbean. But their past still haunts them.

Alec is beginning to remember who he really is, but reliving the torment he went through threatens to destroy his sanity. Is Diego's love enough to hold onto such a broken man?

SONS OF NEVERLAND
A Deliciously Dark Male/Male Romance
Della Van Hise

Set against a backdrop of contemporary culture, *Sons of Neverland* explores the universal questions of love, sex and death - the three most crucial challenges every human being must face. Stefan London is a grieving man, suffering through the loss of his young daughter. When he goes to a science fiction convention in the hopes of meeting her friends, he encounters instead a man who is dangerously seductive. Lured into the night, Stefan soon discovers himself in a world where vampires are real, and immortality is only a kiss away.

But the price of eternal life is high, and as his handsome maker warns, "Through my blood you will learn a secret that will compel you to live forever, yet a secret so sinister it will haunt you for that same eternity."

The secret will haunt you, too.

YEAR OF THE RAM
Della Van Hise

Year of the Ram was described by one reviewer as... "A space-faring gay romance full of love, angst, and longing."

Only after Star Commander Morgan Diego becomes an exile as a result of a Galaxy Corps political blunder does he begin to realize how much he valued the companionship of his second in command - the mysterious Lucien, an Alfarian who is more elfen than human, with peculiar powers & abilities which begin to unfold as he, too, realizes what he has lost.

Separated by circumstance from his former life, Morgan is thrust into a world where he must survive by his wits. When he meets a peculiar little old man calling himself Kim Le, Morgan finds himself in a situation where he is required to master The Art - not only a form of human & extraterrestrial martial arts, but a way of living that will alter his life forever.

At the temple, he is introduced to his new teacher, another Alfarian man who begins to steal his heart - a heart which is already promised to Lucien. Torn and conflicted, Morgan struggles with the world he left behind and the world he now inhabits.

Beginning to believe he may never again return to his ship and to the friends and loved ones he left behind, he is all the more frustrated and heartbroken when a new Master arrives at the temple: a man to whom Morgan is immediately drawn both mentally and physically, a man who is strikingly familiar... yet utterly alien.

Printed in Poland
by Amazon Fulfillment
Poland Sp. z o.o., Wrocław